Art of the Genre represents a huge shared world called *The Nameless Realms*, a place that spans thirteen extraordinary Ages of Man. Each category of fiction in this fantastic world has its own specialized medallion that is 'active' in the upper right corner of each book, thus allowing you to easily tell what specific genre you're purchasing. In the case of **Tales of the Emerald Serpent**, you're about to enter the 5th age of Man, and the shared anthology city of Taux, so the medallion you see above is the symbol for all books in that field.

TALES OF THE EMERALD SERPENT

Edited by
SCOTT TAYLOR

Illustrated by
JEFF LAUBENSTEIN
JANET AULISIO
TODD LOCKWOOD

Tales of the Emerald Serpent
Copyright © 2012 Art of the Genre

Printed and bound in the United States of America 9 8 7 6 5 4 3

Third edition: July 2014

ISBN: 978-1-940528-10-6

Editor: Scott Taylor
Cover: Todd Lockwood
Interior Illustrations: Jeff Laubenstein, Janet Aulisio, Todd Lockwood
Copy Editor Extreme: Joshua Villines
Graphic Design: Jeff Laubenstein
Book Design: John Woolley
Writing Instructor: Terri-Lynne DeFino
Sounding Board: John O'Neill

Art of the Genre
217 Palos Verdes Blvd,
CA 90277

artofthegenre.myshopify.com

Ordering Information:
For details, contact the publisher at the address above.

As an editor, I guess you get to take credit for the anthology you create, so I will do so here. However, I'd like to dedicate this book to John O'Neill, who took a chance on an unknown writer, art enthusiast, and editor long after I'd given up hope that someone would. Without John, nothing I have accomplished in this field, including this beautiful book, would be possible.

I also have to give thanks to the wonderful writers and artists who signed on to an unknown product and helped create a world richer than any I could have imagined when this began. You all made a miracle happen!

I'd also like to put in one last thank you to all the fans on Kickstarter who made this dream a reality with their generous donations. I know I say it everywhere, but it just never gets old. You all are the catalyst that make the imagined a reality.

CONTENTS

FOREWORD

What you hold in your hands began in 1978, when Robert Asprin decided that he'd create a shared world anthology without having any experience or right to do so. A year later, he put *Thieves World* in print, and publishing was forever changed.

As a floundering man in my late 30s, and a struggling writer to boot, I read Asprin's tale of the *Thieves World* creation and decided that if he could do something like this, then so could I. A year later I'd published *Art Evolution; The Study of RPG Art from 1979-2009*, and afterward an entire world opened up.

Having overseen and reconstructed Asprin's vision with art, I decided I could also do it with writing, and in 2011 I began the first stages of what would become *Tales of the Emerald Serpent*. Incredibly, Asprin's simple formula worked again, and here we are at the inception of a mosaic shared world anthology that I hope recaptures some of the lost glory of Asprin's *Thieves World*.

Tales was a true labor of love, and the writers you are about to read dedicated far more brain power to the project than I deserved to create something unique in today's marketplace. The characters in these pages interconnect on a much deeper level than simply sharing a city. With constant correspondence, shared notes, and encouragement, we built Taux brick by brick, and then promptly cursed it!

It is my hope that you enjoy this work as much as we did making it. May your Element be ever strong, and your blade ever sharp! Long live the shared world anthology!

Scott Taylor
June 2012

ACKNOWLEDGEMENTS

Veronique Poulin, Heather Dryer, Molly Hunt, Julie Page, April Steenburgh, Itinerant_vae, Michael M. Jones, Devin Harris, Cody Nelson, Samuel Erikson, Terry Tuttle, Estara Swanberg, Persephone, B. Ross and Sandie Ashley, Shawn Morrill, Tarja Rainio, Erik DeBill, Mary Agner, Kristine Smith, Tony Glinka, Nancy O'Toole, Nancy Steen, Carl Rigney, Adrianne Middleton, Steve Barr, Sheri Larrimer, Gundato, Sally Beasley, Pratchettfan, CE Murphy, Fred Hicks / Evil Hat Productions, Agrimony, Rodney Ramsey, Kelly Maron, Paul Bulmer, Bruce Cordell, Jennifer Stansbury, J.C.Petrovich, Cailleuch, John Bogart, Michael Bowman, Michael Parker, Jeff & Marisa LaSala, Nathan Stohlmann, Nik Hawkins, Margaret Welsh, Andy Molloy, Joerg Ruedenauer, Ncribbin, Nicole, Ted Brown, Sarina, Anthony Paul Frost, Kathryn Young, Rich Burlew, Meghan LaLande, Lauren Sidell, Joseph Hoopman, Lara, Badger, Gawain Lavers, Kai Nikulainen, Lianne, Julian West, Scott Craig, S Gawith, Michele Dainiak, Robert Forbes, Dorothy, Jarrod Coad, Eli Ace Katz, John W. Hicks, Benjamin Read, Gary Hoggatt, Brandon Haase, Laurence O'Brien, Cheryl Morgan, Miles Matton, James Clark, R J Rotscheid, Ted Martin, Nikki, Andrew Barton, Mary Kay Kare, Kate Kirby, Jeff Linder, Tantris Hernandez, Alan Petrillo, Evenstar Deane, Amy Sheldon, Catherine Farnon, Matthew Grierson, Anna Innocenti, Erik Parker, Alexis Darbon, Jami Nord, Thomas Hahn, Wolf, Risa, Rick Cobb, Soli Johnson, Beth Gis, Yago Gonzalez Rozas, Cody Markle, Jenn Ridley, Colette Reap, Jared Trezise, Morgan

Justine Etzkorn, Sam Karpierz, Yileen, Benoit Jauvin-Girard, Jill Valuet, Cassandra Dickson, Jeff Spangler, Nicole Sportsman, José, Barb in Maryland, Edie Evans, Rob Trotta, Gwendolyn McIntyre, Margaret Lindstrom, JP Chapleau, Sara, David, Warren Johnson, Alana Otis

Helen Wright, Marni Cooper, Pat Knuth, Karl Hailperin, Daryl Weade, Ben Lyons, Sharon Vinson, Mark James Featherston, Lisa Evans, Drae Corben, Nurse Minako, Kit Brown, Sheila Lane, Shari Bromley, Poppy Arakelian, Michael Feldhusen, Keith West, Scott Hinckley, KarlTheGood, Greg Clarke, Timothy Cash Durrett, Rob Dooley, Vivian Street, Ann Byassee, Howard Tayler, John Beattie, Richard Strang, Sue Edwards, Brian Monaghan, Jeff Hotchkiss, Anthony W Miller, Jimmy Crase, Lewis, Daetrin, Josh Martin

Heidi Berthiaume, Paul Weimer, Nehar Arora

Kyle Pinches, Chris Thompson, Claire Eamer, Kada McDonald, Kathleen Hanrahan, Kathy Baker, Justin Yeo, Kurt Nolte, Kent Rice, Michael Falcone

Ruth Stuart, Carolyn Coulter, Michael Mock, Henry K. Wong, Temp2264, T M Reed, Christian Lindke, Shane Wheeler, Silevran, Alexandra Cenni, Rule-of-Three, ChrisMcLaren, AD Rutledge, Mary.C.Sutton, Brenda Snyder

Martin Beier

Mikael Olofsson, Wendy Elrick, Igor Zeiger, Marissa Barter-Waters, Rhel, John Idlor, Ryah Deines, Caroline, Ferrex Baldwin, Kirk Hall, Kimberly M. Lowe, Beth Laubenstein, Ingrid Emilsson, Don Bassingthwaite, Peter Halasz, Robert Charron, Derek J. Quinn, Donna L Young, Michael Stackpole, Oliver, David DeRocha, FA OSullivan, Dennis, Jason Simcoe, Andy Tinkham, David Kirkpatrick
Dani Akiyama, Sarah Gruetze, Kent Pollard, The Sand Tiger, Peter M. Poulsen, Joshua Villines, Paul Jarman, Nathan Page, Elizabeth

Maryann Cook, Nathan Morris, Elizabeth Campbell, Jim Goleski

Alanba42, Neil Ferrin, Chiara Pasquini, Kristie Tousignant, Lance Lones, RadiantAbyss

THE INFAMOUS BLACK GATE DISTRICT

ALYSSA FADEN

THE CITY OF TAUX

TALES OF THE EMERALD SERPENT

Illustration by Janet Aulisio

NAMESAKE

Lynn Flewelling

The great city of Taux lay quiet as a spent lover under the silver shades of the Ghost Moon. Shay knew better than to trust it, though. This was enemy territory. Always had been. Always would be. Especially tonight.

"Come on, let's get this over with," Balthazar called softly from the shadows.

But Shay paused, dark eyes narrowed as he looked up at the looming bulk of the great guildhouse atop its stepped platform. Memories nibbled like rats at the wound in his soul. He knew this place all too well. Five years ago, it had been the center of all his hopes.

His eighteenth birthday had begun like every other birthday he could remember, with his mother and her courtesans crowding into his bedchamber at the break of day, bouncing on his bed and kissing him to waken him for presents before they went off to bed.

"My baby boy!" Mama Serene exclaimed, gathering him to her lush bosom in a perfumed, man-scented embrace. "Wasn't it only yesterday you and your sister were playing at my feet? You're practically grown."

"Practically?" Shay grumbled, gently freeing himself.

"I believe you're right, Mama Serene!" exclaimed pretty Will. Flopping down beside him, he ran a thumb across the mere promise of a moustache on Shay's upper lip. "Look at this great thatch."

Lucinda laughed as she pretended to wrestle the velvet and linen bedclothes away from him. "I wonder where else he's growing hair?"

Shay tried to look outraged as he fought to keep them, but he was used to their teasing; the courtesans had been his brothers and sisters, as much as his own twin, Shayla.

She was there too, a special dispensation from her apprenticeship with the Hospitalers Guild. She worked her way free of all the kissing and cosseting to buss Shay on both cheeks. "Happy birthday! And good luck today!"

"Who needs luck when they have skill," he returned with a laugh.

She raised a pale brow at his youthful arrogance. "Even one named after the Saint of suffering?"

"And lust and deceit!" Laughing, he grabbed her and tumbled her onto the bed.

Strangers never took them for siblings. Tall like Mama Serene, he had her soft brown hair, sultry eyes, and that olive skin that turned the color of milk-slaked chocolate in the summer. Shayla was fair-skinned and blue-eyed, with a wild mass of pale curls tumbling over the shoulders of her lace dressing gown the image – those in the know said – of their father, the man Shay knew only from an ivory miniature in his mother's jewel casket, and from a few stolen glances on the streets of Taux.

"Here you are, buried in delectable flesh as usual!" Balthazar exclaimed, striding in. He was dressed in dusty dueling leathers. Two years older than Shay, his friend sported an enviable black goatee and gold earrings that Shayla claimed made him look like a corsair. "Are you going to lounge around fornicating, today of all days?"

Everyone had a good laugh at that. Outsiders made certain assumptions about a young man who'd grown up in the Silk Purse, but the truth was the closest Shay had ever gotten to lying with any of his mother's people was crawling into bed with them during thunderstorms when he was very small.

"Come on," Bal urged, pushing the others aside to haul Shay naked out of bed. "You know how Xavier gets if we make him wait."

"You're not staying for breakfast?" Shayla asked, disappointed at this break in tradition.

Shay kissed her. "Just this once. I'll make it up to you with the best dinner you've ever had at the Golden Monkey."

"Good luck, Cricket. You'll be brilliant!" the others assured him as Mama Serene shooed them out. He gave them all the fig for using the hated childhood pet name.

Bal threw himself down in the armchair by the window. "Get dressed or we won't get a good place on the court!"

Shay pulled on his old practice leathers. "Today's the day, Bal. It all changes today."

The sun was just peeking over the high walls of the Ullamalitzli as they made their way down to the practice court near its center. The streets were steep, narrow, dark, and often as dangerous as the ancient friezes that decorated them, though less so in daylight.

It was still cool at this hour and what honest folk there were who lived here were bustling about their business, shilling milk, beer, fruit, bread, and water from baskets on poles across their shoulders. Fynn, a fiery-haired Eldaryn with a trained monkey, was dancing and lighting firepots for pennies while his woman, Analyse, picked the pockets of those who gathered to watch.

As Shay and Balthazar entered a tiny market square they passed close to a wall, and Shay thought he caught movement from the corner of his eye that wasn't a lizard or hairyfist spider. He quickly spat over his left shoulder to ward off bad luck.

"What's the matter?" asked Bal.

"Nothing."

Few Gate dwellers took much notice of the grisly reliefs carved on every wall, the savage figures lurking in the shadows as if waiting for more victims to butcher in stone. But sometimes the carvings whispered to Shay in their own strange language; sometimes he saw them move, turning to look at him. It almost always presaged bad luck: a broken bone, an unwanted advance from some old sod, the death of someone close to him, and the like.

Soon, thought Shay, carefully keeping his gaze averted, *I'll never have to hear or see any of you again.*

Other people were already at sword practice on the packed earth court, and a few young boys were tossing around a heavy rubber ulama ball. As Balthazar had guessed, old Xavier Crane was already waiting for them. One of Mama Serene's favorite lovers, Xavier had been uncle and swordmaster to both of them. Thanks to him, and a few other swordsmen among the Purse's patrons, they'd mastered not only the Taux dueling style, but the Ebontian Cross Defense and Findalynn Bravo styles, as well.

"About time! The day's half gone," growled Xavier.

"Sorry, Uncle…

"Never mind sorry. Take your positions."

Under the watchful eye of their teacher, Shay and Balthazar paced out the customary starting distance and pulled loose the grubby ribbons that secured the hilts of their blunted practice blades to their scabbards. As long as you kept your rapier hilt tied, no Razor could challenge you. Otherwise, you were fair game.

Xavier took out a handkerchief and held it up. "And…" He let it fall. "Begin!"

The young boys grabbed their ball and retreated up the rows of stone benches to watch as Shay and Balthazar drew steel and began the cruel, intricate dance of thrust and draw. Balthazar scored first, with a painful touch over Shay's heart.

"One dead! One dead!" the young boys chanted.

Shay came back with quick cuts to his friend's thigh and neck.

"Two dead! Two dead!" the boys cheered and some of the others stopped their practice to watch. Shay felt the heat rise in his blood; he knew how good he was, but there was only one person whose opinion really mattered, and Shay was finally going to be able to prove himself.

Balthazar tried to regain the upper hand but Shay caught his blade with his own, and with an elegant twist of his wrist in a envelopment, jerked his opponent's sword from his hand and sent it flying through the air to land point down in the earth while Shay brought the blunted tip of his blade to the hollow of Bal's throat. "Concede."

Bal threw up his hands. "I concede!" As soon as the blade was lowered, however, he grinned wickedly. "This time."

And back and forth it went. The sun had risen an hour's span when Xavier called a halt and clapped them both on the shoulder. A warm spark of Human fire passed between the three of them, their common element and purpose binding them as it always had.

"Well done, boys. Best to save your strength for the test."

"Do you really think we're ready?" asked Bal.

"Of course we are!"

Xavier gave him a sharp look. "Mind that pride of yours, young Shay."

"Nothing wrong with having confidence, is there?"

"By the Saints, you've no shortage of that."

Mama wanted to go with them, of course, and hire a fine litter outside the Gate, but Xavier stepped in and explained that it wouldn't look proper for young swordsmen to appear at the Razor Duelist Guild in such a fashion.

Before they left, however, she drew Shay and his sister aside into her suite of rooms, sweeping ahead of them in her silk and lace.

The sitting room was lavishly but tastefully appointed with velvet and gilt. She settled on the sofa and gazed up at the two of them, but it was Shay she spoke to. "Are you certain you want to do this, my love? I've left well enough alone all these years. Can't you?"

Shay sat down beside her and took her hand. "No, not anymore, Mama. It's my right."

"And what do you say, Shayla? This concerns you as much as him."

The young woman shrugged. "I've chosen my path with the Hospitalers Guild. Shay must choose his."

"Very well." Mama sighed, then went to her bedchamber and returned with a yellowed envelope sealed with a dusty, wax, notary stamp. She held it to her heart for a moment, then handed it to Shay. "Use it wisely, my darling. For once in your life, don't be impetuous."

Shay took it and kissed her on both cheeks. "Don't worry, Mama. I'm not a child anymore."

The household bid them a rowdy farewell from the steps of the Silk Purse as Shay and Bal set off in their fine new dueling leathers, with their rapiers at their sides and practice blades slung across their backs.

At midday in high summer, most of the Gate dwellers were asleep or at least keeping out of the sun. Among the few they did meet were Emil Lacosta, the Zimbolay tome mage who sold love potions to some of the courtesans, and the man's silent apprentice, Mariella. Emil returned Shay's wave with his usual, dignified nod.

As they rounded a last turn, the Black Gate loomed before them. On this side, and that which faced the city outside, it was covered in carvings of skulls and serpents. At its center a huge feathered skull stood out in relief, and travelers milled in and out through its gaping mouth. Shay was careful not to look too closely at any of these carvings, either, but even still he thought he heard a sort of sigh that wasn't anything to do with the gritty breeze blowing over the stonework.

More than mere landmark or waypoint, the Gate was the demarcation between the closed and shadowed world of the Ullamalitzli Stadium District and the wider world of Taux proper. As if to underscore this division, when they emerged from its shadow, someone shouted, "Now, there's a fine pair of Gate rats! Someone fetch the cat!"

Half a dozen young dandies in slashed silk doublets and feathered caps lounged in the shade of an awning in front of a chocolate house, sipping champurrado – a thick, hot drink made with milk, masa harina, chocolate, and anise – from colorfully glazed cups. Only a few wore swords and those were tied up with fancy ribbons.

"I'm surprised your voice is so deep, No Balls," Shay drawled back.

As he expected, the chocolate drinkers shouted more insults but were too lazy or cowardly to actually come after them. Gate dwellers had a nasty reputation in Taux and it often served them well.

The streets' names were painted on the corners of buildings at the intersections here. They strode through the tenements of Division and Milagro, then Shay turned aside onto Ruby Lane.

"By the Saints, Shay, now?" groaned Balthazar.

"We have time."

Ruby led over the canal and up the hill into the Golden Jaguar District, home to high-class merchants of all races and guild leaders. The house he sought was a grand, three-story confection built of pink granite, with white pillars in front of the entrance. It was surrounded by green lawns, with fountains and beds of colorful tropical flowers, all shaded by feathery pepper trees. A tall, spiked iron fence guarded it all from the likes of Gate rats like Shay and Bal.

On one of the lawns near the front gate, some of the resident family were playing Serpent's Head, batting the feathered shuttlecock back and forth with open palms amid much laughter while their nurse sat dozing in the shade beside a wicker cradle.

There were five children in all today counting the baby, but it was the oldest two who held Shay's attention. Robert and Esmeralda would be celebrating their eighteenth birthdays tomorrow.

"Come on," Bal muttered.

Just then, one of the younger children batted the shuttlecock too hard and sent it whistling over the fence to land in the middle of the street.

The twins turned as one. Robert said something to his sister and she ran to the fence, blond curls flying, cheeks flushed. "You there!" she called, giving them a sweet, apologetic smile. "Forgive me, sirs, I don't know your names. Could one of you please toss that back?" She grasped the bars of the fence, like a pretty little caged monkey in linen and lace.

"Of course..." Bal began.

But Shay stepped forward and picked up the toy, made of yellow and green parrot feathers stuck into a little rubber tip. He could easily have crushed it and tossed it at her feet, but instead he went and placed it in her outstretched hand. His fingers lightly brushed her palm as he did so, and he heard her breath catch. She was still smiling up at him, but more shyly now, and the pink flush of her cheeks was a bit darker. He guessed it had little to do with the elemental spark that passed between them; he often had such an effect on girls, even without it. And some boys, too.

"Thank you, sir," she said. "I'm Esmeralda Serata, daughter of Esmer Serata. May I know your name?"

It was so tempting to blurt out the truth, but this wasn't the time or place.

"Balthazar," he replied with his most charming smile. "Balthazar Della Nova."

"Then thank you, Balthazar Della Nova." And with that she ran back to the game. Robert, who'd been looking on all this time, lingered a moment longer, regarding the two of them with what appeared to be more than simple curiosity.

Shay made him a small bow and set off back the way he'd come.

"Lovely pair, that," murmured Bal.

Shay laughed. "Aren't they?"

The huge black stone guild house had been some sort of temple for the city's mysterious previous inhabitants. Rumor whispered it took a hundred tome mages to clear the place of haunts. The flat-roofed building stood atop a stepped plinth and was surrounded on all four sides with square black columns. There had once been carvings and friezes like the ones in the Ullamalitzli, but in wealthy areas most of these had been removed. Shay was particularly grateful for that today.

A large crowd of hopefuls had already gathered at the foot of the east stairs, waiting for the call to enter. Most of them were dressed in respectable silks, but a few, like Shay and Bal, looked to be from the rougher districts of town. There were several proud, hulking Jai-Ruk, a few Aspara women, and even a slate-skinned Kin, his sapphire eyes barely visible under his shaded mask. Shay recognized a few other Gate dwellers among them. The Razor Dueling Guild was said to care about just one thing: prowess.

Shay and Bal joined the crowd, and they were soon comparing blades and intricate hilt designs with some of the friendlier ones.

"You're a handsome pair of fellows," one of the tall, fair-skinned mountain Aspara women said, coming over to join them. Her blond hair stirred around her shoulders and Shay could feel a cool stir of air coming off her skin that had nothing to do with the hot summer breeze. "Do you fight as good as you look?" she asked, looking him up and down in the languid, unhurried way of her people.

Bal made her a showy bow. "I assure you, my dear, we do. And other things, as well."

Shay paid little attention as the flirtation continued, though the woman and her friends were clearly trying to draw him in.

He was saved the trouble of responding when great doors behind the pillars were thrown back and a bell sounded from somewhere inside. A pair of men wearing the silver badge of Second Degree Duelists stepped out to summon them up.

It was cool inside the guildhouse, which was lit by lamps and cleverly-placed, narrow windows that let in light without too much heat. The central room was a spacious practice area with a floor of scuffed, black marble inlaid with white, green and red stone in patterns of serpents and axes. A mezzanine ran around all four sides and dozens of people had already gathered there to watch the fun. More stood ready below to test the newcomers.

Shay caught sight of a familiar face among those on the mezzanine and his heart tripped painfully in his chest. Esmer Serata's long, pale face had aged considerably since the miniature had been painted, but there was no mistaking the tall, spare man. Shay stared boldly up at him until he caught his attention, but the man merely glanced at him before turning to talk with a woman beside him.

Of course he didn't know what Shay looked like. Why would he? He'd never bothered to find out.

At the far end of the room stood something resembling a large stone altar. A bald man in silver spectacles stood behind it with a huge book open in front of him. A large quill, an inkwell, and a sandglass were arranged beside it.

The applicants were first required to present their practice blades for inspection, and to relinquish their real ones, which were carefully laid out on blankets lined up against the wall.

"Form up along that white line," ordered a woman wearing the red silk baldric of a mistress-at-arms, pointing to section of the floor design. "Two arm's span apart."

When they were arranged to her liking, the bell rang again and a group of Razors filed in slowly to take up positions opposite them. Shay exchanged an excited look with Bal. No names had been taken; they really would be judged on nothing but their skill.

Esmer Serata, second-in-command of the Razor Duelists and son-in-law of the Guild Master, came down from the mezzanine and took charge of the sandglass to call the time. One by one, each pair faced off, master duelist against hopeful, and were given the five minute span of the glass or three critical touches.

Most of the hopefuls were quickly dispatched, while others put up a good fight, and except for two draws, the master duelist always won. One by one, the dispirited losers fell back to await their judgment. Soon only two people stood between Shay and his opponent, a broad-shouldered Jai-Ruk with the yellow tips of long lower canines just visible against his upper lip.

The Aspara who'd flirted with Bal put on a good show, parrying and riposting with great skill, but mostly defending until the sand ran out. Then it was Bal's turn.

Drawing his blade, Balthazar bowed and saluted the woman he was paired with. She was nearly as tall as he was, with a long scar down one cheek, though she had little beauty to spoil. Within the first minute they had each scored a touch on the other. Shay could see them sizing each other up as they continued. Bal scored another, and then she did. Shay glanced nervously at the glass; the sand was quickly running out under the bespectacled man's watchful eye; Serata was watching Bal. Shay's heart beat faster at the thought of fighting with that pale gaze fixed on him.

Just as the last of the sand trickled away, Bal lunged under the woman's guard and scored a touch under her heart. The other hopefuls erupted in cheers, but Serata called out "Time ended. A draw. Well done, young man."

Bal gave Shay a wink and went to join the others.

It was Shay's turn, and suddenly his mouth was dry as the dust on the ulama court, but so was the hand he wrapped around the leather grip of his rapier hilt as he drew it and saluted his opponent. The Jai-Ruk flashed him a rakish grin as he returned it.

Shay took a deep breath and emptied his mind as Xavier had taught them. There was nothing but the opponent in front of him, nothing to do but to keep him from scoring a touch. The sounds around him faded away and a great calm descended over him as he met the duelist's first lunge with a skillful parry and riposte.

The Jai-Ruk was a strong, aggressive duelist, but so was Shay and their fight was fast and furious. Shay scored first touch, and the second, before the Jai-Ruk gave him a good poke in the chest that would leave a respectable bruise. Drawing strength from the pain, Shay used the enveloppement he'd disarmed Bal with that morning. His opponent's rapier clattered across the smooth floor, spinning to a stop at Serata's feet.

"Time," pronounced the Duelist officer, as he smiled at Shay. "A winner! Very well done, indeed."

It took Shay a moment to realize what had just happened, but he managed a competent bow and went to join Bal and the others, who thumped him on the back until he nearly fell over.

He was the only winner that day, and later would learn that he was the only one to have bested the Guild in over two years. When the trial was over many of the Duelists came over to congratulate him and those like Bal who'd fought to draws.

"Line up!" The mistress-at-arms ordered.

Esmer Serata himself walked down the line, murmuring his regrets to those who did not meet the standard, and pinning the copper Third Degree badge on the chests of those who had. When he reached Shay he smiled again. "I give you copper today, young man, but you'll have the silver soon enough."

Shay's eyes stung at the approval in his father's voice and he managed a husky, "Thank you, Sir."

Serata left them and went back upstairs. Once again Shay and his fellow new guild members were ordered to line up, this time in front of the stone table. One by one, they gave their names and antecedents to the bespectacled man, who recorded them in his great book.

When Shay's turn came the man peered up at him, craning his neck a little to take in Shay's height. "And who might you be, young fellow?"

"Shay Gatewell, son of Serene Gatewell."

The old man inscribed that in his book. "And your father?"

The breath stopped in Shay's throat

Don't be impetuous . . .

"Shay, no," Balthazar whispered behind him.

But, flushed with victory and dazzled by his father's warm words of approval, Shay blurted out, "Esmer Serata."

The man goggled up at him through his spectacles, quill poised over the page.

The mistress-at-arms stared hard at Shay. "Is this some sort of joke?"

There was no taking it back now. "I— I have an affidavit."

"Give it here."

Shay took the notarized document from his jerkin, which gave sworn testimony from his mother and witnesses that Esmer Serata was indeed the father of her children. The mistress-at-arms didn't open it, but carried it up to Serata.

"Oh, you fool!" Bal groaned.

As he waited, staring blankly at nothing in particular, Shay could feel the gaze of the others on his back, and hear their startled whispers.

"He said *what?*" Serata roared on the mezzanine. Fair face suffused with fury, he strode down the stairs and back to where Shay stood at the table. Shaking the affidavit in Shay's face, he shouted, "What calumny is this?"

"As it says there, sir," Shay managed, though his heart was pounding through his chest as the magnitude of his misstep overwhelmed him.

"The notarized word of a whore is still only the word of a whore!" Serata snarled, ripping the document in two and throwing it in Shay's face. "Look at you. You bear no more resemblance to me than a horse turd does to a steak pie."

Shay felt a stab of heat from the man's hand as Serata tore the copper badge from Shay's chest and flung it away.

"You are a liar, fellow, and we need no liars in our ranks. Get out!"

Shay clenched his hands at his sides to keep them from shaking. "I'm not a liar."

Serata let out an incredulous laugh. "The effrontery!"

"I'm not a liar! I may not take after you, but my sister could be the twin of your Esmeralda."

"How dare you speak her name!" Serata backhanded him, knocking him off his feet and into Bal, who quickly righted him and tried to pull him toward the door.

Shay shook him off and wiped the blood from his lips. "I am not the liar, Sir, you are. I want nothing from you but the truth."

Livid, Serata drew his rapier and probably would have run Shay through on the spot if the Mistress-at-Arms hadn't caught him by the arm.

"Forgive me, Sir. I understand." She gave Shay a look that clearly said she'd though he was trash all along. "But this must be settled properly, with honor." Then, lowering her voice, "This little fish is hardly worth a murder charge, Sir. Do it right."

Regaining his composure, Serata sheathed his rapier. "You have impugned my honor, Shay Gatewell. I demand satisfaction."

Shay lifted his chin proudly, heart burning with a young man's hatred for the man he'd so wanted to respect. "And you have impugned mine, Esmer Serata, and that of my mother, Serene Gatewell. I accept."

"Someone give him a blade," Serata snapped, going to take his place in the center of the great floor.

"I have my own." Bal fetched it from the blanket and Shay buckled it on. "Will you be my second?"

"Of course." His friend regarded him with grief-stricken eyes. "What have you done, Shay?"

The younger man shrugged. "Lived up to my name? Kiss Mama and Shayla for me and tell them I'm sorry."

Just then there was a small commotion by the door, and the cheerful voice of a young woman. It was Esmeralda and Robert with her, no doubt come to watch the new applicants duel. She had on a white sun hat and a white lawn dress, and from a distance looked so much like Shayla in her apprentice uniform it made Shay's heart ache as if already pierced by Serata's blade.

"Papa!" she called, waving from the sidelines. "Have we missed all the fun? Oh, Mr. Della Nova, I didn't know you were coming here."

"Yes, my dear, you have missed it. This is something else," said Serata. "Run along to the confectioner's shop. I'll meet you there shortly. Inez, see them out." He waited until one of the Razors had escorted Esmeralda and her brother through a doorway, then arched an eyebrow at Shay. "Della Nova? Gatewell? Too many names for an honest man."

The man with the spectacles stood to one side as Serata's second, holding up a lace handkerchief. In a very formal voice he announced to the crowd of onlookers gathered around the edge of the practice area and hanging over the mezzanine railing, "This is to be a first order duel of honor, challenged by Esmer Serata, Second of the Razor Duelist Guild, accepted by Shay Gatewell, and witnessed by the seconds—myself, Hector Payson and—"

"Balthazar Della Nova," Bal told him. He hadn't yet been recorded in the book.

"By Balthazar Della Nova and by you witnesses here gathered. Be it known that this is a fair and legal duel in accordance with Taux city law. Do either of you have anything to say before you begin?"

"I have nothing to say to him," growled Serata.

"I do," said Shay. "It's my eighteenth birthday today. You're looking at your firstborn son."

"Liar!"

Payson dropped the handkerchief.

Serata whipped his rapier from its scabbard, and saluted Shay, who barely had time to do the same before Serata was on him. The man was not Second of the Guild because of his name or birth, or to whom he was married. It was like fighting a storm.

Shay tried to clear his mind, as he had before, but instead everything seemed to close in around him—faces, voices, and below it all, like the buzzing of insects in the dark, the alien voices of the lost Tolim souls whispering, whispering . . .

There was no time to wonder what they presaged this time; he had a pretty good idea, and the first moments of the fight did not bode well for him.

The Razor Duelists were so called because they kept both edges of their blades – rather than just the points – sharpened like razors, unlike some dueling schools. Serata quickly scored draws on both of Shay's arms through the leather, and a shallow cut on his left cheek that might have put an eye out if Shay hadn't flinched back at the last moment. But this was not a battle of touches and sand glasses. First Order duels were to the death.

Strong and aggressive as he was, Shay found himself thrown on the defensive, parrying thrust after thrust and being driven backwards down the room. There was no sound but the scuff of their boots on stone and the sharp chime and hiss of steel against steel. He finally managed to cut Serata on the left forearm, but paid for it with a matching cut to his right cheek. He began to worry that the man was only playing with him. His wounds were not serious, but they were painful, and he could feel the blood running down his face and inside his sleeves. Worse yet, he was growing tired, having expended so much energy in the previous duel.

With a skillful snap of his wrist, Serata tried to disarm him, catching and twisting Shay's blade with his own. But Shay managed to hold on, though the effort sent a shock up his arm. Dancing back, he sidestepped, lunged, and cut the other man across the front of the thigh. Serata staggered a little, and Shay could have had him then, but the lessons in honor learned at Xavier's knee kept him from taking advantage of such a moment of weakness.

It nearly cost him his life. The older man recovered far more quickly than Shay expected, lunged awkwardly, but still managed to stab Shay deeply just under his left collarbone. Shay bit back a cry of pain as he jumped back and parried, then his mind seemed to divide. One part registered a flash of white somewhere beyond Serata, at the far end of the room, a flash that should have meant something. The other saw the critical, fleeting gap in the other man's defense. With the voices of the Tolim loud in his ears, he lunged forward and ran Serata – his father – through. For a moment they stood there, joined by steel and a startled gaze, time out of joint, until the spell was broken by a scream.

"Papa!"

That flash of white. Esmeralda had returned from the sweet shop too soon, in time to see her father slide free of Shay's blade and collapse to the cold stone floor. She screamed again as she ran to him and fell to her knees to cradle his head against her white lawn dress. Blood ran from the corner of his mouth to spread a crimson blaze across her breast and thigh.

Shay stood over them with his stained blade, staring into those fading eyes as the man who would not claim him, the man who would rather die than claim him, lay dying.

Even so, Serata managed to raise his hand and point an accusing finger at Shay. Blood bubbled over his lips as he wheezed out, "I admit . . . nothing! You are no son of . . . You are not a Serata!" His eyes went vague and his head fell to one side. A little puff of sparks escaped between his lips with his final breath and winked out.

"By all the Saints!" sobbed Esmeralda. "Papa, please! No!"

Hector Payson knelt beside Serata and closed his eyes. "Honor is satisfied. Shay Gatewell's claim to be the son of Esmer Serata is proven by trial of blade."

"His *son?*" Robert had returned as well, and stood facing Shay, blade drawn. "I will never accept that. You're a liar and a murderer!"

Shay felt incredibly tired. The voices were gone, replaced by Esmeralda's heartbroken sobs. "I didn't come here to fight your father," he told Robert. "That was his choice."

"It's true," said the bespectacled Payson. "There can be no vengeance, Robert. Put your blade away."

"With my father dead at my feet?" he shouted.

Shay wiped his blade on his leg and sheathed it. As painful as his wounds were, he felt numb under it all. "I will not fight your family again. I want nothing from you."

"Kill him, Robert, kill him!" Esmeralda sobbed.

Shay thought of how she'd blushed when he'd given her back the shuttlecock, and the way she'd smiled at him.

Then Bal was there, gripping his hand, pulling him less-than-gently toward the door, down a gauntlet of Razors who'd just watched him kill their Second. They were like the blood-thirsty figures on the Ullamalitzli Stadium walls, ready to carve out his broken heart.

At some point on the long walk home, Shay sat on a water trough and let Bal tie up the wounds on his arms and sponge some of the blood away from his face.

"Guess I won't be needing this." Bal pulled off his copper badge and tossed it to a child who stood watching them from a wary distance.

Shay looked around at the broad, straight streets and fine buildings with their glittering windows and smooth, not-haunted walls. "I'm sorry, Bal. We won! We should…"

His friend shrugged. "It probably would have been boring out here, anyway. And too bright! Too bad about that Esmeralda, though. I wouldn't have minded getting to know her better."

"Don't!" Shay turned away, eyes stinging.

"What?"

"Don't act like you don't care that I just threw away your chance in life, as well as my own!"

Instead of the expected recrimination, Bal placed a hand on Shay's shoulder, letting his warmth flow into him, as it always had. "Whether or not we wear a silly badge on our chest, we're still some of the best swordsmen in all Taux. We proved that today, and word will spread."

Shay let out a humorless laugh as he wiped his eyes with his fingers. "Oh, I don't doubt that."

They continued on in silence. As they approached the Black Gate, Shay looked up at the giant skull on this side. It winked a great hollow eye at him, as if sharing a fine joke.

Shay's twenty-third birthday began much like the last five, waking in the lonely hour before dawn in a cold sweat, wiping the phantasm of remembered blood from his hands on the coarse sheets. Across the room, he could hear Bal's soft snoring.

The corn shuck mattress crackled under him as he rose and crossed the bare floorboards to the room's only window. Shadow upon shadow lay over the Ullamalitzli, with the ball court and the Silk Purse lost somewhere among them.

This was his world and always would be.

The usual summons was waiting for him at the Emerald Serpent when he and Bal arrived for an early breakfast. Written in an elegant, feminine hand, it stated the place and time, always the same.

He watched the carvings all day, but they had nothing to say to him.

The great city of Taux lay quiet as a spent lover under the silver shades of of the Ghost Moon. Shay knew better than to trust it, though. This was enemy territory. Always had been. Always would be. Especially tonight.

"Come on, let's get this over with," Balthazar called softly as Shay paused, staring across the street at the Razor Duelist Guild House. He shook his head and ghosted away after his friend.

The pink granite house on Ruby Lane was deserted, the windows boarded up, flower beds run wild. Dead leaves filled the fountains and had drifted up against the iron fence. No one had played Serpent's Head on the lawn for a long time.

Tonight a few torches had been set into the ground and by that flickering light they could see the man waiting for them. The irony of being able to enter through the front gate, now that the place was in ruins, was not lost on Shay.

He'd sworn the day he'd killed their father that he would never fight a Serata again, so they had simply hired duelists to fight in their stead. Usually it was a First Degree Duelist of the Guild, but last year it has been a clever Corsair who'd come the closest of any of them to killing Shay. There were no sandglasses or dropped handkerchiefs involved, and no rules except kill or be killed before the Sturgeons showed up to stop the illicit fight.

But dueling was Shay's life now, and his livelihood ever since the day he'd killed his father. And every year, on the anniversary of that event—this.

Robert Serata had grown taller, but was still slender as a boy and lacked the steely gravitas of his father. "Well, here he is, our Angel of Death," he sneered as Shay and Balthazar stepped into the torch light. "That's what they call you in the slums these days, isn't it? The killer with the face of an angel, though I'm pleased to see it still bears the little scars my father gave it. And here's your faithful hound, as always."

Balthazar made him a mocking bow.

"Spare me your pleasantries," said Shay. "I haven't had my supper yet. Where is your champion?"

"Here," said a familiar voice, and Esmeralda stepped from the shadows, dressed in dueling leathers and a cloak in spite of the day's lingering heat. A rapier hung at her hip; like Shay's, it bore no ribbon.

"I won't fight you!" he scoffed.

"You won't fight a Serata. But I've forsworn my family name."

"You can't change whose blood runs in your veins, any more than I can. And besides, what do you know of dueling?"

With a hollow laugh, she threw back her cloak to show him the silver Razor Duelists' badge she wore. "I haven't been just sitting around embroidering since that day."

"Why you and not Robert?"

"Because Robert didn't inherit Papa's skill. I did." She paused. "And you. So Robert will carry on the family name, while I avenge it. He is my second." She untied her cloak and tossed it to her brother.

"You can call yourself anything you want, but I'm not fighting you." With that Shay turned to go, but stopped as he heard the scrape of a blade leaving its sheath.

"Don't make me stab you in the back," she said. "I don't want that stain on my honor."

"Go home, Esmeralda."

He started for the gate again when pain lanced through his left shoulder. She'd already leaped back when he whirled around. She stood, left arm raised, in a perfect fighting stance.

"I don't want to fight you," he told her again, grimacing at the pain.

"Then I will kill you for the coward you are," she retorted, and it was no empty threat.

She lunged forward, aiming for his belly. He leaped back and drew his blade; it seemed he had no choice.

He had no intention of killing her, no matter what her intentions were, but instead played a defensive game, testing her style and skill. Her form was impeccable, but she didn't have his experience. And she hadn't spent the past five years fighting the sort of roughs and bravos he had, up and down the Free Coast.

"Stop playing with me!" she snarled, redoubling her effort to get at him.

"As you wish." Lunging and feinting, he drove her back on the trampled grass and into the weeping branches of an overgrown pepper tree. Instead of floundering, she spun under their cover and came out on the offensive.

"You certainly earned that silver badge," Shay remarked as they locked blades.

"The Guild cares only for skill," she shot back, a little breathless now. "They didn't care who my father was."

"So I thought, once."

"You came as an assassin!" She slid under his guard and managed a shallow jab to his chest. He parried, lunged and locked hilts, then thrust her away. She staggered but quickly recovered and rejoined with angry resolve in the set of her jaw.

"Is that what you think?" asked Shay.

"I know it! I saw it with my own eyes."

A blast of heat struck him in the center of the chest and he fell back a step in surprise; few ordinary Humans could concentrate the elemental essence to that degree. "I came for a name, Esmeralda, nothing more. A name I was entitled to. He challenged me."

"You should never have gone there!" she shouted, slashing at him with her blade. "You should never have *been*, you and your whore sister!"

Five years ago he might have forgotten his vow and killed her for that, but he wasn't that green boy anymore. Instead, he dodged her blade and struck her in the face with the knuckle bow of his hilt. Her rapier fell from her hand as she slumped, unconscious, to the ground.

"Esmeralda!" cried Robert, running to her side. "You son of a whore, Gatewell. You've killed her!"

"She'll be fine." Shay sheathed his rapier. "Just a sore head for a few days and a bruise to explain to her friends at the Guild. This was an illegal fight, after all. Come on, Bal. Mama and Shayla will be wondering where we are."

Turning his back on his half brother and sister, he walked away through the iron gate.

"Another year, another supper," chuckled Bal as they made their way down Ruby Lane. "And if that woman's determined to be your opponent from now on, you'll see a good many more."

"She was much better than I expected. She'll get even better with time."

"Then you may have to break your oath about spilling Serata blood one day."

Shay's eyes looked black and empty in the moonlight as he shook his head. "Never."

They walked down the hill through the dreaming streets of privilege and respectability to the Black Gate. As they approached it, the great skull winked a black, empty eye at Shay.

Shay winked back.

Illustration by Jeff Laubenstein

THE ONE THING YOU CAN NEVER TRUST

Harry Connolly

Emil Lacosta did not expect his new prices to please Mama Serene, but he did not expect her to actually swear at him. That is, however, exactly what she did. Being Mama Serene, she did it startlingly well. "I am terribly sorry," he answered her, carefully keeping his voice mild. "Acquiring the materials I require has become quite difficult and..."

"Spare me the apologies of a Zimbolay scholar," she interrupted. "Every learned word makes my purse lighter." She wrote out a bank note, signed it, and handed it to him. It was for the old price. "Next time, I will pay your new, even more outrageous, fee."

Emil nodded and handed the note to Mariella. He turned to the three young consorts sitting on Mama Serene's ornate couch. "Do you accept this spell without coercion, of your own will?"

The consorts said "Yes," in deeply bored tones. One of them added: "because it's making me rich!" They all laughed at him. He had asked them last time, too, and would ask next time. It didn't matter if they thought him fussy. He held out a small vial to the first consort and, after she had spit into the golden liquid, allowed her to take it. He did the same for the others.

They were love potions all. A select few of Mama Serene's clients paid a high premium to be genuinely, or at least magically, adored, even if it was just for a few days.

Their business concluded, Emil and Mama Serene nodded politely to each other. Mariella opened the office door and led Emil swiftly and quietly down the side stair and through the lounge. Emil hated coming to the House of the Silk Purse, hated delivering his product in person, hated knowing the consorts would drink the potion when he was not there to watch over them. But the money was good. Very, very good. With luck, he...

Two men seated in the lobby rose out of their chairs and moved toward him. They seemed to have been waiting for him, and Emil stopped immediately and drew back. Mariella stepped around him, her hand on the ribbon tying down her sword. There was an odd expression on her face.

"No no!" the taller man said, his empty hands raised. "We mean only to talk."

He was near thirty, blue-eyed and deeply tanned. His clothes were satin and leather, and his black hair and long mustache was oiled into curls. He dressed like a dandy, but the amount of sun he'd gotten and the corded muscles in his wrists suggested *pirate* or *merchant*, not that there was always much difference.

His companion was small and slender, and his skin was as black as Emil's – darker, even, because Emil spent long hours in his basement lab. The tattoos on the man's face marked him as a dock thug or cutpurse from Zimbolay. Emil felt a pang of homesickness at the sight of him, but of course he had nothing in common with such a person. "If you want to talk to me," Emil said mildly as he tried to move around them, "come to my shop during shop hours."

"That is impossible," The merchant said. "Please, let me buy you a drink and I will explain why I am so desperate."

"Shop hours," Emil said, moving slowly and carefully around him. "Thank you."

"My friend," the merchant said. His tone was still light, but there was an undercurrent of threat. "I am trying to handle this respectfully."

Emil stopped heading toward the door. Mariella had skill with her blade, but she was no Razor and certainly no bodyguard. Besides, she was burdened with his tome. Emil, of course, had no weapon. "I don't need your respect," Emil answered.

"What about my money? Eh? Aha! I see that got your attention."

"I already have more clients than I can accommodate."

"I will double your price."

"You don't even know what my prices are."

"I am desperate," the merchant said again, although he managed to include a trace of condescension in his voice as he said it. "And you are insulting me."

Emil sighed. Mariella and the cut purse had their hands on their blades, but this merchant, whoever he was, had not tied off his own rapier with a ribbon. Since he was clearly not stupid, it meant he was not afraid to be challenged in the street by a Razor. That meant he was very, very good.

Getting killed was bad for business. Emil turned to Mariella: "You'll have to complete your errand without me today. I will meet you back at the shop."

"As you say, sir." She left.

"Let me introduce myself," the merchant said as he led Emil into a booth near the back wall. The lamplight was dim there. "I am Rene LeCroix, Captain of *Broadbelly* and *Tide Dancer*, merchant, trader, shipper, and bearer of tidings good and ill."

"Good day to you, sir. My name is Emil Lacosta."

"That is a Findalynn name, is it not? But you are Zimbolay, like my friend here."

"It's true," Emil said. "It's what my people call a 'public name.' We have private names which are just that."

"It is good for you that you are a scholar of obvious breeding," Rene answered, smoothing his mustache, "or no one would do business with you. When my friend here gives his name, the Sturgeons accuse him of using an alias."

The cutpurse smiled, making the knife scars around his mouth turn grey. "I am called Increase Coin," he said.

"An auspicious choice," Emil said politely, inclining his head slightly. It was common for men of low class to choose such names.

Rene continued. "Still, it must be difficult for a black man in Taux, yes? Even for a man of privilege like yourself."

Emil nodded to acknowledge the comment, then turned the conversation to business. "There is something you should know from the first, Sir: I will not sell a potion or powder to make some unsuspecting person fall in love with you. What's more, do not think you can purchase a potion under some pretense and use it on an unsuspecting person. The magic will work on one person only and be directed toward one person only, and I will not cast such a spell without the express permission of the person it will be used upon, not even under pain of torture."

"You misunderstand me, Sir. I do not wish to make someone else fall in love with me. I want you to make me fall in love with my wife."

A young girl came to the table carrying three wooden cups and a red clay jug of wine. Increase poured their portions, but only he and Rene drank.

Emil waited until the waitress had left before he spoke again. "That is an unusual request. So unusual, in fact, I'm tempted to refuse you outright."

Rene gave him a crooked smile. He was really quite a handsome man, and he knew how to use his charm. "Hear me out first, please. I beg you. I am in your hands." Emil could tell he was trying to sound sincere, but he was too arrogant to excise all of the sarcasm from his tone. "Three years ago, I married. I did not love her, but what difference did that make? I was a Captain, good with a sword and doing quite well for myself. She was young—but not too young—and impressionable. Also, her family is tremendously wealthy. How perfect, yes? She wanted me, and I wanted her money. Do you recognize me now? Surely you have heard the gossip."

"I have not," Emil admitted. "I spend much of my time in my laboratory, trying to keep up with my clients' requests."

Rene laughed and turned to Increase. "By the Saints, the first man that I hoped would recognize me is the first who does not."

Increase laughed hoarsely. Emil could see that Rene felt slighted in some strange way. "Please accept my apologies," Emil said mildly. "Affairs of the heart do not hold my interest." Remembering Mariella's expression, Emil realized that she must have recognized the Captain immediately. Perhaps he would ask her at the end of the day.

Rene waved his hand as though brushing away a fly. "It does not matter, my friend. In any event, things have changed. My bride no longer blushes when I look at her. In fact, she sneers. I fear we are about to divorce, which will ruin me."

"In what way?"

Rene drained his cup, then slammed it onto the table. He noticed that Emil had not touched his own drink, and his grin became crooked. "There were certain... contracts I was obliged to sign. We had eloped, you see, and when we returned that great fat fart Daddy Oswald – my beloved bride's father is Oswald Burgunzi, so you see what I mean about wealth – had me dragged from my own wedding bed and brought to him in chains. You see, I had convinced my precious little one that I loved her with all my soul, but her father was not so easily fooled. So, with a knife at my throat, I signed. I am pledged to adore her in all things for her long life. If I do not, we divorce and she will get half of everything that is mine. Half! If that meant she would take just one of my ships, I would consider it, but she has told me she intends to collect *half of each ship*. She would have them cut down the middle. I would be ruined. You see, she hates me because I am a man, with all the appetites of a man."

"Why not just set sail, then? Isn't it the privilege of the man of the sea to venture onto the ocean and leave his troubles behind?" Emil asked.

Rene shook his head, his lips pursed in distaste. "Were I to leave the city, her father would call it abandonment – a petition for divorce, essentially

– and I could never again do business in a port where the Burgunzi family are established, else they have my ships seized. In truth, I cannot even take on cargo and ply my trade upon the waters! Even discussing a trading voyage that would see me back in her bed in a mere six-month brings talk of 'abandonment.' You see, Taux is a free city for everyone but me. I am trapped."

Increase spoke suddenly and urgently: "We cannot remain."

Rene gestured toward him. "You see? My own crew – the greatest friends a man could ever hope for – long to abandon me and my ships. I still pay their wages and ask nothing in return, but they do not want to linger."

"Only a madman would live in this city of ghosts," Increase said. "Only a fool would stay here when the doom that befell Taux might return at any time."

Rene pointed to his companion as though he was a proof of a complex philosophical theory. "You see? My time in this city is short. However, I have a plan: Were my wife to request this divorce herself, as I'm told she is close to doing, I could refuse. I am her husband, after all. The matter would go to the court."

"The Burgunzi family has many friends among the magistrates," Emil observed.

"True! But if I truly loved my wife, if I protested against this separation openly, before the bench, I believe they would dissolve the marriage – and the contract – in my favor. The agreement states that she can take half if I spurn her love, not if she spurns mine. I would keep my ships and regain my freedom."

Emil shook his head. "You do not need magic for this. Just profess your love in court."

"I could never pull it off," Rene said, leaning back and sighing. "I would have to perform for days, and my nature is too ironical. I must convince everyone, even the most skeptical, that I love her..."

"...more than himself," Increase finished. Both men laughed.

"Yes, you see? Exactly." Rene gestured to his own face as though presenting a work of art. "I am a prideful man; I am not ashamed to admit it. It is my great flaw. At some point in the trial, I would smile sardonically, or make a snide remark under my breath, or roll my eyes. It is not just the magistrate I need to convince, it is also her whole cursed family. I am a great man capable of many things, but wooing a woman in front of her mother, father, and a whole room full of strangers? After I've already bedded her? I could never manage it."

"No one would be hurt," Increase said.

"He is right. No one would be hurt," Rene said, his voice low. "You would only be helping me out of a bad spot. And now you know why I could not come to your shop, where anyone might see. Do you understand my predicament, my friend?"

Emil was silent a moment. "In my time, I have made a few potions that would save a marriage, but none that would save a divorce."

Rene got a canny look. "Does that mean you will do it?"

"Will I have to deliver the potion to you here?"

"Yes, absolutely."

"Then the price will be two and a half times normal, payable by a bank note. I will not carry coins inside the Black Gate."

Rene turned to Increase. "That... can be arranged. I am told the writ will be delivered soon but do not know exactly when. If your potion works for three days as rumored, I will need two dozen doses."

Emil shook his head. "That's not necessary. The short-term doses are for the consorts who work here. For you I would create a different formulation that would have longer effects. The price would also be much lower than twenty-four doses."

"Ah! That is good news! How long would it last?"

"It depends on the person. The average time is about two years, but some people with a weak will or a powerful sense of self-hatred can feel the effects for the rest of their lives."

"So, in Rene's case," Increase said. "It will last a month." He and Rene laughed again.

"No," Emil said. "Even for a man with a great pride, the spell should persist for longer than a year. I should warn you, though: The one thing you can never trust is love. People in love can be unpredictable. Your heartbreak, when the object of your devotion rejects you, will feel entirely real because it will be real. Your pain will be great."

"My friend, I am counting on it. You need a lock of her hair, do you not? I cut it myself while she slept." He passed a folded square of red velvet across the table. Emil opened it, saw three times as many straw-colored strands as he would need, and pocketed it.

Then Emil wrote a price on a scrap of paper and passed it across the table. Rene seemed almost delighted by it. They made arrangements to meet the next day to complete the transaction. Emil and Rene shook hands on it, clicked their cups, and drank.

"We have, of course, been seen here," Rene said. "If asked, I intend to say that I wanted a potion for my lovely bride."

Emil nodded. "I will neither confirm nor deny anything. Discretion is part of the service. Be aware that the potion will make your body temperature run high for a day, while your spark seeks a new balance, and that might give you away. Is our business concluded?"

"I must ask you something, my friend. Forgive me if I seem to pry. Can you really stay in business when you operate in this way? One man to another, are there really so many people longing to fall in love—at these prices—that you can afford such fine cloth and bracelets of gold?"

"No," Emil answered after a slight hesitation. "No, there aren't. It's a common misconception, though. Along with the ability to create love comes the ability to destroy it. The great bulk of my business involves purging people of painful infatuation and heartbreak."

"Is that so? I had not realized. You destroy love? That sounds terrible. Isn't it a great tragedy to take love out of the world?"

"Perhaps. But it is not just the money that keeps me in my lab, working long hours into the night. When a young wife comes to my shop, weeping over her unfaithful husband, and her mother shows me the knife scars on her wrist…"

Rene quirked his head at this.

"…and the young woman swears she will try again," Emil continued. "I cannot help but feel I perform a great service. Because truly, this happens more often that I can say."

Rene and Increase looked at each other in a strange way, as though recalculating their price. Finally, Rene said: "You are more honorable than I expected."

Emil slid out of the booth and bowed to the two men. In his mildest, most polite tone, he said, "I do not need your respect."

Then he went through the doors of the House of the Silk Purse into the blazing day.

Emil climbed the stone stairs that lead to the walkways above the Ullamalitzli court. The walls along the stairs were carved with horrifying images of murder and Human sacrifice, but above the court the limestone walkways were mostly bare. The only company he had was the neglected corpse of a Razor, bloating in the sun. The new residents of the city killed as often as the old ones. They just didn't record the deeds in stone.

The ball court was empty for the moment, and there seemed to be fewer people milling about by the Black Gate. Emil made his way down another flight of stairs, hurried through the gate and turned south, away from the tombs of the city.

The unexpected meeting had delayed him so much that the midday sun was already high and hot. He was a madman to live here in this so-called free city; Increase was correct. Every building he passed was covered with images of war and bloody ritual, and the doom that had come to this city, the one that had left it an empty shell to be ransacked by vicious white traders, whatever it was, it would come again. He was sure of it.

By then he hoped to be back home with his wife and daughter, living on his family's hilltop stone estate, trading gold, fur, and ivory. He only needed a little more money. Just a little more.

He passed down the narrow, shadowed street that lead to his building, went under the two corbelled arches that marked the entrance of his plaza, and strode across the grass toward his shop. In Zimbolay, this mud and grass would have been replaced with smooth blocks of close-fitting stone, but in Taux the streets were full of weeds crushed under square-heeled shoes.

Mariella was already waiting for him in the front room. The house, being one of the original stucco and limestone buildings, was cool inside. Best of all, the walls were bare; Emil had long ago erased the carvings inside his shop with acid. Those with ties to the Element of Earth told him that it did not silence the voices of the souls contained within, but at least he could concentrate on his work without having to stare at the images of their torment.

He stopped in the doorway, letting the door swing shut behind him. Something was wrong. "Mariella, did you deposit the note?"

She didn't answer. Emil felt a little tingle. His apprentice was especially sensitive. Sometimes, when she sat alone in the dark, she heard whispers.

"Sir?" she finally asked, her long, pale face looking morose in the lamplight. "Do you think they were better than us?"

He didn't need to ask who she meant. He glanced at the wall, where he'd burned away a scene of a slave being ritually knifed. "They killed, we kill," he said. "But we went into their Ullamalitzli Stadium, the ball court where they played sacred games, and we built a whorehouse. They could hardly be worse. Come on. We have work to do."

They worked together in the basement lab for the rest of the day creating the love potion. The next morning, Emil met with Rene in the market, as planned. They exchanged bank note for a vial in an herbalist's shop, and Emil had no cause to think of the matter for half a month.

The days were growing shorter as the autumn equinox approached, and even dried spring herbs like woodruff had become dear. Emil had spent long hours haggling in the market over a bundle he absolutely had to have for the long winter, but the asking price was ten times what it should have been. As a result, he did not return to his shop until after dark, and he was irritable and distracted.

As he hurried down the narrow street toward the double corbelled arches leading to the little plaza in front of his shop, he noticed too late the squelching footsteps of the man following him. Emil glanced back and saw a tall pale man in a quilted vest only a few paces behind. The man's right hand lay on the hilt of his undrawn rapier, but his dagger was naked in his left hand.

Emil broke into a run, knowing there was little hope the man was alone. He ran under the arches into the muddy plaza and was met by three men. All their rapiers were drawn.

Emil sidestepped, backing into an alcove. The stone wall was rough against his shoulder-blades... carvings pushing against him. He had bumped against the ceremonial art that covered so much of the city. These were a scene of war, he suddenly remembered, just as the moonlit blades moved toward him.

There were two men standing close, and two behind them. Emil raised his hands beside his face so his sleeves would slip down, showing his golden bracelets. "There's no need for violence. I will turn over my valuables without a fight."

The man who'd followed him down the alley came close, the point of his blade aimed at Emil's heart like a long needle. "Oh, we'll be taking your valuables, and I don't expect much of a fight." The other men laughed nastily, moving closer.

So be it. Emil pressed his left bracelet against his mouth and, snapping a latch open with his teeth, blew into it with all his strength.

A cloud of fine powder billowed out, engulfing all four men. They gasped and shook their heads, staggering a little. Their swords dipped toward the mud.

"By the Saints," the nearest one said. He sounded dumbstruck. "I...

"You love me," Emil said. "All of you." None of them disagreed. They just stared at him, enraptured. "But I'm terribly sorry to say that I can only love one of you in return."

There was a pause while his meaning sunk in. The first to understand was a man at the rear; he plunged his rapier into the back of the one who'd followed Emil into the plaza. The man's death scream shocked the others into action, and their swords slashed and clashed against each other.

Like most fights, it was over in seconds. The first man to be struck had been pierced through the heart and was stone dead. The man who'd killed him lay in the mud, his slashed throat bleeding fiercely. The one who'd cut his throat had managed a short fight with the fourth man, but the fourth had pierced him three times before he'd managed to thrust his knife under the man's chin and into his brain.

He took one unsteady step toward Emil, then collapsed. "I'm dying," the killer said. "By the Saints, I just found you. I just found you and I'm dying!"

Emil knelt beside him. If he'd known healing magic, he could have saved the man, but there was no hope. "My love," Emil said. The man's spark, fueled by the magic in the powder, made him feel feverish. "You fought so bravely."

The man looked deeply into Emil's eyes. The moonlight was dim, but Emil could see that he had a square, ugly face, bulging eyes and a squashed nose. The face of a thug. "I just found you moments ago, and now I'm going to slip into the next world without you."

Emil laid his hand tenderly against the side of the dying man's face. "Do you think anything could come between our love? Even death?" Tears brimmed in the man's eyes and he laid his hand on Emil's, but his strength was fading and his arm dropped into the mud. Emil lowered his voice to a whisper. "Tell me, my sweet, who sent you here?"

"Oh!" the killer said as though suddenly remembering he'd done a great wrong. "Oh what have I done?"

"Sssshhh," Emil said, laying a finger on his lips. "You could never do anything to harm me. I know it. But someone told you to come here and hurt me, yes? Please, my sweet, tell me who it was."

"It was my Captain, Rene LeCroix. He didn't tell me why..."

"That doesn't matter now. Don't trouble yourself over trifles. Not now."

"I'm so cold! By the Saints, I just found you, and now I'm going to die!"

Emil caressed his face tenderly once more, feeling it grow cool as his fire spark dwindled, then bent low and kissed him. When he raised his head, tears streamed back over the killer's temples. Emil stayed with him a few more seconds, looking tenderly into his eyes, until he died.

He stood. The man with the cut throat had already died. Emil checked the latch on his bracelet, then shut it.

He glanced back at the carvings behind him, but they were too deep in shadow to make them out. They could hardly have been worse.

He went inside and barred the door. Mariella had already gone to sleep, so he woke her and sent her onto the roof, where she lit the lamp that would catch the attention of the city guard.

Within the quarter hour Emil unbarred the door long enough to admit a pair of the blue-cloaked Sturgeons. He knew these men well—he'd done business with one of them some years back, and they did not treat him as though having a public name was the same as being a fugitive. He needed very little time to explain what had happened, but much longer to answer all their questions. By the way they spoke, he could tell there was something they weren't telling him, but of course the city guard didn't share information.

After they left, Mariella brought him a cup of tea. "Sir..." she said, and hesitated.

"If there's bad news," he told her, "I want to hear about it immediately."

"Well, sir, you've been so busy preparing for the winter, I didn't want to distract you, but Rene LeCroix was arrested for murder last week, and he was released today."

Emil slumped in his chair and rubbed his face with both hands. "Murder? Of his wife?"

"Yes, Sir. It seems she had taken a lover. He surprised them abed and slew them both. The Sturgeons arrested him, of course, but the magistrate burned the writ against him. He was found innocent because..."

"...because it was a crime of passion." Emil stood out of his chair and paced around his little shop. Even the Burgunzi family wouldn't punish him for a scandal like that. Not openly. In fact, they had probably offered him a full purse to sail away. "Damnation! I've been such a fool!"

"Now that word is out, though, the Sturgeons will arrest him again."

"For the death of a Burgunzi?" Emil realized that Rene had never said the girl's name, almost as if she didn't matter. But with a family name like hers, she would matter very much. "The whole Razor's Guild will be called out to hunt him. And I will be pleased to testify against him, discretion be damned."

"Assuming they bring him back alive."

Emil nodded. There was that. He opened the shutter a crack. There were no Sturgeons or Razors in the little plaza in front of his shop, but once word spread some number would arrive, to lie in wait in case Rene tried again.

"There's nothing we can do," Emil said. "The doors are locked and the windows shuttered. We'll sit tight behind stone walls until the morning, and we'll find safer lodgings then, until his men are all rounded up."

"Thank you, Sir," Mariella said.

She went to her room in the basement, and Emil climbed the stairs to his small room at the top of the building. He checked all the shutters twice and the roof hatch three times before stretching out his bed.

Sleep was impossible. A young woman was dead, and it was his fault that her killer had been set free. Scandal was the best thing that could happen to him, and the worst was to be hung as an accomplice.

After several hours, Emil heard a chair move downstairs. Thinking Mariella must have been having a sleepless night of her own, he went down to find Rene LeCroix sitting at his dining room table, naked blades lying before him.

"Don't try to run," Rene said. "And don't move your hands."

Emil stayed very, very still. "How did you get inside?"

Rene shrugged. "Does it matter? I am here. I've snuck into better defended homes with less motivation than I have tonight."

"It's too late," Emil said. "Even if you kill me, you will be a hunted man in every port from here to Thalonia. What you did is known."

"By whom?" Rene asked. "A pair of stuffy old guardsmen with aching feet and feeble swordplay? They never had the chance to tell anyone." He gestured toward the corner of the room, where a pair of swords identical to those the Sturgeons carried leaned against the wall.

Emil forced himself to take a breath. No one knew what Rene had done. "I must admit, my friend," Rene said, "I underestimated you. Not only because you killed four of my best men, but because you were so damnably right about this potion of yours. My heart is aching with the loss of my bride – sometimes I start weeping uncontrollably. Me! I can't fight off these feelings, even though I know they're counterfeit."

"Because they're not counterfeit."

Rene took a deep, quavering breath and released it. "Be that as it may, this heartache would be reason enough to cut your throat, even if I did not need to silence you. Don't move! You cannot imagine the things I could do to your horse-faced apprentice downstairs. If you try to use a potion or powder on me, I will make her an anvil for my grief. If you let yourself be taken quietly, she will die in her sleep, peacefully." He stood. "So make sure your hands are empty."

"You're right about one thing," Emil said as Rene moved toward him, rapier held high. "I need a potion, fume, powder or salve to make someone fall in love. But I don't need any of that to destroy love."

Emil spoke a short, powerful incantation.

Rene staggered, his sword clattering to the floor. His eyes went wide with horror, and his mouth twisted in revulsion. He cried out in disgust, and then cried out louder.

Emil moved toward him and took his dagger. "Every Human being has a mix of self-love and self-loathing, *my friend*, but your arrogance has been like a suit of armor, has it not? Any self-doubt, and twinge of empathy, any speck of conscience has been swept away and drowned by the deep and abiding love you feel for yourself." Emil moved close to him. "Or should I say the love you *used* to feel for yourself."

"By the Saints," Rene said. "By the Saints, what have I done?"

"You've murdered the only person in this world that you loved, Sir. Have I mentioned that I met her? I didn't recognize you at first, no, but I recognized your wife when you mentioned her family name. She came to me in tears, wounds on her wrist, and twice now I thought I was helping her be rid of you. Sir. To think that you imagined yourself a great man. Sir."

Rene suddenly shuddered as though he wanted to jump out of his skin. "I can't bear it!" he shouted. "I can't bear what I've done! Help me! Please!"

"There's only one thing that will take away your pain," Emil answered, and tossed the dagger onto the table.

Emil backed away and went down into the basement to wake Mariella. She was a strong young woman, and he would need her help to move the corpse.

Illustration by Todd Lockwood

BETWEEN

Todd Lockwood

*T*he Emerald Serpent seethed with everything Torrent hated most about Taux. The Jai-Ruk smelled of dirt and the things dirt covers; the Lowl, when they were in their cups, reeked of dog. The Kin were as inscrutable in their daytime masks as in their nighttime shadows. And the Humans were ever *doing*, never at rest; even in relaxation they gamed or chattered or fought. The whole city stank of wasted lives and frustrated ambitions.

It wore her out. She wanted nothing more than to return to the sea that had given her birth. Her people, the Corsairs, carried the salt of the oceans in their blood. Even at its most torrid the ocean moved with tempo and cadence. It soothed. Uplifted.

It was so close. When the wind blew in from the North, its salty tang cleansed Taux's fetid air.

For the moment, however, she could not escape the stench of Taux. Almost a month ago now, her erstwhile employer, Rene LeCroix, had killed himself over some failed love affair. One of his ships vanished the next morning with half its crew, most of his wealth, and all his officers. The courts impounded the rest of his fleet against the suit of the family whose daughter LeCroix killed before taking his own life. Torrent wouldn't give a hanged cat for any of them, except that cursed Taux now harbored a surplus of seamen and a shortage of berths. She was no swab—her sword was what she sold to any ship that would have her. But that didn't matter. There was no work to be had.

So she found herself in the Emerald Serpent, across a rough plank table from a burly longshoreman with a shaved head, her coin on the table to her right. He hoisted a tankard of ale—his sixth, by Torrent's count—and laughed. "Ye don' look so tough to me, sea sprite! I think you've prolly had a few too many if ye challenge me in me own demesnes!" He gave out a great booming *HAR!* and scanned the tavern for support in his mirth. His companions cheered drunkenly.

Torrent gave him half a smile. "If you doubt my intent, I can increase the ante," she said, placing another silver coatl atop the first.

Together they represented the sum of her wealth.

"I feel sorry for ye, I do, but far be it for me to stop a woman who wants to give her money away." He slapped his tankard down on the planks and extracted two coins from his purse, then arranged them on the opposite side of the table from hers. He leaned across, grinning wickedly. "Because I am a fair man, I might be of a mind to let ye earn your money back afterwards." And he winked, dropping his gaze to her breasts. One of his friends tittered like an old lady.

Sometimes the marks set themselves up. Torrent smiled her most sultry smile. "What makes you think that two silver birds would buy you a night with me?" She leaned closer. His breath stank of garlic and beer. "I'll throw a night with me into the pot if you'll add four more coatls to your stake."

The dock man's eyes grew wider, then squinted in rheumy drunkenness, then wrinkled up with glee. "Y'r on, ye raven minx! Six for your two and a night ye'll ne'er forget!" Clearly enjoying himself. "I knew tonight would be lucky!" He fumbled four more coins out of his purse and stacked them with exaggerated care atop the others.

She gave him the whole smile now, spat in her hand, and held it up for him to clasp. He spat dryly into his own palm, and they grasped each other's thumbs, wrists crossed, elbows planted firmly on the rough-hewn planks. She only needed to mingle his water with hers. The sweat of his palms would be enough, but saliva worked better still.

He didn't know it, but he'd already lost.

The barkeep and de facto referee approached, wiping his hands on his apron. Torrent concentrated on her opponent. She had the touch, same as her mother before her. Perhaps there had been a Wizard somewhere in their ancestry—Torrent didn't know if that was even possible, but unlike Humans, and all but a very few Corsairs, she could manipulate water in small, but meaningful ways.

The dock man's pulse throbbed under her fingers, hurried by alcohol, which only made it easier for her to sense the liquids in his hand, his arm, his shoulder. Liquor had dried him out. This would be simpler than she thought.

The barkeep placed his hand atop theirs. "You'll begin when I say 1, 2, 3, go."

She grinned wider, which made the longshoreman burst into laughter. "Ye cocky wench! I'll have y'r coin in a heartbeat! And then I'll have y'r—"

"1, 2, 3, go!"

The longshoreman's entire arm clenched in a spasm. Torrent slammed the back of his hand to the tabletop and snatched his coins before the first tear of pain squirted out of his eye. He doubled over, clutching his arm to his side. "Me arm cramped!" he insisted, but his friends erupted into jeers and laughter. Torrent took the longshoreman's tankard and held it up, as if to toast him. "Because I am a fair woman, you're welcome to try to win your money back at any time." The dock man shrank beneath new peals of laughter.

She took his tankard to a quieter table in the corner. Normally she'd have made more of a show of it, to entice the next patsy into a match. But her gambit had paid off well enough. She'd won sufficient money to wait out this dead air, to stay fed until new opportunities blew into the harbor.

Hopefully, this wouldn't last longer than another week…

"Up to your old games, eh, Torrent?" She looked up to see dark hair pulled back in a ponytail, a perfectly trimmed goatee, rakish clothes on lean swagger, a charming grin. A familiar sinking feeling hit her stomach.

"Savino. How nice to see you."

The rogue slid into the seat across from her. "I heard you were back in town. Just can't stay away, can you?"

She tried to smile convincingly. "The winds of fate are stalled. I wouldn't be here if I had a choice."

Savino settled back, studying her, allowing his eyes to linger perhaps a little too long. "Ah, but it's good to see you again, my dear water sprite. You look…well. Taux hasn't been the same without you."

"You seem to be getting by just fine."

"It was better when you were here. We were quite the team."

She nodded slowly. "I smell a pitch coming."

Savino laughed, hearty and melodious. His theater background informed his every move. Suave charm came as naturally to him as breathing, and had tempted her more than once.

But she'd given in only once, only to learn that air and water don't always mix. Of all the people Torrent knew in Taux, his winds blew with the most intensity. Dashing, scheming Savino always had an angle, a ploy, a mark. For a time she found it irresistible, and they combined their talents— Torrent's subtle ability to manipulate the water in a body she had touched, and Savino's deceptive swagger and stage artistry. He posed as a duelist, though his skills with the blade derived only from stagecraft, the mock fight. He could never have won an honest fight.

But then, he never engaged in an honest fight. His opponents always seemed to tire quickly, or pass out from the heat, or suffer a painful cramp or blinding migraine at a critical moment. Then he and Torrent shared the winnings—there were always wagers on the side—until finally few would challenge him; his reputation ended many duels before they began.

Eventually Torrent wearied of the game, the stench of the low streets, and the energy it required. She took a position on a LeCroix merchant ship headed to the Carribé, glad to be quit of Taux and its many poisons. The Saints only knew what Savino had been doing in the meantime.

"You read me too well," he smiled.

"So you are up to something."

"Let us say rather that the winds of fate have blown an opportunity your way."

"How did you get by without me?"

He shrugged nonchalantly. "A potion here, bravado there, the convenient accident in other places… I have more tricks than you have curses by which to name me."

She couldn't help but smile at that.

"But when I heard you were back in Taux, I saw a way out of a predicament." His smile vanished, his face fell ever so slightly, if only for a moment—but his normally dark complexion paled, even in the dim lantern light of the Emerald Serpent.

Savino never let his guard down. This could only be bad news.

She leaned toward him. "What have you gotten yourself into?"

Savino never failed for words, either, but his mouth worked against silence.

"That bad, eh? Whose daughter did you bed unknowing?"

She'd meant it to be sarcastic, but Savino whispered, "Yaotl Vash."

Torrent felt the color drain from her own face. "You. Are. Fucked."

"She was slumming it; I had no idea who she was. Raven-haired, like you—"

"You would be wiser to flee town."

"If *you* could leave town, don't you think *I* might have left town?" He swallowed.

"True. Point won. But you have managed to offend the one member of the Vash family who is also a member of the Razor Guild. And no pushover."

"Trust me, I know."

"I won't be able to get near him. Worse, he'll have protections, and bodyguards. How do you think I'm going to perform the old magic?"

Savino squirmed uncomfortably in his seat. "Believe it or not, I have a plan..."

She laughed a gallows laugh. "But of course you do! I hope it's a good one."

He glanced over his shoulder, then leaned closer, his eyes wide with fear... or was it excitement? The two were often joined with Savino. "You have no idea." His eyes twinkled with something that bordered on manic glee.

Her brow pinched into a frown. "I'm listening."

"You won't have to get near him. But you will use your talents, in a way you've never used them before. In fact you won't even be there. Yaotl has summoned me to the Baymourn Bridge at midnight tomorrow. You will be across the harbor by the Whispering Shoals, beyond sight..."

She shuddered. Rumor made the Whispering Shoals a place of slumbering magics better left undisturbed. "By all the Saints, why would I—"

"Just listen. You'll be completely safe. All you have to do is perform one very simple task."

"And that is?"

"You will freeze the harbor, for fifteen minutes between the chime for the watch change and the twelfth bell of the midnight hour. I've timed it out; it works perfectly."

Torrent knew her mouth hung open, but she could not find rationale to wrap around the words he had just spoken. Seeing her astonishment, Savino summoned up his charm and grinned broadly. She shook her head as he broke into nervous laughter.

"Some sort of parasite is eating your brain," she said at last, and Savino laughed all the more.

"I know! It sounds insane. But I have done all my research. There is a way. And as you know, I hate to back down, I hate to lose a fight—"

"You've never *had* a fight—until now. This may be the one that undoes you. I can't help you. I couldn't freeze more than a pail of water, let alone the entire harbor. What you need is a Wizard."

"Ahh, but I have the next best thing; I have you." As Torrent started to shake her head, he reached into his doublet. "And I have this."

He opened his lapel just enough to reveal a canvas bag, out of which peeked a large red gem set in a simple flourish of gold.

"Holy Saint Erik, what is that?" She whispered. The ambient noise no longer seemed sufficient to obscure their conversation.

"It's a focus item, a tome-mage's tool, something that will channel the energies of the Afterglow Sea in major ways... in the right hands. And the right hands, in this situation, dear love, are yours." With an over-the-shoulder glance, he cupped the bag in his two hands and extended it across the table. She took it with equal caution, trembling, and opened the drawstrings. She touched the stone.

Its power struck her like a thunderclap, a deep, pulsing *boom* that roared outside of normal senses. The gem felt hot, but equally and simultaneously cold; fragile, but incomprehensibly strong as well. Its presence expanded to fill the tavern, the way her hands had felt in a fever dream as a child; vast, but empty, light as a feather, but cumbersome and wild. There, but not there.

She'd experienced something like this only once before, not two days ago. A certain lady, Cenoté of the grim mask, stirred Torrent's unease when she saw her from time to time. She sensed the water at the very first sighting. The Lady was almost certainly a Wizard—water knows water. But this particular morning the Lady's litter passed so close that the rush of recognition took Torrent by surprise. The city became illuminated somehow, as if it were a pond, and the ripples in Cenoté's wake revealed glimpses, lens-like, of everything beneath the surface.

So it was now. Glimmers of light moved behind her eyes, in her mind, mingling with threads of black, all tied to something else, a distant glowing source.

In shock, she zipped the drawstrings closed, and hid the bag with her hands. "Where did you get this?"

"Well, you don't really want to know that."

"Then I'm out."

"Torrent, it's for your own protectio—"

"No. Tell me or you're on your own."

Savino started to chortle in nervous humor. "Dethocrates acquired it for me this very night. You remember Thock, right? It used to belong to Pelantus, the Arch Pyromancer to High Man Tlacolotl Vash himself!"

Torrent could only stare in disbelief.

"The irony is so rich I can barely stand it. As far as the Vash family knows, it was destroyed in the mess yesterday—what a miracle that was! I might almost believe I am beloved of the gods. " He winked. "We'll use Tlacolotl's tool to defeat his own nephew Yaotl."

Torrent pushed the bag back across the table at him. "No. Sorry. I'm not messing with the Vashes."

"Torrent—they know nothing about the fate of the gem. When this is over, we can do whatever you like: sell it, return it… or ransom it back to them for another hefty turn of coin."

"No. No chance. You're in way over your head this time, breeze-for-brains."

Savino left the bag on the table where it lay. "Oh Torrent, Torrent. Don't you see what you're passing up? Dethocrates is already laying wagers on our behalf. We are going to make So. Much. Coin. You'll be able to buy a ship of your own. How would that be, to put back to sea, in your own craft for a change? To be your own master?"

"Oh, there's that tongue of yours again…"

"I know you're not happy here. Look at you: trapped between the jungle and the sea, between your last meal and your next scam. You never even made up your mind between men or women."

She glared at him.

"You're stuck *between*, Torrent. Your whole existence here is between one thing you hate and another you can't have. This is your chance to break free."

She studied the tabletop in front of her, blood pounding in her ears. Carved graffiti covered it, years of defilement that echoed the frenzied life of Taux. *Increase Coin is a faggot* said one. Another offered only an address below crudely scratched naked breasts—a come-on from a street prostitute. A regular pattern of nicks and gouges suggested games of *finger fillet*, complete with bloodstains. It was all Taux: ugly, disrespectful, filthy, brazen.

In the center of the table sat the little bag. She had to admit, she wanted to touch the thing again.

"What makes you think this item will work for me?"

"It only needs a conduit. It won't work for me. It requires someone who can touch the Afterglow. Torrent, you do it almost without thought. It might not do for you everything it did for that little red pustule, Pelantus, but anything you can do with water, it will amplify. That's its job; to take your intention, connect it to the Afterglow, and make it real."

"Why the Whispering Shoals?"

He squirmed. "Situated strategically, in case the range of your magic is limited. Taking no chances, but keeping you out of harm's way."

"And when I do this deed for you—what happens? Why freeze the harbor?"

Savino's odd humor left again, and the ashen fear touched him. "Let me worry about that, won't you? If I told you, you wouldn't believe me—"

"It's harder to believe than…than…" She indicated Savino, the bag "… all of this?"

He laughed again, but this time without the theatrical pretense. It was the first genuine laugh she'd heard from him tonight. Perhaps ever. "It's probably better if you don't know. I have it all worked out. All you have to do is your small part. You have tomorrow to practice with the focus item and to get in position."

She scowled, watching the bag on the table as if it might jump into her lap.

"Please, Torrent. I'm begging you!"

A shadow fell across the table, and she looked up.

"I'll have another go, ye cheating hussy. And this time we'll not be spitting into our hands." The dock man stretched and curled his arm, still working off the cramp she'd given him. "And I'll have me tankard back. That wasn't part of me stake."

Torrent sighed and handed it to him.

"That's more like it," he said, and took a long swallow. "Now bring me coin and set y'r fine ass down at the match table." He leaned close, his sweaty face mere inches from hers. "It's not y'r coin ye'll reclaim on your back tonight, but my good will."

Torrent had done more than drink from the man's tankard. She'd spit in it, too. She touched his sweaty arm for just a moment, feeling the water in his body and all its courses. He groaned suddenly, and then a look of horror elongated his face as a wet stain spread across the front of his trousers and a blast of wet air ripped behind him.

He fled the tavern as quickly as his hunched gait would allow, but the hot odors of urine and loose feces filled the air. Pointing fingers and jeers chased him out.

Savino held his sides and howled with laughter, but Torrent's face burned.

She plucked the bag off the table and slid it into her doublet.

Even though she headed out early, it took Torrent most of the next day to cross the city of Taux. The vibrant quarters were all within walking distance, but the westward arm of the harbor was a good hike away. As she passed the final empty, disheveled quay adjacent to the paupers' quarter, she realized sunset would be upon her soon, the night half done before she would return to the Black Gate district.

That wouldn't do. She wanted a place to rest after this evening's work, and a place to get her mind focused beforehand. That meant finding a night's lodging in the poor district. Not a pleasant prospect—its denizen's named it the Ghost Quarters for a reason—but it couldn't be helped.

Unemployed sailors haunted the poor quarter, but Torrent found a waterfront hostel facing the stony expanse of the Baymourn Bridge—the very spot Yaotl Vash had chosen to exact satisfaction from Savino. She understood the choice: it was isolated, connecting only the very poor to ruins that held nothing any sane person would desire. There would be little risk of the Sturgeons—or anyone else that mattered—witnessing their illegal duel here.

But that was later. First things first.

Two coppers secured a bed. The innkeeper, a wiry old Jai-Ruk woman, led her up rickety stairs to a small room containing only a hard bench for a bed, a nightstand with a clay ewer of water beside a metal washbowl, a cracked chamber pot in the corner, and a vanishing scurry of cockroaches. Torrent thanked her, tipped her another copper for a promise of privacy, and closed the door.

A single window looked out across the channel to the harbor island beyond. The Whispering Shoals were at the far end, on the point of the island. Beyond, she could just make out the Temple of the Sun in distant haze. Savino's answer to her question, *Why the Shoals?*, leapt into her thoughts: *Situated strategically, in case the range of your magic is limited.* The Whispering Shoals were across the harbor from the Baymourn Bridge; how was that the center of his little operation? Surely his plans didn't involve the Temple of the Sun… that would be true insanity.

No, no, she corrected herself, that would be Savino.

Blessed Saints, what have I gotten myself into?

For some reason, she kept picturing Savino's charming smile… meeting her fist.

She closed the window shutter. It was time to experiment with this magical stone. She poured some water into the washbasin, no more than a cup or two. First: a test with her own, native abilities, for comparison's sake. She dipped her finger in and concentrated on making it freeze. After a few seconds it grew extremely cold; she swished her finger once and ice crystals formed, streaking away from her finger. Within a second the water froze solid. She nodded, pulling her finger out and leaving a digit-shaped hole. With another small bit of effort, she thawed it again. After some consideration, she poured the rest of the water from the ewer into the basin.

Then she took the bag containing the stone from her belt, held it, stared at it. Finally, she wiped a bead of sweat from her brow and pulled the drawstring open.

The ruby pulsed with a subtle illumination, like a cat's eye in dim light. She didn't recall it glowing last night. Interesting. Even without touching it, a taught feeling of *potential* rippled through her skin, at once exhilarating and terrifying. She held her breath. Could it really be as easy as Savino made it sound? Pulling one of the drawstring loops over her wrist, she stuck two fingers into the bag and touched the stone.

Instantly the roar of cold, untapped possibility surrounded her senses, as if she had plunged into a deep and turbulent pool. The close walls of her tiny room retreated, the space between filled with swirling shapes like heat shimmer. At the boundaries of her perception were flames, air, stone. They were beyond her reach—perhaps someone else with a different connection to the Afterglow could have touched them. But water presented itself everywhere: in the air, coating every surface, permeating every pore of fabric or leather. Once again she sensed more than saw the tendrils of light connecting all to a luminous source.

With shaking hand, she reached toward the water in the basin again.

Before she'd quite formed the thought or touched the surface, it hardened with a crack; the bowl rang as swirls and florets of frost dashed up the sides, inside and out, across the tabletop, ending with a snap against walls suddenly dusted with glistening ice.

With a cry of surprise, she dropped the stone, and it dangled in its little bag from her wrist.

"Saint Erik's balls!"

Bright motes of crystallized water hung in the air, and her exposed skin stung with the bite of cold. At the same time, she felt a light twinge in her right arm, the slightest of aches. She shook it off, but made note of it. *What price does the "conduit" pay for channeling such energies?*

She had no idea what sort of power she dealt with here. Did Savino? What made him think she could freeze the entire harbor? Was he mad?

Ha… No more than she was for trusting him. Her stomach churned with that old sinking feeling again; too often in the past Savino's machinations had led her into trouble.

She imagined his smile. She imagined her fist.

She pulled the drawstring closed again, poked the bag into her shirt, and took a deep breath. The sun would be down soon, and she wanted to get there early. Perhaps she could experiment again with a tidal pool…

As she pulled the door to the hall closed behind her, voices rose from the entry below.

"Ye can't bring that… that whatever it is in here." The old Jai-Ruk woman said.

"Step aside, old girl," said a husky male voice—gravelly, like another Jai-Ruk. "We're only going to have a look around."

"You're not Sturgeons, you can't tell me what to do."

Scuffling noises.

The old woman, angry now, said, "You pay to go up these stairs! No coin, no stairs!"

"Out of the way, hag," another voice, with the growling tonality of a Lowl.

Something crashed, and Torrent pressed back against the wall. The old woman shouted a name, and more footsteps clomped into the room. "What's going on here?"

A shout, a stifled groan, and a scream. A crunch. Something heavy fell to the floor.

Then silence.

Followed by strange snuffling, dry and raspy.

"What did you do that for, road-filth?" The Jai-Ruk voice. "They weren't going to—"

"Shush," said the Lowl. "Look, the dweoler have picked up the scent again."

Torrent stiffened. *The what?*

She slipped back into her room as quietly as possible, closed and barred the door, then listened as footsteps creaked on the stairs, accompanied by scrabbling and clacking. They paused outside and for a few moments she heard only that sickly snuffle.

She pushed the shutter on the window aside and swung her leg over the sill. As she dropped down to the street below she heard the door crash open and the rattle of debris. She hit the ground, rolled, sprang to her feet and dashed to the side. At the corner of the building she pressed flat against the wall and chanced a look back around the corner.

A Jai-Ruk head stuck out the window and looked down the street in the other direction, then two Lowl poked their heads out too, scanning both ways. One of them pointed and shouted, "There!" Torrent cursed and dashed down the side street as a cry erupted behind.

"Whitey!" Shouted the Jai-Ruk. There came a more distant answer, then, "We've got something!" More shouts came from the direction of the Ghost Quarter, and crashing from inside the hostel. Torrent ran for the closest narrow alley and ducked in, bowling over a beggar as he shook his cup. She turned left in another alley—a dead end—spun about and hurried across the other way.

At a juncture she paused in deep shadow, crouching behind a rain barrel. Pounding footfalls approached, then two Jai-ruk and a Lowl sped past the far intersection. Black livery: Vash colors. These were Tlacolotl Vash's goons.

How many of them were there? And what in Saint Erik's codpiece was a *dweoler*? They must have been right on her heels all day long. *The dweoler have picked up the scent again*, the Lowl had said. The scent of what? Tlacolotl couldn't know anything about her...

The scent of *magic*?

As soon as the word crossed her mind, she knew it must be true. Whatever the dweoler were, they knew the "scent" of Pelantus' gem. They were tracking it.

She pulled the ties on her sword, releasing it. *Please, good Saint Erik: if you truly love vagabonds and scoundrels, let there not be a tome-mage among them.*

A glance at the sky showed orange clouds and the evening flight of crows. The sun had set; soon it would be dark. She couldn't play cat and mouse all night in the Ghost Quarter—she needed to get across the Baymourn and down to the Whispering Shoals. But she had to shake these vermin first.

The sounds of pursuit dwindled, so Torrent tiptoed down the alley to the next juncture and peeked around the corner.

"Here!" cried a Lowl, not forty feet away, and charged. Another came from between two wagons and joined him.

Torrent sprinted back the way she'd come, but two more Lowl spied her from the far end of the street and came running. She ducked into a side alley, only to find another dead end.

She pulled her slender, curved sword and readied her stance. Footfalls thundered closer as she studied her surroundings, planning her defense. Cramped, her only cover the...

Rain barrel!

With all her strength she heaved against it, tipping it, slowly at first, but then spilling it all into the intersection of the two streets. As the first of the Lowl charged from her right, she knelt down and touched the water in the road with the knuckles of her sword hand, while sticking fingers of her left hand into the bag with the gem in it.

Freeze, she thought, as her sensory world expanded.

The two Lowl tried to turn the corner, but slipped and fell on the sudden skating rink and slid into the legs of the other pair rushing in from her left. She ran the nearest through as he struggled to rise, ripped her blade free, spun, slashed through the neck of another as he lurched to his feet. The remaining two were entangled, the one on top with his sword arm on the ground, seeking leverage. Torrent pinned his blade with her boot as she stabbed the Lowl beneath him, then let go her sword long enough to grab his face. With a thought, all the water in his head boiled. He dropped without a cry, steam hissing out of his nose, mouth, ears, and eyes.

Panting, she pulled her blade free, shaking her head in disbelief at what had just happened. Her right arm ached, and her fingers stung from contact with boiling flesh. More running footfalls and shouts spurred her to action. As she ran down a fourth way, she pulled the loops of the drawstrings around her wrist and stuck her entire left hand into the bag with the stone. When she needed it, she could grab it. Until then she would let it dangle just out of reach.

She imagined Savino's smile, missing teeth.

She moved cautiously in the direction of the bridge, pausing at every intersection to peek around for her pursuers. Stars began to flicker awake in the deepening sky before she made it back to the waterfront, where only an open courtyard separated her from the bridge. She pressed back against a wall as the watch bells began to chime from the far end of Taux. Listening for tramping feet, she counted the peals. …seven…eight…nine…

Nine bells. Time grew very short. She should have been halfway to the Shoals by now.

There was nothing for it. She sprinted toward the bridge. A cry, another cry, then footfalls and a clacking rattle. Torrent glanced back over her shoulder as she reached the Baymourn Bridge. Two Jai-Ruk and a Lowl raced across the courtyard, led by an abomination that made her gasp in horror.

The dweoler ran with a strange, loping gate on all fours, arms longer than its legs, the body and limbs like twisted driftwood bound together with thorny vines. Long spikes protruded from shoulders and knees, arms and thighs, and from the knuckles of the hands or forefeet, like talons. For a head it bore the skull of a dog or Lowl, bound to the misshapen torso by more entangling vines. A construct of magic, a golem.

And it gained quickly, outpacing the other Vash toughs—halfway across the bridge as Torrent reached the island. She wouldn't outrun it, but this was no place to make a stand. She dashed for the lip of the high-tide plateau and leapt in desperation to the beach fifteen feet below. The wet sand, hard as stone, drove her knees into her chest and the breath from her lungs.

She scrabbled to her feet as the dweoler tumbled down the steep earthen embankment after her. Jai-Ruk appeared on the top but paused to look for a way down. The Lowl passed them and jumped without hesitation, as the Jai-Ruk called back to more Vash men somewhere behind.

Torrent gasped in a breath of air and dashed for a tide pool in the rocks ahead. She splashed through it to the far side and turned even as the dweoler leapt into the water. Pulling her feet clear, she gripped the gemstone and froze the pond instantly, trapping the creature in mid stride by one forelimb. It flipped forward, crunching onto the ice.

She'd intended to freeze it along with the pond, but wood and bone contained no water to freeze. A thin shell of ice shattered off its surface as it struggled upright again, tugging on its trapped limb. Dog-skull jaws snapped and bit without voice. Runes were carved into every surface of its flesh, even on the skull; those around and inside its nasal cavity were filled with paint and precious metals. It scratched and clawed at the ice, trying to pull free and claim its prize.

The Lowl caught her eye, skirting the pond on her right. She backed to a smaller puddle and dipped her left hand, bag and all, into the water. The Lowl slowed uncertainly, eyes darting between Torrent and the dweoler. He turned his head slightly, keeping Torrent in sight, and shouted "Whitey!" An answering holler came from beyond the lip of the plateau. "She's down h—" Torrent swung her arm up and out of the puddle, sending a thick fountain of water toward him. It turned to steam as it reached his face and he screamed in pain and anger, but Torrent's blade ended his cry before he could clear his eyes.

She left the dweoler thrashing on the ice and moved along the beach. Rocks broke the shoreline, but she sprinted along every sandy stretch. She needed to recover lost time; the tide rolled in quickly. Soon she would be forced to abandon the beach and join "Whitey" on the high ground above.

She pressed on, gasping for breath, both her arms throbbing. At last, forced to catch her breath and shake out her arms, she slumped against a boulder to assess her situation. She pulled her hand out of the bag and looked inside. The gem glowed clearly, brightly. It definitely hadn't done that last night, and not to this degree earlier in the evening. That both confused and alarmed her. What did Savino know about this thing that he hadn't told her?

From across the harbor, ten bells sounded.

She pushed herself forward again. The Ghost moon provided just enough light to navigate by, but the path became difficult as the high tide rolled in and the shoreline grew rockier. Finally, with some trepidation she found a spot to scramble back up over the embankment to the island proper. There were no Jai-Ruk or Lowl in sight, and no dweoler, praise the Saints! Ruins crowded the shoreline —plazas of tightly knit pavers now overgrown with grass and creepers. Stone buildings covered with intricate carvings of odd, square-headed beasts, feathered serpents, men dressed as spotted cats bearing weapons lined with shark's teeth. Vines crawled over everything; the jungle already tried to reclaim this land.

An ancient road followed the shoreline where the waves hadn't undermined it. She made better time, always listening for the sounds of pursuit. Where were they? No doubt still close on her heels, for as long as the dweoler snuffled for a scent of the gem.

Sooner than she expected it, from Taux eleven bells rang.

With a curse, she picked up her pace. The headlands drew near as the moon put the Star Tower into silhouette above her. Impossibly tall, it whorled out of the center of the harbor like a waterspout cast in stone, seamless and featureless as blown glass.

The Wizards inside would have a great view of the show she put on… if she succeeded. Not a comforting thought.

At long last she sprinted along the narrow strip of the headland toward the Whispering Shoals. The end was in sight. Waves caressed the stony tip of the island, which broke up into smaller isolated rocks and islets. At low tide they'd be pillars marching into the mouth of the inlet. Now, at high tide, they barely surmounted the level of the sea. She had seen them from the decks of ships many times, on entering or leaving Taux, but standing here now she became aware that they weren't entirely natural. The tops were perfectly flat, the sides almost perfectly vertical. All were covered with more of the carvings and runic decorations that marked the buildings of Taux. The promontory – even without the embellishments – would have served the harbor as a seabreak; the purpose of the runes defied knowing.

And then she heard the whispers.

As each gentle wave receded from the rock faces, voices murmured. More than the mere hissing of foam and spray, they spoke in a lost tongue, or in many at once, ghostlike. She half expected to see shapes in the mist of each wave. It soothed in a way she didn't expect… or perhaps *soothed* wasn't the right word. Entranced… Or beguiled… She could nearly sense what they…

The clattering gait of the dweoler broke through her reverie.

She spun even as it leapt at her. She ducked, but one thorny paw raked her shoulder, catching her doublet and pulling her over. The creature tumbled as well but sprang lightly to its feet, then charged at her again. She stabbed, but her sword did no more than nick a thorn from its driftwood torso. The golem drove her to the stone, clawing her legs, tearing at her doublet. She held its bony jaws from her face with the hilt of her sword, but the teeth raked her hand and snagged on her sleeve. She rolled over and gained the upper position, leapt clear, sidestepped as it charged again, hacked at the beast, but with a weapon designed for flesh, not wood.

Her elemental magic seemed equally useless—the thing contained no water she could manipulate. She crouched, sword leveled, as it circled her. As much in desperation as anything, she took the moment to thrust her left hand into the bag with the gem again, though she didn't know what she would do with it.

As before, the link to the Afterglow exploded in her mind, enhancing her kinship with water. And suddenly she understood the voices in the Whispering Shoals: not ghosts, but water elementals, bound to the rocks. They spoke to the waves in a language of rain, and tides, and deep currents. Even all these decades after the disappearance of the Tolimic people they guarded the harbor, bound by some arcane and ancient covenant. Though she didn't know the words, through the agency of Palentus' gem and her own ties to the sea, she perceived the intent. They negotiated with the seas, calming the swells as they rounded the seabreak.

Inspiration struck her. She focused on the water in the harbor, allowing her sense of the elemental language to inform the shape of her will.

She ran across the surface of the waves.

The dweoler sprang after her, but splashed into the water. Torrent stopped on the first of the islets and turned. The golem, clearly not designed for swimming, clawed at the water and would surely have sunk were it not made of wood. She knelt, touched the surface, and caused the waves to dash it against the rocks until only splinters of bone and wood remained.

She collapsed, her arms and legs and mind throbbing with pain. She wanted to release the stone, but she knew she wasn't done.

The water told her that a boat approached, and she looked up. From the direction of the harbor island came a rowboat bearing two Lowl, three or more Jai-Ruk, and a dweoler perched at the prow like a dog on a carriage ride. Every dip of their oars caused the elementals to chatter. A Human stood behind in the billowing robes of a tome-mage, all in white, with an astounding shock of white hair standing straight up from his head. *Gods, what else would you call such an ostentatious poof but "Whitey?"*

She walked out across the swells to the furthest islet, arriving as the Ghost moon attained its zenith directly overhead. Torrent looked around to see that where she now stood aligned almost perfectly with the Temple of the Sun on her right, the Wizards' Star Tower to her left, and with the Black Gate across the harbor in Taux. Coincidence? The water didn't know, but it thought not. She looked into the bag; the gem now glowed so brightly she averted her eyes. Whatever else was true about the Whispering Shoals, they were a power nexus of formidable scope.

She kneeled down to wait. The boat bobbed closer and closer. She might yet have to contend with these pests the hard way.

Then came the chime from the city, a single bell that marked the changing of the guard.

11:45, and all's not at all well.

She focused her mind, asked the ocean for aid and forgiveness, and touched the water.

Power exploded through her body, in every direction outward. The harbor boomed as a circle of ice fled from her touch like a tidal wave. The stone under her feet shivered. Pain gripped her and she cried out. The ice crackled and shone, heaving as the deep currents beneath it were disrupted by the expansion. She hung her head and braced herself with her other hand, desperately clinging to her equilibrium. She started to shiver with the exertion, quelled it only through force of will by crying out again. She lost her balance, expected to fall into the harbor, but landed on ice, pushed herself upright, gasping. Somewhere behind her the ocean ice heaved and cracked. Looking up, she saw whole sections of harbor ice lifted up as if something gigantic moved beneath, in the direction of Taux.

It finally occurred to her to check on the progress of the Lowl, the Jai-ruk, the dweoler, and Whitey.

They'd left their boat locked in the ice and approached on foot. Whitey and his minions tested each step; the dweoler scrabbled frantically in a mechanical need to run, even though its feet weren't designed for such a slick surface. They would be upon her soon.

Hang on a little longer, she told herself. *Savino is depending on you.*

But the dweoler made progress too quickly, and now Whitey shouted with joy; he'd spotted her at last in the darkness, and reached into his robes.

"Oh, fuck all," said Torrent, removing her hands from the ice.

With another thunderous crack, a black tide of unfrozen water raced away from her position like a wave. Whitey, the dweoler, and all his henchmen dropped into the harbor. The instant they were all submerged, she plunged her hands back into the swells and pushed the ice outward again. Pain bludgeoned her every sense as a third stupendous boom shook the harbor, but she maintained concentration, encouraged by the whispers, buoyed by mere contact with the sea. She hoped that temporary hiccup wouldn't destroy Savino's carefully laid plan.

Then a blessed sound: the first peal of the midnight bells.

"*Saint Erik be praised*," she panted.

The second bell rang out. Twelve o'clock, and all is weird.

Thumping noises caused her to look up; a Lowl banged on the underside of the ice, eyes wide, cheeks distended.

Three bells…

She noted that ice encased Whitey's head. His shock of white hair stuck up above the surface like an odd desert plant. Below the ice he didn't move at all.

The dog skull of the dweoler also protruded above the ice, jaws still snapping. With a thought and a little concentration, she moved the tides and ripped the body off of it from below and tore it apart.

The bells pealed. She began to shake. Eight bells? No, nine.

The Lowl floated face-up beneath the ice. Jai-Ruk were notoriously bad swimmers, sadly for them, and she saw no sign.

The Afterglow roared in her mind. Anguish coursed through her arms and legs.

The twelfth bell rang. Torrent released the stone and collapsed upon the rock.

She awoke to whispers. The Blood Moon now hung low in the west. She smelled the sea floor and knew the tide had gone out again. The actual sandy shoals would be visible now.

All her muscles screamed when she sat up and stretched, rotating her shoulders, flexing her arms. Without the gem in her hand, it seemed odd that the whispers were merely strange noises, imparting no wisdom, stripped of their beguilement. She opened the bag and pulled the stone out. Not only had it lost its inner glow, it didn't penetrate her awareness or crash into her senses. She'd heard that some tome-mage's foci were good for but a single use, while others could be recharged, and a rare few would recharge themselves over time. This one was clearly spent, for now at least.

Whatever kind of focusing tool it was, Tlacolotl wanted the thing back badly enough to send two constructs, a mage, and a small army in search of it.

Perhaps more than one.

Vash would keep looking; she knew that with certainty. Should she give it back to him? Dispose of it?

Or keep it?

Her first instinct was to fling it as far out into the harbor as she could. But it certainly had been a useful thing last night. A self-recharging magical gem… She shook her head. The Vash family never forgave. She might well need it again. If she had been trapped *between* before, she was deeply, deeply *between* now.

Torrent sighed heavily. It was still a damned big ruby, if nothing else. She would keep it for the time being, and figure out what to tell Savino.

Savino…She couldn't begin to imagine how all of this related to a Razor's duel. *I wonder how he made out*, she thought.

She found enough toe and finger holds in the rock face to climb down to the sandy bar below. She saw no sign of Whitey or his retinue, though the dweoler skull lay half buried in the sediment. She crushed it under her boot and started toward shore.

Walking helped to work the stiffness out. Soon she felt better.

I hope Savino is alive and well, she thought.

She balled a fist up at her side unconsciously.

She wanted so badly to see his smile.

Illustration by Jeff Laubenstein

VENTURE

Juliet E. McKenna

Zhada woke to luxuriate in the warmth of his feather mattress in this coolest season of the year. As usual stirring among the four-storey tenement's other inhabitants had roused him. Other races talking and moving quietly – above or below – was still more than loud enough to cock a sleeping Lowl's sharp ears.

He rolled over and looked at the gear he had set ready the previous evening. Sturdy thigh boots stood beside his backpack by his room's bolted door, leather breeches and a long-sleeved jerkin draped over it, with a clean shirt and underlinen on top and his sword and dagger laid on the floorboards.

Zhada threw off the coverlet and sat up. Rising, he took a step towards his washstand before recollecting himself. He crossed to the broad-silled window instead and looked into the earthenware pot standing there. Passing a hand over its wide neck reassured him that all was well. The gentle heat he had summoned within it was holding constant, palpably warmer than the air in the room. He breathed a silent prayer in, his mother tongue, to Vitcoska, demon queen of the Crucible's molten crater, the greatest of the fiery mountains watching over ancestral Lowl islands:

"My fervent thanks for granting your chosen people a spark of your Elemental Fire. I ask for your blessings on my quest."

He washed and dressed, brushing his black fur and slicking down an unruly tuft between his ears with wet fingers. Locking his door, he made his way down the stairs and along the hallway.

Mistress Talleran saw him through the kitchen's open door. "Master Jada!"

Like most Humans, she could only manage an approximation of Lowl names. Unlike all-too-many in the city's more prosperous and orderly districts on the other side of the Black Gate, she didn't assume that just because the Lowl looked like a Human with a dog's head, that they had no more wits than such an animal.

"Will you take some breakfast?" She bustled around the well-scrubbed table. "Will you be wanting dinner this evening?"

Ducking his head politely, Zhada settled for answering her first question. "No thank you. I go to call on a friend, and will eat there."

"You can take the edge off your hunger as you walk." She hurried after him to the double-fronted building's entrance, pressing a folded and fried pastry into his hand.

"Thank you." He ducked his head again as he opened the door and went down the steps. He passed the sunhawk-carved pillar left by the priests who'd once shared the tenement, and strode through the crowds in the lane leading towards the practice ball courts.

The brooding bulk of the Ullamalitzli Stadium rose beyond them. A veil of mist softened the topmost towers and hid the hovels and hucksters' stalls now built on the terraces where tens of thousands of the original inhabitants of Taux had once watched the fast and furious game played.

The Emerald Serpent loomed larger as he walked towards it. It was Zhada's destination, though he had no interest in watching any ball games on either side. While he had watched a few contests, both in his younger days and since he'd returned to the city, it couldn't compare to the thrill of a Lowl hunt, pursuing spiral-horned elk for endless leagues across the vast plain far to the north.

Perhaps the sport had had more meaning when it was played under the auspices of the priests who had once ruled this sacred district, in the days before the inexplicable disappearance of all the city's inhabitants left Taux empty and open to whoever dared profane its mysteries and brave its lingering ghosts.

Zhada was heading instead for the Serpent, first and most famous of all the Black Gate's taverns. Whoever had first claimed that half of the long viewing palace had known a trick or two about keeping customers coming back even more readily than they visited the neighboring Silk Purse and that house's fragrant courtesans.

The pastry triangle in Zhada's hand was still warm and plump with hotly spiced meat and fruit. He wolfed it down, relishing the bite of the pepper pods. So much Human food was tediously bland to Lowl tastes, but Mistress Talleran was Taux-born and accustomed to using all the Free Coast's bounty in her cooking.

"Here comes a hound for hire!"

Zhada halted as he rounded the corner into the wider thoroughfare called the Silver Circle that ran the full interior of the stadium's centre.

"Varrach." He let his hand rest lightly on the hilt of his sword. "Don't you find the day a little chilly?"

Like the rest of his followers, Varrach was shirtless despite the season. Zhada noted that three more had now followed his lead and gone under the needle for tattoos. At first glance the ink extended the Lowl pelt covering their heads and necks right across their Human-framed shoulders and down their chests. A closer look would show they were no more furred than any particularly hairy Human.

He also saw Varrach's gaze drop to check that knotted ribbons secured his sword's hilt to its scabbard, to signal that Zhada had no intention of duelling today.

The tan-furred Lowl squared his impressively muscled shoulders and stared straight into Zhada's eyes. "I choose not to soothe the Humans' fears through wearing their clothes."

"Then shouldn't you be going bare arsed?" Zhada's riposte was as swift as any blade.

Varrach clenched a fist beside his tattered ulama trousers, the loose cotton fabric cut short above his knees and bare feet. "And throw the ball straight into the Merchant Guild's hands? Their Sturgeons would chain me like a cur in their lock-up for goading Humans into unsanctioned fighting. Who would challenge their claim on this city then?"

"But you don't care to challenge them in their own language." Zhada interrupted with a gesture towards the men and women walking past, fewer than half of them sparing curious glances for this exchange in incomprehensible, Lowl speech.

Varrach's scarred muzzle wrinkled as he drew dark lips back from his canine teeth. "I have nothing to say to such stunted specimens, as good as deaf and noseless."

Zhada cocked his head. "Why do you feel so threatened when Vitcoska's blessing has given us so many advantages over them? She chose to form us from Humanity. Doesn't denying that kinship insult her? Don't you see it every time you look in a mirror?"

Truth be told, he wasn't speaking to Varrach now but to the pack of younger Lowl loitering behind him. He noticed that a couple of those fool pups had done something to their eyes. No longer manlike, their gaze was as dark and featureless as any beast's.

The fur on the back of Zhada's neck bristled with irritation. He took an angry step towards the closest, ready to grab his scruff and shake some sense into him. "What are you going to do next? Cut off your thumbs so you're left with useless paws and start scurrying around on all fours?"

Varrach moved to intercept him, both fists clenched. Zhada halted. He didn't have time to waste on this nonsense or on trying to explain himself to the city's blue-liveried guards.

Taking a swift sidestep to wrong foot Varrach, he went on his way without another word.

Taken by surprise, the tan-furred Lowl settled for shouting a last insult. "Be sure they reward you richly for putting their leash round your neck!"

Zhada ignored him, lengthening his stride. He didn't want to be late for his meeting and the sun had already risen above the vast stadium. He hurried into its shadow, heading straight for the Emerald Serpent.

When he entered the tavern , he saw Lareo already deep in conversation with some Human. Zhada approached nevertheless, to make sure that the aging Eldaryn had seen him. The diminutive individual was barely two thirds the height of most Humans, even sitting on his tall stool.

Catching the Human's scent, the Lowl's nostrils flared. Magic. A Tome Mage. One of those cheats peddling magic-wrought fakery on the basis of some supposed kinship with true Wizards. As if such mountebanks had any link with those scholars who lived unseen in the Star Tower across the harbor!

"Zhada, good day to you." Lareo waved to him over the Human's shoulder.

The Lowl shucked his backpack and dropped it on the floor to land with a solid thud. The man turned around in his chair, startled.

"Good day." His smile widened. "Ah, I am looking for one of your kinsmen. Do you know a—" he hesitated "—one called Durrau?"

Zhada had the tome mage's measure in an instant. Newly arrived in the city from one of the New Kingdoms, probably Dravaria. While he'd have heard of Lowl he'd never have seen one beyond the seas. He didn't know how to pronounce their names, just as he didn't realise that Zhada now baring his teeth was nothing akin to a Human smile.

"No." He barely managed not to snarl the word.

"No matter," the mage assured him. "Perhaps you might be interested in my wares?" He reached into a pocket. "An amulet of illusion, to let you walk the wider city without drawing undue attention," he explained with feigned delicacy. "Anyone looking at you will see a wholly Human visage—"

"You'll excuse me, Master Mage, but my friend and I have urgent business." Lareo spoke quickly, before Zhada could snap his furious refusal. "I will be in touch," he promised.

"Good day to you." Zhada leaned over the mage with unmistakeable menace.

"Good day, good sirs!" As the mage slid out of his seat and backed away, Zhada smelled the tang of fear in his sweat.

He was tempted to take a swift step after him, to bark a savage Lowl curse, maybe even see if a full-throated howl would make the charlatan piss himself.

"You're late," Lareo observed, sliding his eyeglasses down his sharp nose to peer over their tortoiseshell frames.

Zhada took the vacant seat, the impulse to pursue the mage fading as the man fled. "Varrach." He knew he needed to give no more explanation. He frowned. "Is that fraud selling his tricks to those tattooed fools?"

Tome mages had no shame, so why wouldn't they sell one deceit to the Lowl who wished to look more like a beast while selling another to those like Durrau who had inexplicably become ashamed of their dual nature.

"What? Oh, no." Lareo adjusted his eyeglasses with a long nailed finger and opened the rosewood coffer on the table beside him; a marvel of unfolding drawers and cantilevered trays. He found a little silk drawstring bag and shook two shining discs into his wrinkled palm. "See? Just colored slips of glass worn inside the eyelids."

Zhada winced at that notion as Lareo replaced the pointless trinkets. "Swear you won't tell that leech where to find Durrau?"

The Eldaryn leaned back and folded his arms. "Why should I forego a finder's fee?"

His eyebrows bristled, as bushy and fiery red as Zhada remembered them, even if recent years had seen Lareo's hair fade from burnished copper to pale gold.

"Wouldn't it be better for Durrau to buy a harmless illusion," the Eldaryn continued before Zhada could reply, "instead of succumbing to worse temptation, to be found dead in a midden like Calouf?"

Zhada had no answer to that, choked by recollection of the young Lowl who'd sworn to all and sundry that a true Wizard had promised to transform him entirely. The following day he'd been found, lifeless, vilely poisoned.

"I thought we were here to do business ourselves." Lareo grumbled.

"We are. Do you have the map?" Zhada made sure to speak sufficiently slowly to pronounce the word properly. The *m* sound wasn't as problematic as the *b* and *p* sounds that littered the Human language but it still didn't come naturally to a Lowl.

"I do." Lareo made no move to produce it though. "If you're still sure you want it. I have any number of merchant houses and trading guildsmen who would pay you handsomely to sign on as their guard captain. You've built a reputation since the start of the year that men with ten times your experience must envy."

"And those traders would doubtless give you a handsome finder's fee." Zhada's long jaw sagged and his tongue lolled in a Lowl's true smile, to show Lareo that he meant no insult. "Forgive me, old friend, for not filling your coin chest further."

"You'll give taking such a hire some thought though, when you come back?" Lareo persisted. "And make sure you come back safe, you fool pup," he added roughly, "otherwise your father will eat me for breakfast and your mother will crack my bones for marrow for her supper!"

"I will watch every step I take and return whole," Zhada assured him, "as long as you give me that map," he added pointedly.

Lareo sighed. He opened the bottommost tray of his cunning coffer and took out a folded parchment. "The quickest routes and the safest paths when you get there, as far as anything can be considered safe."

His hand rested on the open drawer, one leathery finger tapping something still within it. "I can offer you a little more help?"

Zhada glimpsed an Eldaryn firestick. Not magic, whatever the Humans believed. Eldaryn alchemists mingled sulphur from the Crucible's crater with charcoal and saltpetre to make their famed black powder. Tamped down inside the long hollow of a firestick, the substance could hurl a deadly lead pellet the length of an ulama court with lethal speed, once an Eldaryn's element ignited it.

Their race's innate spark of Fire was far stronger than any Lowl's. Shortest and slightest of all the peoples found on any sea's coast, the Eldaryn had long since devised various ways to level the odds so often stacked against them.

"The Candon could still be dangerous," Lareo urged, "even if they're supposed to be sluggish at this season."

Zhada yielded. "Thank you."

Lareo nodded, barely mollified, as he folded the map around the ebony stick and handed them both over. "You come back safe," he repeated, "or I'll kick a hole in the Shadow Plane myself and box your ghost's pointy ears."

Zhada couldn't help a yelp of laughter at that prospect.

But the old Eldaryn might have to try making good on his joke, he thought grimly the following evening. Zhada consulted the map yet again. Granted, the Black Swamp was, self-evidently, a swamp but the paths which he was finding bore little resemblance to the peripheral routes which had long been charted, supposedly enduring on ground above the vagaries of the seasonal floods.

He had no doubt in his own abilities to find any path, not after being raised tracking prey by the merest dusty scuff marks or a few bent blades of grass. Just as he had no doubt that Lareo had given him the best information which any Eldaryn could buy, borrow, or bamboozle out of some unwary source. No, something untoward had happened here, to make such a nonsense of this map.

Still, he was well inside the fringes of the marshland now, so his chances of spotting his quarry should be improving with every step as long as he didn't go too far and find himself in the truly trackless morass of ash sands and tar pits, where he would undoubtedly become hunted rather than the hunter.

Zhada looked warily around. This dense vegetation wilted and blackened in the cold season rather than dying back to fall away entirely. He searched the gloom beneath the twisted trees' leathery leaves for any hint of movement.

The merest shiver of a fern caught his eye. Zhada stood motionless. A second mottled frond shifted and then a third. Something was moving through that undergrowth, keeping low to the ground.

He took a stealthy step forward, sliding his booted foot through the litter of decaying flotsam. Better to risk some banded snake breaking its fangs on the thick-oiled leather than to tread on a stick whose sharp snap would send his prey fleeing. Or worse, the sound would draw far more unwelcome attention his way.

Zhada studied the shadows intently for any hint of scarlet. Even travellers who hadn't set foot within a hundred leagues of this swamp had heard of its Death's Kiss; beautiful flowers somehow borne of death and corruption and the dark magic that oozed from the heart of the mire. Since no one could agree if the vine's malice reached as far as arm's length or even a long stride, he wouldn't be going within slingshot of any such blooms, not if he could help it.

No, there was no hint of red amid the shifting black and green, only that same sustained ripple of movement advancing through the lowest leaves. Zhada took another pace, then another, his movement adding barely a whisper to the soft rustle of the breeze through the contorted branches.

His pricked ears angled this way and that, alert for any hint of more purposeful movement amid the eerie lack of birdsong. Anything hereabouts used to hunting Humans would soon learn how much more difficult it was to sneak up on a Lowl.

The breeze shifted and Zhada licked his nose. As the odors surrounding him instantly strengthened, his heart beat faster. Faint but unmistakable, he remembered the scent of the belt which his grandfather had shown him so long ago. A Lowl only needed one sniff to fix an aroma in their memory lifelong.

That belt had the same smell which he caught on the wind, but this wasn't dead and faded. This was a living, breathing lure firing his blood for the hunt. Zhada looked ahead, tracing the most likely path for the creature he could now hear sliding through the knotted tree roots.

The dull daylight glinted on an oily slick of water. That's where it was heading. Once it gained the water, he would have lost it. He kicked a silted clot of broken twigs without caring about the noise. Glancing back to the fern-clad tree roots, Zhada saw sudden stillness. Good. Looking back down to be sure that nothing venomous lurked in the debris, he stooped and grabbed a handful of spongy sticks in his off hand. His sword hand reached for his belt, not for his blade but for the braided leather hanging looped against his thigh.

He threw the dead wood hard and sure at the cluster of frayed leaves where his prey had stilled. The black serpent instantly sprang forth, swift and deadly. Alas for the inexperienced creature, it found Zhada still hanging back, too far away for its strike.

Standing half as tall as a man, the serpent reared up, just as the cobras of the plains would do. Mouth agape to display ferocious fangs, the black swamp snake batted its stumpy wings as angrily as a jessed hawk. A juvenile, it couldn't yet fly and escape him that way. On the other hand, it had outgrown the caution of its first few seasons. More than ready to fight, it hissed a vicious challenge, daring Zhada to come within reach.

Swinging the strangling cord around his head, once, twice, the Lowl felt the familiar pull of the stone-weighted leather balls at the weapon's ends. His people might have taken to fighting with Human swords and daggers as readily as opal otters took to water, but they still hunted with the weapons that had served them for time out of mind. He hurled the weighted cord. It spun through the air, fast and true.

The black-winged serpent's hiss was cut comically short. Its weaving head was yanked backwards by the flying cord looping around its neck. Zhada was already running, drawing his dagger.

The black-winged serpent was thrashing in panic. Avoiding its muscular coils as thick as his forearm, Zhada planted one booted foot solidly on the leather rope. The serpent's immediate attempt to strike up at him was foiled by the unyielding tether.

As it strained against the strangling bonds, he thrust his dagger underneath its gaping jaw. The blade sliced through the soft skin and tiny scales. He drove the point upwards into its brain. The winged serpent collapsed, as lifeless as the loops of weighted cord which entangled it.

Though the combative light in its eyes died, the rainbow glimmer on its scales shone as alluring as gemstones. The sheen of its feathered wings rivalled the most sumptuous shot silk.

Something rustled behind him. Zhada whirled around but there was nothing to be seen. An incautious gust of wind? He could only hope so. Regardless, there was nothing to be gained by any further delay. He'd got what he had come for, so the sooner he left this swamp, the better.

Dropping to one knee, he cut the winged serpent's head clean off. As its coils writhed in one last spasm, he looked cautiously in all directions. Satisfied he was unobserved, he began skinning his kill. Zhada worked as swiftly as possible, shutting his nostrils as best he could against the rankness of the creature's black blood. He hadn't imagined it would smell as bad as this. Worse, the teasing breeze would carry such a pungent odor all too far and wide.

But he had come this far and he wasn't about to leave without his prize, nor was he going to ruin it with incautious haste. He bent to his work, easing the blade between the serpent's scaled skin and the black-streaked pale meat. The dead chill of the thing numbed his fingers.

Something rustled, and this time it rasped against a tree's knobbly trunk. Zhada froze, seeing the waving tops of a tall cluster of reeds over beyond a slick of water. Judging the distance, he took a steadying breath. As well as the fetid stream, there was a decent expanse of open ground between him and that undergrowth. He should get a clear sight of whatever it was, when it chose to attack him.

He continued flaying the serpent, finally wrenching the scaled hide free of its blunt tail. Standing up, clutching the skin and his strangling cord in one hand, he snagged the slimy corpse with his dagger.

The furtive creature erupted from the reeds. Malevolent crimson patches shone like fresh blood on its black scales. It was a Candon, still low to the ground as it raced towards him, razor-toothed maw gaping. Zhada guessed it had been hunting on all fours when it caught wind of his kill.

An ignorant traveller might mistake such a beast for a gaudy crocodile, and that would be the last mistake he would make. These were no more witless lizards than Zhada was a dumb hound.

Crossing the slick of water with a few strokes of its muscular tail, the Candon reared up on its stumpy hind legs, ready to challenge Zhada's sword and dagger with its own teeth and talons. Its dark eyes gleamed with cunning. So much for assurances that these creatures only lived in the heart of the swamp, still less for them being slow and lethargic in the cold season. This one was awake and hungry.

Zhada threw the winged serpent's naked remains straight at the Candon's face. The beast snatched the bloody carcass out of the air with a chilling clash of teeth.

For an appalled instant Zhada feared it would toss the carrion aside and continue its attack in hopes of warmer meat. Then the Candon spun around, tail gouging an arc in the mud. This time it ran sure-footed through the water, head held high to keep the dead serpent clear of floating scum. It vanished into the feathered canes where it had been skulking.

Zhada breathed a sigh of relief and sheathed his dagger. Turning around, he slid his backpack's strap off one shoulder, ready to stow the serpent skin safely for his journey.

Ahead, something hissed. Something large, judging by the size of the shadow under the creeper-strangled trees. Zhada let his pack slide to the ground, dropping the serpent skin and drawing his sword. Whatever that thing was, it warranted a longer blade. He dropped into a duellist's crouch, Ebontra style.

The creature burst through the topmost leaves, soaring upwards to wrongfoot him entirely. With a wingspan as broad as Zhada's own outstretched arms, this winged serpent had no difficulty flying. It lashed at his head with its tail, brutal as any cudgel. He barely managed to dodge the blow, with no chance of landing his own blade at all.

Why was this creature awake? Everyone knew that winged serpents of any color slept through this season once they were full grown. Zhada had been counting on it when he planned this hunt.

The Lowl's indignation was nearly the death of him. The winged serpent lashed with its tail a second time, landing a bruising blow on his shoulder. He went staggering across the damp ground, his sword arm numbed. The great serpent twisted bonelessly in midair. Its gaping mouth shot straight towards his face, venom glistening on its grooved fangs.

He barely saved himself, ducking sideways, at the cost of losing his footing on the soft ground. Zhada rolled over and over, desperately clinging to his sword. Painful spasms wracked his fingers as he flailed wildly with the blade. The serpent's hiss sounded almost contemptuous as the next sweep of its tail knocked the sword clean out of his hand. The finely-honed edge was no match to its impenetrable scales.

Zhada scrabbled backwards, digging his heels into the mud until he felt a solid tree trunk at his back. Whatever might hide in the undergrowth was surely less of a threat than that cursed serpent. Now the creature hissed with frustration, unable to strike from above, unwilling to land and fight him on the ground - for the moment at least.

He clawed at the side of his boot with his un-numbed hand. The Eldaryn firestick was sheathed where he usually carried a second dagger. He wrenched it free and pointed the open end at the hovering serpent.

Vitcoska save me.

He reached for the spark of fire which all Lowl carried in their heart, enough to light a candle or an ember. There was nothing there. He tried a second time, only to sense with growing horror the all-pervasive water magic of this sodden marsh dousing any thought of his own flame entirely

The great winged serpent hissed again, but this time it was turning towards the malodorous stream which the Candon had crossed. Rasping cries echoed across the swamp. The lizard man was returning and he had brought allies. The great serpent flapped closer to the water, tail lashing with insensate fury.

Zhada seized his chance to flee. Risking his life one last time, he snatched up the juvenile serpent's skin and his strangling cord. Before the winged beast could react, he was racing away down what remained of the path. His backpack and sword lay behind him, abandoned.

A dagger and the cord should suffice to see him home. As long as they did, the serpent skin in his other hand should more than repay him for his losses.

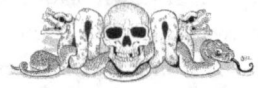

"And you couldn't spark it?" Lareo shook his head, mystified, as he examined the firestick in a discreet corner of the Emerald Serpent. "Sorry, no refunds."

Zhada knew the feeble joke for the old Eldaryn's gesture of apology. He could smell Lareo's contrition.

"I don't imagine there's anything wrong with it," he said hastily. "It was drowned by the magic in the swamp. But I don't want to keep it around me, not with what I'm carrying."

Lareo's gaze followed Zhada's down to the two cloth bags on the floor by the Lowl's chair.

"Has your quest prospered then?" he asked delicately.

"That remains to be seen." Zhada carefully retrieved the bags and stood up. "I should know one way or the other before sunset."

Lareo nodded. "Come and let me know."

Zhada answered with a smile before heading out of the tavern. Skirting the stadium, he headed for the Black Gate itself. Squaring his shoulders, he walked out through the gaping mouth of the great carved skull, not looking to left or right. After his experiences in the swamp, just seeing the winged serpents writhing across the gate's mysterious reliefs sent a shiver down his spine.

He headed towards the harbor. Halfway there, he cut through an alley to follow a northbound high road. Unsurprisingly, his presence was soon turning heads. Out here in Taux, fewer than one man or woman in twenty was anything other than Human.

That didn't bother Zhada. He'd grown used to the stares when he'd lived here as a child. His father had been the first Lowl to buy a house in the modestly prosperous Turquoise Turtle District. His mother had been the first to worship at the local shrine to Saint Erik of the Thousand Faces. Vitcoska wasn't a jealous goddess, and it never hurt to keep local demons happy.

Zhada took a side street to look at his childhood home. The house itself was still in good repair; the shutters recently painted and the fruit trees in the garden had been pruned back. Satisfied, he nevertheless made a mental note to visit his father's man of business down by the docks, to make certain that the current tenants had already been warned they should not take their lease's renewal for granted.

He followed the long lazy curve of the street around until he reached a house seemingly some good distance away. However, Zhada knew this dwelling's long gardens reached back to join the grounds where he had once played.

How much simpler life had been then. When Human children wanted to know if a Lowl pup really had a tail as their nursemaid claimed, they had simply asked, as readily as Zhada himself had dropped his trousers to prove it was a lie.

As he went up the steps to the house's door, his mouth was so dry that his tongue felt like a length of matted felt, and he could feel his hackles bristling. He hadn't felt so scared when he'd been facing that winged serpent in the swamp.

Well, all that foolhardy bravery would be for nothing if he didn't see this through, whatever the outcome might be. Drawing a deep breath, he yanked on the bell pull.

A lackey appeared so swiftly that Zhada realised his approach had been noted from some upper window.

"Yes?" The servant looked him up and down.

"Good day." Zhada bore the scrutiny with composure. He was dressed in his finest clothes. "I wish to see Master Mesare." Though he could have wished for an easier name for a Lowl to pronounce.

"The master?" The servant queried.

"Correct," Zhada said crisply.

"Enter, please." The servant retreated to allow him through the door into the cool, tastefully tiled hall. "I will see if he is free to receive you."

"Thank you." Zhada dared allow himself a little hope. After all, he could have been left standing out on the steps. He gripped the necks of the bags he carried, feeling the sweat from his palms dampening the creased cloth.

The servant quickly reappeared at the door which he had vanished through. "This way, if you please."

"Thank you." Zhada followed him into the light and airy chamber where Master Mesare sat behind a broad table piled high with ledgers and scrolls.

The bald merchant looked up as the door closed behind the departing lackey. "It's Icael's friend, isn't it?" He was clearly intrigued.

Zhada was impressed. So few Humans could reliably distinguish between two Lowl with the same color fur. He nodded. "Good day to you, sir, and I hope that your son prospers?"

"He does indeed." Mesare's eyes strayed to a fat leather bound book before he looked back at Zhada. "But he's not here at present. He's learning our family's business over in Thalonia."

"So I had heard." Zhada carefully set the bags he carried on the polished wooden floor.

Mesare frowned, puzzled. "I thought your family had returned to Lowl lands."

"We did," Zhada agreed, "Though my father retained the properties which he owned in this city."

"Properties?" The plural caught Mesare's attention. "So you've come to – what? Manage them for him? Sell?" His eyes brightened.

"We have no wish to sell," Zhada said, apologetic, "nor any need," he added. "I have come to Taux to trade as my grandfather did." He looked around the luxuriously appointed room. "Like your forefathers and your son."

"Trade?" Mesare rubbed a thoughtful hand over his expertly shaven chin. "What do you have to trade from the North?"

"Not from the North." Zhada hunkered down and loosened the first bag's drawstring. "From the Black Swamp."

He lifted out the black winged serpent's skin and laid it carefully on top of the bag. The hide was not yet cured but a touch of Zhada's own fire had dried it sufficiently not to rot and summon every hungry rat in the city with its reek.

"A black—" Mesare stared, rapt, at the treasure. "What are you asking for it?" he demanded abruptly.

"Who knows what it could fetch across the ocean?" Zhada shrugged. "I am content for one of your ships to carry it, then to split whatever coin it brings us equally, especially if Icael is to sell it." He couldn't help a loose-jawed grin at the notion of his childhood friend's astonishment.

Mesare nodded slowly. "An equal division of profits—"

Zhada raised a polite hand. "Equal division of the coin earned. I know you have your ship's costs to cover – still, I also have my expenses."

Mesare stared at the iridescent scales, at the shimmering beauty of the wings, doubtless picturing the New Kingdom's wealthiest men flaunting belts and boots trimmed with the glittering leather, their ladies' high-piled hair secured with combs dressed with those astonishing feathers.

The corners of his mouth twitched in what might have been a rueful smile. "Very well. An equal division of the price paid, and that will be a handsome sum, I'm sure."

Zhada didn't doubt it. He knew just how much the Human traders paid for winged azure serpent skins from the estuaries where the Hilani rivers met the seas near the Opal Gates, and for the cinnabar serpents' scales and feathers from the far side of the fire mountains in Dravaria.

Mesare looked up. "Can you get more of these?"

"I think so," Zhada said cautiously. "I wish to hire some Lowl to hunt with me." He wasn't going back to that swamp without someone to watch his back, and besides, what better way to show the likes of Durrau or Varrach's lapdogs how a Lowl's dual nature gave them advantages over Human and hound alike.

Mesare pursed his lips before nodding slowly. "Then I believe we are in business, my friend."

He rose from his seat and came around the table, offering his hand to Zhada. As he did so, he looked acquisitively at the second cloth bag. "Do you have more wares to trade?"

Zhada looked Mesare straight in the eye. Among Humans, this promised good faith. Among Lowl, it was a challenge. Both suited him well enough.

"It is a gift for your daughter."

"My—" Mesare was more taken-aback than he had been by the serpent skin.

"May I speak with her?" Zhada didn't drop his gaze, tucking his hands behind his back so he could clench his fists unseen.

This time Mesare took an age to make up his mind. Finally he nodded, his faded eyes hard as agate. "You may give her your gift."

He turned to the table and rang a crystal bell. The lackey opened the door so fast Zhada guessed he'd been listening at the keyhole.

"Please ask Asalyan to join us," Mesare said tersely.

"At once." Wide-eyed, the lackey fled.

As the silence in the room lengthened Zhada tried to recall the layout of this house. How far away could she be? How long would it take for her to decide if she wished to obey her father's summons? Were her curls still as golden as they had been? He'd noticed how Humans' hair often darkened as they grew older. Not that it would matter to him.

He looked down at the cloth bag with the bulk of the earthenware jar inside it. What would he do with that if she didn't come?

"Father?"

After a seemingly interminable interlude, Asalyan appeared in the doorway. As she took a step into the room, her hazel eyes softened with recognition.

"Zhada? You've come home?" she whispered.

Mesare stepped forward. "We have some business together. Zhada was good enough to bring you a gift."

He only had eyes for Asalyan. She had remembered him. Better yet, she had remembered his name which her father clearly had not. What else did she recall of their games in the garden? Or their later conversations, with Zhada perched in the tree overlooking the garden wall and Asalyan sat on the grass on the far side. When Zhada had explained so much of Lowl nature to her. Had he ever told her that his people only ever chose one true beloved, lifelong?

"A gift?" she prompted, her delicate lips twitching with amusement much as her father's had done.

"Of course." Fighting to stop his hands shaking, he drew the earthenware pot from the bag. As he removed the lid, a glorious perfume sweetened the room.

"Roses? You remembered?" Incredulous, Asalyan came close to look into the pot. "At this season?"

"A tiny rose tree, such as the Lowl keep, for when we move from place to place." Zhada shifted slightly so that Master Mesare could see the miniature shrub.

The merchant looked puzzled. He passed his hand over the vessel's wide mouth and his face cleared. "Ah, you use a touch of fire to keep it warm."

Asalyan frowned, concerned. "I cannot do that. Will it die?"

Zhada strove to answer as casually as he could. "Not if I help you tend it, when I have cause to call on your father."

Then he could court her as steadily and as patiently as he had ever pursued any quarry.

He couldn't help looking at Mesare though. Now was the time for the merchant to shatter all his hopes as surely as a dropped pot. He wished he could sense something from the man's scent but the rose's perfume was filling his nose.

Did the merchant guess that Zhada was determined to be as much a pathfinder as his father the merchant, and as his grandsire, the leader of that first expedition sent to discover why letters and envoys from the city's merchants had ceased so abruptly?

Zhada didn't care that the notion of Human and Lowl pairing was only the stuff of tavern tales, from the sentimental to the obscene. There had to be a first couple to walk the streets hand in hand, unashamed.

Mesare ran ink-stained fingers over his bald pate. Though he didn't turn his head, his eyes slid sideways, as though to look at the black serpent's skin still lying on the desk.

"Since we will have business together, that should present no problem," he allowed. "Provided that's acceptable to you, Asalyan?"

"Most acceptable," she assured her father. She took the rose jar from Zhada's hands. "Why don't we take this to the conservatory now and you can tell me how best to care for it."

Mesare pursed his lips again before nodding. "Very well. I'll join you when I've dealt with my correspondence."

"Of course, father." Asalyan's glance shared her amusement with Zhada. "I'll send for a pot of Champurrado and some cakes."

"Go on with you then." Mesare couldn't help a fond smile as he dismissed her with a wave of his hand.

Zhada was still tongue-tied as he followed her into the hall. But if he truly had had a tail, he would have been wagging it.

Illustration by Jeff Laubenstein

THREE SOULS FOR SALE

Michael Tousignant

After nearly a full day of scrambling through the dark, slimy abyss with only a torch and his paranoia for company, Syrtuno had assembled an extensive mental catalog of unpleasant sensations. The dampness and constantly looming shadows were mere annoyances; the sounds of skittering insects, and the bat dung under his fingers, were much more distasteful. Now, Syrtuno added yet another sensation to his list – a nauseating stench, growing stronger as he progressed. Still, he had expected such discomforts when he slipped into the dank caverns that ran beneath Taux's bay, and as long as he could find what he sought, it would be worthwhile.

He became aware of a soft, off-key humming, coming from further up the tunnel. Syrtuno doused his torch in one of the many puddles in the cave and crept around the bend. There, the stone opened into a large chamber, dominated by a stagnant, softly glowing pool. This chamber, he knew, sat directly beneath the Star Tower of the Wizards. He had arrived at his destination.

A Wizard was seated next to the pool, working on what appeared to be a loom suspended in midair. The Wizard's features were concealed by a hooded robe. It was black, trimmed in gold, and must have been impressive once, but it was worn and tattered now. The Wizard's hands moved skillfully over the loom, but with a great stiffness.

Then the figure shifted slightly, and Syrtuno knew that the Wizard had sensed him. His chest felt chilled, and his breath came in short spurts. He was trained in the ways of magic, but the being before him had a direct connection to the sorcerous energies of the distant Afterglow Sea. Syrtuno felt the subtle flame within him giving way before the vast oceanic power within the Wizard. Inside he felt the weight of the waters of the bay above his head, and the magical might of the Wizards in their tower. The two oceans threatened to wash him away.

"It is not often," the figure said, "that I am plagued with visitors."

The Wizard spoke in a low and raspy voice, and Syrtuno couldn't tell if they were man or woman.

Syrtuno took a deep breath, regretted it as the cavern's stench filled his lungs, and spoke, carefully. "It took a great deal of effort to find you, honored Wizard. Knowing you prefer your privacy, I have obscured the path behind me. Any parchments I consulted were burned, any signs altered, any tongues removed."

"This is appreciated," the Wizard said, the reply oozing out slowly, word dripping after word. "So, why have you come? For my pets, I suppose?"

Syrtuno nodded. "You are a Wizard; I am a lowly tome mage. Everything born into your blood, I must struggle for. You call them pets, and gain them effortlessly; to me, they are crucial ingredients, all but impossible to obtain."

The Wizard ceased working at the loom, and slowly stood. "Not two hundred feet above this cavern, my brothers and sisters sit in their Starry Tower, a much more accessible location. Am I to assume that they were, shall we say, less willing to work with you?"

"None must know my business," Syrtuno said. "Not until after the fact. Besides, even amongst Wizards, you are one of very few who traffic in souls."

"Souls," the Wizard repeated. "Of course." With a raised hand, he conjured a flock of small, barely-visible wisps of cloud, which rose up out of the pool and circled the cavern in a slow, dignified orbit. "I hope you brought something to trade – and not gold. The last ones brought gold. I laughed for hours, and it took them a long time to drown."

Syrtuno could not hide a smile as he reached into his pouch and pulled out his most precious cargo – an egg, six inches in length, yellow in color, with blue spots.

The Wizard turned to face the prize. Syrtuno could barely perceive flashing eyes within the depths of the hood. Then slowly, stiffly, it walked towards him; he could hear the Wizard sniffing the air.

"Where," the Wizard asked, after some time, "did you get that?"

Syrtuno grinned. "Let us just say that, comparatively, finding you was easy."

The barely audible sound of lips being licked escaped from beneath the hood. "And how many souls," the Wizard said, after a great silence, "will you require?"

Syrtuno carefully set the egg down on the ground, then reached into his pack again, pulling out three clear orbs. "Three shall be sufficient for my purposes, honored Wizard. I have brought my own means of transporting them."

The Wizard slowly bent down to take the egg, which vanished into the voluminous robe. He then inspected the orbs, one by one. With another waved hand, the circling wisps floated closer to Syrtuno. "I shall allow you to choose two," the Wizard said. "The third, I shall choose for you."

As the misty forms approached, Syrtuno could perceive faint images moving within them. Lives routine and wondrous alike played out before him, and he watched carefully. Soon, he spotted the image of a man on a ship, fighting his way through the dozen men surrounding him; then, another image, of a man coldly torturing a prisoner. He pointed at these two images. The Wizard nodded, and summoned the two clouds to him.

The Wizard picked up one of the orbs, and regarded the man on the ship. "Captain Archibald Blood," the Wizard said. "You may have heard of him. Scores were sent to the depths of the sea at his hands and those of his crew. He plundered the coasts of four continents in his day, but the wealth slipped through his fingers like sand. In the end, he gambled away his soul to a passing stranger, all in the hopes of buying one more dram of his beloved whiskey."

Syrtuno nodded, recognizing the name. Over the years, many foolish explorers had tried looking for Blood's hidden hoard, not realizing it had never existed.

The Wizard then turned to the other floating soul. "This one was Kalanar Creed, a ruthless crime lord. He ruled kingdoms from the shadows, and the streets ran red with blood at his displeasure."

"I've heard of him," Syrtuno said. "Supposedly, he was a horrible glutton. One day, the story goes, a young man interrupted one of his feasts, and Creed had him tortured to death. Of course, the young man's mother was a Corsair-blooded witch, and a low-water curse from her tore Creed's soul from his body."

"There is some truth to that," the Wizard said. Then, with deft movements that Syrtuno couldn't follow, the Wizard drew the two souls into the orbs, before setting them on the ground. Syrtuno reached down to pick them up, and saw scenes continue to play themselves out within.

"Thank you very much, honored Wizard," Syrtuno said, placing the orbs in his pouch. "And the third?"

The Wizard took no time for consideration. Gestures were made, and, while the remaining orb still sat on the ground, a soul was drawn into it. Confused, Syrtuno reached down and picked up the orb, looking into its depths. Within, he saw what appeared to be a child playing in the streets, clutching a cloth doll in her hands.

Syrtuno looked back at the Wizard. "What exactly is this?"

"Mystina Oceotl," the Wizard said. "She lived in this very city, some centuries ago. She was sweet, innocent, and beloved, until a plague took her life. I honestly have no idea how I came to possess her, but now, she is yours."

"Are you mocking me?" Syrtuno asked, his voice raising in volume. "I come here for killers! For souls dark and bloody! And you give me a child?"

The Wizard's head titled slightly, and Syrtuno found himself unable to breathe again. He could hear the sea around him. He idly wondered what it would feel like to drown in Afterglow.

"Have a care, mortal," the Wizard said. "You have exhausted the audacity that your offering purchased for you."

Syrtuno fell to his knees. "Forgive me, honored Wizard," he said, choking out the words with shortened breath.

The Wizard turned his back on Syrtuno, shuffling towards the loom. "You made no demands as to the quality of the souls given you, and you already have claimed two of my best. A child's soul has little will of its own. It should be easy enough to control, and will follow along the lead of the other souls. They will suffice you. Now go, and tell no one what you have seen."

Syrtuno found himself able to breathe again. He placed the third orb within his pouch, turned, and ran from the chamber. He didn't pause to light another torch for several minutes. The anger and fear he felt within the chamber soon subsided, and he smiled, thinking of the precious things he took with him out of the caves of the apostate Wizard. Soon, vengeance would be at hand.

Even in the old days, the open courts of the Ullamalitzli Stadium beyond the Black Gate had been arenas, where ball games were played before the populace. In hushed tones, credulous barkeeps and mischievous grandfathers told lurid tales of how the losers of such games would be led off to horrid deaths to honor the city's rulers, or the old gods, in what was now the Raised Market. Whether innocent or bloody, such times were long in the past. The city of Taux was in the hands of a new populace, new Saints, new games, and new rulers – and it was, in fact, those new rulers that walked through the arena this evening.

That afternoon had seen a match between the Snakes of the Black Gate District, and the Jaguars of the Golden Jaguar District, with victory going to the Jaguars. The Jaguars were the favorite team of Tlacolotl Vash, possibly the richest – and almost certainly the most powerful – man in the city. To celebrate the game, the wealthy Red Pillar threw a lavish party that night right in sight of the court itself.

The city's elite gathered on appropriated grounds, along with the members of both teams. Long tables were filled with exotic food and expensive drink. Servants picked up trays from the tables and walked strategic routes through the crowd, so that nobody would be too far from refreshment. Vash even provided artifacts from the time before the disappearance – items left behind in the mysterious vanishing of Taux's old owners, and looted in the mad scavenging dash that followed, now tastefully displayed as works of art. Of course, the images of the old gods carved on the walls of the arena had been covered up, obscured by tapestries of the Six Saints. Vash himself remained in his private box, smiling down at his assembled guests.

By an hour after sundown, most of the guests had arrived. The sounds of laughter and spirited conversation did not quite drown out the music. Vash's personal guards, dressed in black and gold livery, stood solemnly around the perimeter. The rich and the beautiful danced, ate, and engaged in deep conversation. The most heated of these discussions was between Chaplain Damon, devout follower of Saint Amanda of Virgins, and Lady Enalya Paige, known to support the ways of the Old City, and rumored to worship the Death Cult of the Moon in secret. She was dressed somewhat scandalously; wearing a long skirt, but with only a piece of silk to cover her top, in what she claimed was the style of the old ways. Few of the young males watching questioned her historical accuracy. One such male found himself so enveloped in the discussion that he stopped paying attention to where he was going and slammed into a nearby servant, knocking to the floor the two serving trays the poor man had been carrying.

This sent Wenintal, Major-domo to the Vash family, running over. Wenintal was a Kin, and looked exactly like what many would picture one of the Earth-touched Kin to be – short and stocky, skin dark as an opal, with pearl-white swirls running in patterns up his arms. His eyes, sapphire-blue, had a tinge of rage to them, though his bald head didn't have a drop of sweat on it. He helped the clumsy onlooker to his feet, and then glared up at the unlucky servant as the scent of newly tilled earth pervaded the area around them.

The servant in question was a Jai-Ruk, and did, in fact, look just as many of those gathered would expect a Jai-Ruk to look. He was tall, muscular, and square-jawed. His eyes had a somewhat vacant expression to them, and his mouth hung slightly open, giving a glimpse of the small tusks that were a telltale mark of his race.

"Oaf!" Wenintal hissed, standing a few inches away. "Be more careful where you tread!"

"Sorry, Boss," the servant said, looking down at Wenintal.

"Well, I suppose it can't be helped," the Kin said. "What is your name, servant?"

"Me Thock, Boss," the servant answered.

"Right, Thock, very well. I need you to clean this mess up."

The Jai-Ruk smiled. "Aye, Boss."

Wenintal shook his head. "And it is not 'Boss', it is 'Sir'."

Thock knelt down to start clearing the mess. "Aye, Sir Boss."

Wenintal sighed, then turned towards the sound of nearby giggling. Several of the female servers were gathered around a fetching young man, also dressed as a servant, who was amusing them with his conversation. Fuming under his breath, Wenintal walked away from Thock and grabbed the man by the arm, spinning him around.

"Am I missing something important?" the Kin asked.

The young man's cheeks flushed red, as the girls he had been addressing swiftly found other places to be. "Ah, Sir. I was just, you see, making sure these young ladies knew their duties."

"Ah! So you enjoy management, do you? Good. Go over there and manage to help good mister Thock clean up the mess. Make sure he doesn't eat any of the food – or silverware - either, would you? Very good lad." Wenintal gave the young man a hard shove towards Thock, then resumed his rounds, on the lookout for the next looming crisis.

The young man shrugged, and bent down to help gather the errant bits of food. The Jai-Ruk glanced over at him.

"How long do I have to maintain the illusion of complete imbecility, again?" Thock asked the young man.

The handsome servant shrugged. "Hopefully not too much longer, Dethocrates."

The Jai-Ruk coughed. "Please, Andril. Not until the job's over."

"Sorry," Andril said. "I wouldn't worry, though, 'Thock.' You're giving a great performance."

Dethocrates smiled. "I'm not even all that sad that Taux's rich and powerful see a Jai-Ruk and expect an idiot. The only one I was worried wouldn't fall for it was Wenintal – and actually, I'm still a little worried. For all we know, he's gathering some guards to throw us out."

Andril turned a platter right side up, and started piling food on it. "If so, we'll deal with it as it occurs. Any sign of Pelantus yet?"

Dethocrates shook his head. "Nothing. I'm growing concerned about this plan of yours."

"He'll show," Andril said. "Don't worry, Dethocrates. We'll have the rubies and be gone before anyone's the wiser."

Dethocrates grabbed up the dirtied plates and walked through a nearby entry reserved for servants. "I'd at least feel better if I had my bow."

Andril followed with his own armload. "If all goes well, there will be no need for weapons. Besides, if you were so worried, you could have smuggled in a sling or something."

"I hate slings," Dethocrates sniffed. "Useless little trinkets, not good for accuracy or penetration, just for annoying people. Might as well fight a Razor with a butter knife. I swear I'll kill Savino when I see him…"

"What?" Andril asked.

"Nothing," Dethocrates replied.

Andril shrugged and they arrived in a room filled with water basins and dirtied plates. Andril set his down, and said, "Even without weapons, we're always armed. You have your wits, and I have my luck."

Dethocrates groaned. "Why can't you be like a normal scoundrel and simply claim to be the greatest swordsman in New Kingdoms?"

"Because I'm not," Andril replied. "I'm competent with a blade, fast on my feet, good with my hands and tongue, yes. But my best trait, as you well know, is my luck."

"Then why is it," Dethocrates said, becoming quieter as they returned to the courtyard, "that you never seem to win at gambling? Or that your horses run away, or the myriad of other unfortunate happenstances you've come across?"

Andril waved a hand. "Unimportant. When all depends on it, when my life or others' lives are in the balance, Saint Erik watches over me."

Dethocrates rolled his eyes. "Not once have I ever seen you pray to the Saint of the Thousand Faces."

"Even so," Andril said, "He must be with me. I even won a duel pitting my luck against another!"

"Please, not this again."

"Why does it bother you? He and I were both hanging from ropes. They both snapped at the same instance. I landed on branches about ten feet down, and he plummeted into the canyon."

"That," Dethocrates insisted, "is *not* a duel!"

Before the conversation could go any further, trumpets rang out, and they could hear Wenintal's voice echo through the courtyard.

"Presenting the Wise and Esteemed Pelantus, Arch Pyromancer and Magus to Red Pillar Tlacolotl Vash!"

Andril and Dethocrates's eyes turned toward the other side of the courtyard where the guests entered. Not quite able to see from their position, they drifted through the crowd until they were close enough to observe the man in question. Pelantus was one of the Eldaryn, which made him difficult to spot; he was smaller even than Wenintal, though his fiery red hair, spiked straight up and touched with blue at the tips, helped him to stand out. His people were attuned to pure Fire, just as the Kin were attuned to pure Earth, and Pelantus dressed to remind people of this; he wore elaborate red robes, golden rings studded with topaz and sapphire, and a necklace of nine rubies around his neck.

"He's wearing them, just as you predicted," Dethocrates said, his eyes on the larger central-most ruby in the chain.

"Remember, only the central one is magic – the rest are just expensive. Though I'm sure that even without it he's got all he needs to cast his spells in case of an emergency," Andril observed. "Most tome mages do."

"I just don't get, given how quickly Vash goes through mages – Pelantus, Gezel before him, Syrtuno before that – and how limited the abilities of a tome mage are, why doesn't he just try acquiring the services of an actual Wizard?"

Andril smiled. "You want to row out to the Star Tower and convince one of the Wizards to concern himself with mundane matters, in exchange for mundane currency? Best of luck to you."

Dethocrates chuckled. "Good point. So, the plan is, I sneak up and obtain the rubies, and you provide a suitable distraction to enable our escape?"

"It'd be best if you could get the whole necklace off of him. If that can't happen, just get the center ruby and we'll..."

At that moment, a hideous shriek sounded in the night air. Out of the blackness of the night, a creature descended on leathery wings. The thing had the color and stench of grave dirt. Aside from its wings, it also had four legs, with sharp talons on the front pair. Three long, sinewy necks extended from the front of the creature, and at the end of each was a gruesome head, dominated by bulging eyes and a maw of fangs. Guests and servants alike scattered as it landed, some knocking tables over in their haste. Red Pillar Vash was pushed to cover by his guards, but he quickly shoved past them to keep watching.

Atop the creature, a man rode a makeshift saddle of leather and petrified bone. He dressed in a blue robe that was, at one time, formal and opulent, but had become soiled and torn. His hair and beard, black with a touch of gray, was neatly trimmed, though his flight had put them in disarray. With one hand, he held the reins; the other hand, he swept about him, encompassing the affluent crowd.

"Behold," the rider said, "the return of Syrtuno! Banished unjustly from your polite society, and now come back to destroy his enemies!"

Even though more than a few in the crowd seemed ignorant of the declaration's meaning, many in attendance gasped. Wenintal cursed, and then ran to gather guards. Andril and Dethocrates took cover behind one of the upturned tables. Pelantus, rather than be cowed, moved to stand defiantly before his predecessor.

"We had wondered," the Eldaryn said, "whether you would show your face in Taux again, after the charges were made against you."

Syrtuno glared down at the Eldaryn. "Ah, the unworthy charlatan who has taken my place. For you, I have nothing but mild disgust. My rage is reserved for Vash, and all the others who cast me down."

Pelantus reached into his robe and pulled out a wooden wand and two vials of unknown substance. "Disgust or not, you shall have to pass through me before earning your vengeance. I have prepared myself with a charm, making me strong against any magic you could send at me. If you were wise, you would fly your ugly mount back to whatever hole you crawled out of."

At that, he raised his wand up to begin an incantation, but Syrtuno merely cackled. "This is no mere mount! This is my weapon! A thrice-souled instrument of my revenge!"

Pelantus stopped at that, looking at the beast, confused. He did not have a chance for realization to dawn, or for panic to grow within him; the three heads simply extended themselves, side by side, and a blast of black fog poured out at the unlucky tome mage. At the fog' touch, what once had been flesh and bone was dissolved like sugar in water, then siphoned into the creature's maws. Three breaths later, there was only an unrecognizable mound where he had stood.

Syrtuno cackled again. "It would seem the 'Arch Pyromancer's' flame has been snuffed out!"

By this time, Vash's guards had assembled. Though the city guard was undoubtedly aware of the disturbance, Vash's men were in no mood to wait for the Sturgeons to take the glory from them. Valiantly, they drew steel and charged the creature from behind. The beast was slow to turn around, but their weapons had little effect on its hide. A beat of the wings sent several flying, while one of the beast's necks swept half a dozen off of their feet, Syrtuno laughing the whole time.

Behind their table, Dethocrates and Andril watched all of this.

"I'm not sure what surprises me more," Andril said. "That creature out there, or Syrtuno's cackle. It's very impressive."

"He said it had three souls," Dethocrates said. "He must have *built* the creature himself, and then managed to acquire souls to bring it to life – putting one in each of the heads."

"Does that make it more mystically potent, or something?"

Dethocrates shrugged. "Possibly? I'm mostly guessing."

Syrtuno and his beast turned, moving towards the box where Vash stood, calmly watching the proceedings. As the creature advanced, one of the Jaguars grabbed a spear and charged towards the rightmost head. It snapped down on him, and he found himself without weapon, or weapon arm. He fell to the ground, clutching the stump and screaming in agony.

Andril steadied himself. "Well, I guess it's time, then."

Dethocrates looked over at his companion. "Time for what? You're not seriously contemplating-"

Andril sprang onto the table, and started running. "I'll distract it! Get moving!"

Dethocrates cursed, but made his move.

Andril ran atop the tables until he was closer to the melee. The guards had fallen back, trying to rally for another push, but the creature now ignored them, and continued moving towards Vash's box. Looking down at the table he was on, Andril grabbed a bottle that had been left out, and hurled it at the heads. It struck the leftmost one, and shattered, red wine dripping onto the grotesque face. The head turned towards Andril, ready to kill, when a long tongue darted out, and licked up the liquid. An odd look of reptilian glee came to its face, and it slithered closer to Andril but didn't attack.

Confused, but desperate, Andril grabbed up another bottle, and threw it. This one, the creature caught within its mouth; Andril heard the crunch of the glass as the head bit down, then a satisfied gulping noise. Quickly, the thief grabbed up more alcohol and tossed it to the head, which gulped down each as quickly as it could. After a dozen bottles, plus a few half-filled goblets, the head clumsily swung back and forth in the air.

A frowning Syrtuno, his cackle now quiet, gripped the reins tighter. Runes carved into the bone of the saddle glowed, and the leftmost head held itself straighter. Meanwhile, the rightmost head dove at Andril, who fell backwards off the table, barely avoiding the head as it smashed the table to splinters.

By this point, the guards were advancing again. Several tried throwing spears at Syrtuno, but none even came close. In response, Syrtuno pulled forth a tube from his robe and aimed it in the direction of the guards. From the end of the tube shot forth a shower of brilliant, multicolored motes of light. The motes slowly changed from simple rainbow light into angry rainbow hornets that flew at the guards. Some were chased off, but those that stung the men exploded in fiery bursts of violet and green and gold.

Syrtuno cackled again. "Fools! The magic I have at my disposal does not end with my mount. I have been preparing for this night for years. Your only hope against me was lost with Pelantus!"

While Syrtuno ranted, the rightmost head continued to snap at Andril. He jumped out of the way four times, as it got closer. Finally, he jumped over a table, and the head bit through it. In doing so, it swallowed whole the roast pig that had been sitting on the table. The eyes of the head lit up, and it took another bite out of the table, swallowing an entire tray of finger food. As Andril regained his feet, he saw the head gorging itself without any prompting.

Seeing that Andril had distracted another of the heads, Syrtuno snarled. "That is quite ENOUGH!" he shouted, pulling out a silver orb. He tossed it into the air, and it flew forward and collided with Andril. He was knocked back, slamming into the side of the courtyard and tumbling into one of the Old City art displays. Syrtuno grabbed the reins and ordered the creature forward, ignoring the few guards that hadn't run, he positioned the middle head right above Andril's prostrate form.

"You've done very little, compared to the others," Syrtuno said to this middle head. "Eat him, and do me proud."

Andril's vision was clouded and red. *Something very bad is about to happen*, he thought shakily, *and I don't think I can do anything to stop it.* Desperately, he felt about him, for anything that could be used to help. He grabbed the first thing his fingers touched and lifted it in front of him, showing it to the beast. So, as the head closed in, maw gaping open, it found itself looking at...

A small, cloth, child's doll.

The middle head paused, staring at the doll. Then, it let out a surprised screech and bobbed up and down, excitedly. Through a blurry haze, Andril looked from the head to the doll.

"Do you want the doll?" he asked groggily.

The head nodded, and its maw extended in what seemed to be a grin. Andril weakly tossed the doll to the side. The head turned after it, causing the whole beast to shift in that direction. Syrtuno wavered back and forth before snarling again, taking the reins in both hands.

"Stop it! Stop it! Listen to me, you stupid lumbering thing! I am your master! You do as I command! And I command you to DESTROY HIM!"

Immediately, the three heads snapped to attention. Dethocrates, meanwhile, had maneuvered through the crowd, and now stood with several onlookers a dozen paces away from the beast, with a silver goblet in hand. He watched as, at Syrtuno's command, the beast turned, slowly and deliberately back towards Andril, who appeared too dazed to rise. Dethocrates glanced around, and noticed that Lady Paige was crouched next to him. With the quick, precise movements of a master thief, he undid the knots of her Old City top and pulled it off of her. Paige yelped in shock, wrapping an arm about herself and ran for cover.

Syrtuno cackled again, "The souls will dine well on you."

"I hate slings," Dethocrates muttered. As the heads reared back to breathe death on his friend, the Jai-Ruk placed the goblet within the top, spun it around several times, and loosed.

The goblet sailed through the air, in a beautiful arc. It struck Syrtuno on the temple. The force of the blow made Syrtuno lose his balance and with a cry, he fell from the beast landing on the ground.

Freed from the tome mages' control, the beast became confused, each of the three heads pulling towards their various desires. The body shifted back and forth while the long necks darted around, heads snapping at each other. With a hideous ripping sound, the beast tore itself apart.

The leftmost head flew off of the body, leaving a bloody stump behind, and slammed into a barrel of ale, smashing it apart. The rightmost head, likewise, became unattached from the body, and landed on one of the tables, sliding into a collection of pies and cakes. Both heads greedily consumed the substances they had landed amongst, but after a minute or so, their movements slowed, and they eventually lay still.

The middle head remained attached to the body. It snaked through the air, looking for something, before spotting the doll. The beast walked forward and gripped the doll in its talons, uttered another shriek of unearthly delight, and took to the skies, flying off into the night with its prize.

All was silent in the courtyard for several moments, the gathered people uncertain what they had witnessed. This silence was broken when Syrtuno pulled himself to his feet.

"Fools!" he shouted. "Do you think this will stop me? It was but one of my…"

Which was as far as he got before Wenintal clubbed him from behind. The mage crumpled to the ground again, and a group of Sturgeons, who had finally arrived, moved to take custody. Servants resumed moving through the party and began to clean up the sizeable mess. The conversation started flowing again between the guests. The remainder of Vash's guards, meanwhile, had moved over to the beast's heads, discussing where best to display them as trophies.

Dethocrates moved to help Andril to his feet. As he did so, Wenintal walked over to them, smiling.

"Well done!" he said. "The two of you have helped to detain a dangerous madman and, I daresay, saved several lives in the process! I don't know how the household of High Man Vash can repay you!"

Andril coughed. "Oh, Sir, it was nothing that any…"

"Actually," Wenintal continued, "I suppose the best way to repay you would be by not throwing you to the Sturgeons for masquerading as servants and sneaking into the party with intent to steal. Instead, you'll simply be escorted out. Guards!"

House guards that Andril did not remember being there during the fighting manifested all around Wenintal. Andril was not in any shape to resist, so he meekly threw his hands up. Dethocrates saw this, sighed, and did the same. The guards grabbed them both and lead them towards the exit.

"Wait," called a voice.

The guards and their prisoners turned, and saw Lady Paige walking towards them. She wore a tablecloth draped over her, and looked rather cross. Dethocrates sighed as she walked over to him. He extended the silk top, still in his hands, to her.

"My Lady," he said, now employing the perfect diction of a high noble, "I wish to thank you for your valuable contribution in the saving of this city. I return your possession to you, and hope you will remember the valuable service that the garment has rendered on all assembled here."

The lady took the garment, but her fire-spark filled the air with heat. Dethocrates braced himself to be slapped in the face, and thus was caught unawares by her rather vicious right hook.

"It's completely unfair," Andril said, sometime later. The two of them were sitting on the ground beside one of the Black Gate fountains, not far from where they'd been ejected from the celebration.

"It's more favorable than rotting in a cell," Dethocrates replied, holding his swollen eye up to a cold stone recently removed from the well.

"But we were the heroes of the day!" Andril insisted.

"Not by the time the guards are done with the story," Dethocrates said. "Besides, our contribution was almost certainly luck."

"Damn it all, what do I keep telling you? My luck is an asset!"

Dethocrates slowly rose to his feet. "After seeing you survive all of that, you may have a point. Come on – the Emerald Serpent's certainly serving, and I could use a drink."

Andril stood up, stretching. "We can't even say that we saved Tlacolotl Vash's life as I don't think he was really in danger."

Dethocrates shook his head. "I think he stayed up in his box, just watching, for a reason. But whatever the case, I'm almost glad that his party was so disastrous."

"I suppose," Andril said, as the two walked away. "People scared, property smashed, several guards killed, a few dozen more injured or crippled, and the Arch Pyromancer utterly destroyed, with nothing remaining."

At that remark, Dethocrates chuckled. "A night like tonight gives a person a chance to learn new things. That hideous fog the thrice-souled beast spat out, for example. It has a truly horrible effect on living beings, but what effect does it have on, say, precious minerals? Perhaps none at all?"

"Some of us were, indeed, wondering about that," Andril said. "Does that mean that you got something valuable from all this?"

Dethocrates stopped walking, standing in a shadow obscured from the light of the Ghost Moon. "I imagine that a normal roguish adventurer, when he says 'I'll distract it,' is implying that his companions should find a way to destroy the beast they are confronted with. You, of course, are not normal, so I stuck to the original plan."

At this, he reached into his tunic and pulled out a small bag, handing it to Andril. The smaller man opened it up, and gazed down at several golden rings.

Audril frowned, "Well, it's no ruby necklace, but it's still a sight better than empty pockets and a black eye."

Dethocrates nodded. "After we give the Nightmen Guild their share, we should have enough to settle the tab at the Serpent, pay off an outstanding debt or two, and leave us a bit of spare coin to waste."

"And waste it I will – eagerly," Andril said, picking up one of the rings and noting that it was somewhat sticky. "Hold on. There's a red, sticky substance on the rings, and in the bag – isn't that bits of…"

"Don't waste a moment's thought on it," Dethocrates said. "It might ruin your drinking mood."

"Fair enough. After all, whoever we sell them to certainly won't ask questions about a bit of grime."

"Very true," Dethocrates agreed, discretely moving a hand to make sure that the other bag – the one containing the central ruby – was secure inside his tunic. "Our clients like to keep things as discrete as possible."

Illustration by Jeff Laubenstein

REVENANTS

Martha Wells

"Jelith."

"Hush, I'm busy." His awareness of the chamber had faded until there was nothing but the rock.

"I have a job for us."

"We already have a job. I'm doing it now." The stone under his hands echoed with rushing waves of voices, their words incomprehensible, coming and going like the edge of the ocean. The temptation to listen was a mistake; they could draw in the unwary and sink them forever. Jelith fought past the waves to the stone itself, and sensed the cavity. At first it was smooth, but he winced as he sensed sharp edges. For a long moment it seemed like a promise fulfilled, then it narrowed to nothing. Disappointed, he drew his awareness back up to the surface. "Ah! Damn."

"Not a room?" Despite her distraction with jobs, Kryranen's voice was tinged with disappointment. They had had high hopes for this spot, now dashed.

"No." The taste of old blood filled his mouth and Jelith had to clear his throat to make the word understood. All the stone in these catacombs, the bedrock of the city above, tasted as if it was drenched in blood. "It's too irregular to be constructed by sentient beings, even those of such odd tastes as once populated Taux." He stepped back from the wall and dusted rock fragments off his hands, his dark skin briefly mottling with the sandstone color of the stone.

Jelith took a seat on his folding camp stool and lifted the small wooden box that he used as a lap desk. He dipped his writing stick into the inkstone to fill it, then began to note the dimensions and characteristics of the cavity. If they were lucky, this information would eventually form some small vital part of a greater whole. More likely it would just serve to remind him of what he had done today.

This tunnel was in the outer ring of the concentric circles of catacombs beneath the city, deep enough underground for Jelith to feel the weight of rock and stone buildings overhead, to taste the living earth in the back of his throat past the blood-drenched stone. Kryranen, oblivious to the sensations of stone, leaned one shoulder casually against the wall. She was a muscular Jai-Ruk, with skin similar in color to the sandstone lining this passage, and onyx-dark hair. Only the tips of her lower tusks were visible above the line of her pursed lips.

They made an odd pair for a number of reasons, but one was that she was tall for a Jai-Ruk and he was short for a Kin. They were dissimilar on all counts, except for their interest in the past, in strange myths, and mysteries, and how the world had looked before they set foot on it. They talked of things no one else cared about. Rather than an odd pairing, everyone thought they were just odd.

"This is a job that will pay us well," Kryranen said. "Up in the Gold Jaguar District." She added unnecessarily, "Where people like the Vash live."

"You're supposed to be keeping the notes," Jelith pointed out. Most inhabitants of Taux assumed Jai-Ruk were too brutish for scholarly pursuits, but Kryranen's handwriting was better than his. Her hands were large but her fingers were slender and dexterous; his notes looked like the scratchings of a child next to her elegant script.

She leaned forward to look at the book and her grimace suggested she agreed. "I'll recopy it later." Exasperated, she said, "You just don't like working for money. It's too bad we can't eat history."

"You would eat history if you could," Jelith felt obliged to say. It was true.

She folded her arms and gave him the long-suffering look.

He sighed. "What is this job?"

"They want us to lay a ghost."

Jelith stared. "Are you out of your mind?"

These prospective employers were not expecting them until later in the day, so Jelith made Kryranen buy him dinner at the Emerald Serpent. He wrapped up in the hooded cloak that he used to protect himself from the too-harsh light of Taux's sun, and they left the catacombs. They entered the old ball courts through the single entrance, the Black Gate carved with skulls and serpents and other symbols of the former inhabitants of Taux. Jelith would have given much to know the full meaning. There were two remaining sunken courts, the wide stepped stone bleachers around them now covered with makeshift shacks and dwellings, the crowded residences of Taux's less-prized citizens.

They took the stone ramps up past the ramshackle dwellings. The place was noisy and thick with thieves, mercenaries, and every sort of criminal, but no one bothered them. They blended in well, and the casual inhabitants assumed they were mercenaries. Their work often involved hard labor, moving stone or digging, so they were always covered with dust and sweat. Sometimes newcomers learned they were scholars and challenged them, to find that the appearance of ferocity was not a deception.

They passed the Silk Purse, where the prostitutes were too discrete to shout at passers-by, and turned into the dark entrance of the Emerald Serpent.

There were tables of different heights, designed for all the varying races that now inhabited Taux. Since Jelith was under four feet tall and Kryranen topped six, none was truly comfortable for them. As this was occasionally a matter of hilarity for newcomers to the Emerald Serpent, Jelith stood by their table and surveyed the room while Kryranen found stools of the right heights. There was some sniggering in the back among a group of Opal Gate mercenaries, but the regulars ignored them and no one spoke, so Jelith didn't have to cock-punch anyone.

When they were seated, Kryranen leaned back against the dingy wall and said, "They think the haunting is caused by a burial secreted somewhere inside the walls of their house."

"Madness, madness. You are a madwoman." Taux's stone was rich with spirits as it was; anyone who would bury a body within a house wall was asking for worse than trouble.

"They need someone to locate the body so it can be removed and set to rest. It will be simple."

"Simple? You are simple to think we should do this."

"I thought I was mad." Kryranen eyed him. "And if you say that again I will break your jaw for you."

Jelith decided not to say it again. Everyone knew much of Taux was haunted, one way or another. When the foreign newcomers had first moved into the deserted city, the wealthy had tried to turn the empty temples into palaces, but had been forced out by the sheer volume of strange and sometimes deadly supernatural occurrences. Such incidents in the more quiet Gold Jaguar District, which had always been residential, were more rare, but not unheard of. "It could be dangerous. Why don't they hire a Wizard?"

"They say the ghost has hurt no one so far." She shrugged one shoulder. "And they're afraid of Wizards."

As an answer it was woefully inadequate. And it also had the mark of Kryranen's vivid imagination. "Did they tell you this or did you make it up yourself to explain their inexplicable behavior?"

"I made it up myself," she admitted. "But I think it's true. I think they're afraid that the Wizard would tell their enemies of their trouble."

Jelith reluctantly conceded that that made some sense. "But they aren't afraid we will."

"Who cares what we say?"

This was true. No one associated with the powerful merchant clans or Red Pillars would be much interested in Jelith or Kryranen's opinion of them. "How much money?"

She told him, and he almost spat fermented grain water across the table. That would be enough to pay their living expenses until winter, and allow them to spend most of their time on their explorations in the catacombs, not in the hunting and selling of artifacts. "I see," he muttered.

Kryranen leaned back against the wall, giving him a self-satisfied look. "Am I a madwoman?"

"No. No, you are not." He spread his hands on the table. It was wood, and dead to his senses. "How did you hear about this? Surely they did not advertise in the market."

"The major-domo of their trading business approached me outside the Black Gate. He said he had been asking the dealers of art about Kin who would take commissions to search for things, and they directed him to us." At his expression, she added repressively, "I checked with the dealers, and he spoke the truth. I also spoke to some of the sellers of luxury goods, and they knew the house, and recognized the major-domo."

Jelith was still dubious, at best. "But when people with wealth hire people like us for mysterious jobs involving the supernatural, it never ends well."

"I know." Kryranen leaned forward, intent. "But the spirit may have learned something of old Taux, buried as it is within a wall. We could question it! And think what we could do with this money."

He sighed. No one would think it from her manner, but Kryranen was as big a fanatic as he was; she just hid it better. "The spirit will probably eat us."

"I would not say 'probably,'" Kryranen disagreed, but it didn't matter. She had heard the assent in his voice.

It was growing dark by the time they reached the Gold Jaguar District, and the warm lights in the windows of the tall stone houses did not far fall enough to light the street. In a way this was good, as their prospective employers did not wish for attention to this errand, and doubtless would not have appreciated it if Jelith and Kryranen became obliged to explain their presence here to the Sturgeon guards.

They had both stopped at their quarters to wash and put on cleaner leathers. There were wealthy Kin families who lived in this quarter, and hopefully, in the dark, they would be taken for a Kin merchant and his Jai-Ruk bodyguard, and no questions would be asked.

At first they passed others, fire-spark Humans, wind-born Aspara, a few earthly Kin, some traveling with personal guards and most carrying lamps, all clearly on their way home or to the entertainments being held in the more brightly-lit houses and the gardens surrounding them. Then the streets grew less busy, passers-by few and far between. There were few lighted windows, no music or voices drifting from walled courtyards or open doors. With less distraction, Jelith became more aware of the stone under his feet and in the walls. It echoed – all of Taux echoed – but there was less distortion from the everyday activities of current residents. He caught the edge of voices that came from no living being, and tasted old blood in the back of his throat.

"Why are ghosts hunted at night, and not in the day?" he asked.

"They aren't as likely to come out in the day," Kryranen said. "We want to speak to it before we tell them where the body is, remember? That's the point of all this. Besides the money."

"Yes, yes," Jelith grumbled. He could not quite believe in this ghostly conversation Kryranen had her heart set on. He thought they would find a moldering body, hopefully be paid, and go home as ignorant as they had started. The spirits of Taux were many, but they were never cooperative.

Kryranen found the house with difficulty, having to retrace their path twice. The near unbroken darkness and silent houses leaning over them wore on Jelith's nerves. Not sure whether he was more worried about being stopped and questioned by guards, attacked by street robbers, or assaulted by some mythical creature of the night, he said, "I thought you knew where this place was!"

"I was given the direction, but it's hard to mark the way in the darkness of the abyss," Kryranen said, annoyed. "Wait, I think this is it."

It was a stone-walled yard looming out of the dark, a bulky structure rising behind it with odd angles and a few windows visible only as dimly-lit squares, light leaking sporadically out between tightly-closed shutters. At some point, an elaborate iron rail had been added to the top of the already tall stone wall, to further discourage intruders. Kryranen pushed the heavy wooden door of the gate and it squeaked open to admit them.

They crossed an outer courtyard, all tree shadows and the rustle of leaves, the scent of flowers, the trickle of water and the smell of dust on the path. Kryranen led the way through to another arched stone gate, to a smaller stone-floored court lit by two hanging lamps framing the large double doors of the house. In their light, Jelith could see that the house had four levels at least, in the blocky square stone construction that was common in this part of Taux, with bands of carved ornamentation running across the face of it. It was not nearly as large as he had supposed, as the other houses of the Gold Jaguar District. Perhaps because it was so near the edge of the burrow, or perhaps it extended further back than it seemed.

Before Kryranen could approach the doors, one of them began to open. Jelith admitted to a slight flutter of unease, but the door revealed a lamplit entryway and an elderly Human male in a servant's plain clothes. The man said, "You are the Kin Jelith and the Jai-Ruk Kryranen?"

"That is us," Kryranen replied. "We are here about the...spiritual problem."

The servant stepped back. "Please enter and follow me."

The servant led them through a series of small but high-ceilinged chambers, fitted out as receiving rooms.

Jelith had thought the family must have acquired the house only recently, discovering it was afflicted with a spirit sometime afterward. The furnishings were very rich, as expected, chairs and tables of fine dark woods, inlaid with ivory and mother of pearl, but rooms were small and the walls of smooth unornamented stone, like the walls of many of the common structures in

Taux. It was not nearly as fine as what was usually found in the Gold Jaguar. But all the structures in Taux, except for the new ones of wood constructed by recent arrivals inside the Black Gate, were re-purposed and often oddly laid out for whatever use their new inhabitants put them to.

Then they entered a last waiting room with an archway that opened into a large space, unlit and shadowy. Jelith could see heavy square columns, carved with the angular designs, and a very finely polished floor of red granite.

The servant said, "Wait here, please," and started toward a smaller door in the sidewall that led off into a different part of the house.

Jelith asked, "Wait for what? May we not simply get started?" The house seemed larger than he had thought at first and the sooner they began to search, the better.

The servant turned back. "My Master wishes to speak with you first."

"Your master?" Kryranen asked, a trace warily. "I thought the arrangement already made. We will locate the source of the disturbance, free it from whichever wall or floor it is buried in, and you will pay us."

The servant inclined his head. "That was the arrangement, but my Master wishes to deal with you directly."

Of course he does, Jelith thought. The better to assess whether or not they could keep the house's secrets.

As the servant moved away, Kryranen surveyed the room. "It doesn't seem haunted."

"You mean there are no shrieking demons climbing out of the cracks." Jelith stepped to the nearest plain wall and put his hand to the stone. Unlike the underground, its echoes were muted, blunted by uncounted years of simple daily life, much like the stone of the streets they had walked to reach this place. He frowned at the much more richly-decorated room visible through the archway. It made a strange contrast to the rest of the house. He took a step toward it.

"Not yet." Kryranen added, "But I don't want shrieking demons, I want an original inhabitant, a chatty one eager to speak to..." She spun around, drawing her sword in one smooth motion.

Jelith flinched and reached for his blade, but Kryranen faced a corner of the room, occupied by nothing other than an ivory chair too delicate for anyone to sit on. "What is it?" he asked.

"Something touched me." She eased a step back. "A cold touch, on the back of my neck."

"It seems we have not mistaken the house," Jelith muttered. He leaned against the wall, torn between sending his awareness deeper into the stone and watching Kryranen. There was still no hint of a disturbance in the wall. The corpse, wherever it was concealed, must be hidden behind a different stone, something that did not share echoes with this wall. *Or the haunting is caused by something else...* "I think—"

He forgot what he thought, for a dozen dark shadow figures melted out of the far wall and charged them.

Jelith drew his sword, blocking a swing aimed at his head. He half-expected his blade to pass through the specter but it connected so solidly it rattled his bones. He ducked a second blow, caught sight of Kryranen surrounded by shadows, her sword moving like a bright flash. He feinted, stabbed, but as his blade entered his shadowy opponent's chest, the thing surged toward him and seized his throat. The force of it choked off his breath and cracked bones and... it was gone.

Jelith stood in the center of the room, his sword held limply in one hand. Kryranen stood a few paces away, breathing hard, her sword still raised in guard. The air was icy cold, and Jelith's exhaled breath came out in a steamy cloud.

Their eyes met in mutual consternation. She said, "I apologize for persuading you into this job."

"I forgive you," he told her.

She hesitated. "Do you want to leave?"

Jelith considered it, then said, "All the benign powers help me, I do not."

"Me neither." Kryranen's prominent incisors flashed in a brief grin.

They heard the servant's quiet footsteps, and a moment later he stepped into the doorway. He took in their martial stances with a raised brow.

Kryranen cleared her throat and sheathed her sword. She began, "There was a... We believed there was a..."

With an air of weary resignation, and the first sign that there was a personality behind his façade, he stopped her. "There is no need to explain, believe me. Come this way, please."

The servant led them through another maze of small reception rooms, then upstairs and through a door to a somewhat larger sitting room with a balcony looking down onto a dark inner court. The room was lit by many lamps, and occupied by five Humans. They were speaking, rather agitatedly, and the room was warm with the restrained power of their Element. They stopped as the servant opened the door.

Jelith saw immediately that three of them could be discounted. They were a young woman and two young men, all dressed richly, with the tattoos fashionable among the later generations of newcomers to Taux. They must be family members but had obviously been relegated to the sulky fringe of the conversation. There were two main players, the first an aged woman sitting in an armchair as if it might have been a throne, her expression that of an emperor dealing with a particularly difficult vassal. The vassal in question was a young man, handsome, pacing impatiently before the balcony. They had a family resemblance in their sharp, stubborn features, their light brown skin and dark straight hair.

The young man looked up at their appearance and ceased his pacing. "You are the-…"

He stopped, at a loss for the word. Jelith wasn't sure what to fill it in with, either. None of their occupations seemed appropriate for the occasion. He said, "We are. I am Jelith, and this is Kryranen."

The young man said, "I am Cerran Vatel." He nodded toward the older woman. "My mother." To the others as a body. "My wife, my brothers." The mother was the only one who acknowledged the introduction, giving them a grim nod of greeting.

Vatel said, "Did my major-domo tell you about the… problem?"

"Something of it," Kryranen admitted cautiously. "That there is a disturbed spirit, which you believe is buried within a wall."

Vatel said, "We acquired this house from another merchant family, some five years ago. After a time, it became apparent that there was a spirit here. There had been rumors of some sort of foul activities in the house, that the daughter of a lesser merchant clan had gone missing here." He folded his arms and turned away. "Everyone believes her corpse was hidden in the walls of the house somewhere, and that the spirit disturbances are caused by it."

Jelith said, "When did the spirit's more violent appearances start?"

Vatel tossed him a frown. "Does it matter? Do your work, find the thing and get rid of it."

Kryranen raised a brow. Jelith said equably, "It does matter. I wonder why anyone would spend much time living in a house with a restless spirit. Everyone knows that in Taux, the consequences could be dangerous."

Mother Vatel glared at her son. "Tell him."

Vatel paced away, and forced the words out. "We are a prominent family." This seemed aimed at the old woman more than anything. "If we don't take our place among the other merchants of our class, we will be ignored, ridiculed—'...'"

"Quiet! I'll tell him, then." The old women sat forward. "Do you know where this house is?"

Jelith exchanged a look with Kryranen. It seemed a trick question. She answered, "I know it's in the west end of the Gold Jaguar District, but we're not familiar with this area."

"Correct. It is at the far west end of the Gold Jaguar District, near the old temples."

Kryranen let her breath out in a hiss of dismay. Jelith clapped a hand to his eyes. He said, "I think I see where this is going, madam." And he didn't wish to. Only the very poorest of Taux's residents could be found within the walls of the old temples because of the haunting.

Mother Vatel nodded. "When our family claimed this house, we were one of the least important traders in the port. Securing this house, at the edge of what was to become the Gold Jaguar District, allowed us access to more important trading contracts. We ignored its unsavory antecedents, and the disturbances were no worse than what is common is much of Taux. But while the façade of the house is impressive, the interior was small for the area, with no impressive assembly rooms. We could not hold the entertainments important to gather attention and favor with the other wealthy families. A few months ago it came to my son's attention that there was a closed-off room behind this house, a large, elegant chamber. He said he had heard stories that the former owners had had it walled off. So he had workmen break through the wall at the back of this house to open it again." Her jaw hardened. "That was when the spirit began to attack us in earnest."

Grim, Kryranen said, "This chamber extends across the border. You think that was why it was walled off in the first place."

The old woman sat back. "You understand."

"Only too well," Jelith said. He controlled the urge to say something more sarcastic. Only a spoiled fool could think this large comfortable house somehow inadequate, and look what the Vatel's' greed had led to. "But I have a question for the young master."

Vatel turned, reluctantly, sulky guilt writ clearly on his features.

Jelith said, "How did you know the chamber was there, behind your house?"

Vatel demanded. "What do you mean?"

"Did someone speak to you of it?" Jelith asked. Mother Vatel was frowning, but he suspected she was entirely on his and Kryranen's side in this matter. "You have no affinity of Earth. I would say you were low Fire, as is the rest of your family. Did a Kin, or some Jai-Ruk with a greater degree of Earth tell you of it?" The young man's expression showed increasing confusion, and Jelith felt the pit of his stomach turn hollow. He had suspected this, but the confirmation was more frightening than he had supposed. "How did you know it was there?"

"I don't... I don't know."

Mother Vatel obviously followed his reasoning, for her expression betrayed consternation now more than annoyance. She said, "You believe something...influenced him, from behind the wall."

Kryranen answered her, "It – whatever it is – may have used the Human spirit remaining here with the body as a conduit. It may have been working for years towards this."

Jelith added, "That chamber may have never been part of this house at all. It may be part of a temple, buried among the other buildings of the quarter, walled-off for some ritual purpose by the original inhabitants of Taux."

Everyone stared at them in horror. Mother Vatel said, "What is your advice?"

Jelith said, "Leave this house for the night, and summon the stonemasons immediately."

Vatel protested, dragged his heels, and otherwise resisted, but his mother carried the day. She was old enough to have heard firsthand the tales of the newcomers who had tried to take Taux's temples for their own homes, and what had happened to them. The idea that her son's mind had been compromised by a spirit's influence firmed her resolve to iron.

As the family members and servants scrambled to decamp for the night, Jelith wrote down a direction for her. "Send a servant to these stonemasons. Tell them Jelith said it is an emergency and they will understand, and come."

While they were speaking, the lamps in the room fluctuated all at once, the flames shrinking away nearly to nothing, then blossoming again as one. It sped everyone on their way.

Before leaving, Vatel rallied long enough to order the older servant who had let them in and three much younger, sturdier men to arm themselves and stay to guard the house, in case Jelith and Kryranen decided to loot the place in the family's absence. "I wouldn't touch a thing from this demon-ridden place," Kryranen muttered to Jelith.

"I hope they keep their coins elsewhere," he told her.

Once the family was gone and the wary servants posted in the front entrance, Jelith and Kryranen held a brief consultation.

Kryranen said, "So we have to find the corpse that started it all, wherever it is, or sealing off the temple chamber won't work."

"Exactly."

"So where is it?"

Jelith had thought about this, while everyone was coming and going. "If one wishes to hide a murdered body, presumably one doesn't put it in a wall where one can stare at the spot for years afterward."

"So not in one of the family rooms." Kryranen tapped her chin. "It must be in one of the service areas. Not the kitchen; kitchens are seldom empty long, and one presumes the guilty party didn't want an audience while hiding the woman's body."

"A chamber used for storage." Jelith looked around thoughtfully. "We need to find the service rooms."

There were several chambers below street level, reached by a stairway down from the kitchens, situated in the court in back of the house. They took lamps from the kitchen to light the cool darkness, and as they went down the stairs the light shone on a simple stone-walled room, with an archway leading into another, and another. The slight separation from the stone and walls of the main house explained why Jelith had felt no taint of organic rot there. But apparently the spirit could jump the gap with ease.

In the second room, Jelith found a lighter patch in the smooth gray-brown stone. It looked as if a section of the wall had been knocked away and replaced. The patch was clumsily, and perhaps hastily, wrought. "This is not Tolimic masonry." He placed his hand on it.

He sensed it immediately, a faint echo of rot in the stones and the mortar between them. He pushed a little deeper and found the narrow vault just on the other side of the layer of stones. It was a very small vault, barely big enough for even a small Human body. Jelith just hoped the woman been dead when shoved into the space. "Here," he said, his voice low with concentration. "We dig here."

He began to withdraw his senses. And something caught hold of him, like a hand wrapping around his wrist. "Kryranen," he said, only that, but the change in tone was enough.

She grabbed his free arm to yank him away from the wall, but a pressure pushed him forward into the stone. He felt his Element drawn out of him and his body followed. "Jelith!" the Jai-Ruk shouted, an echo down through the ages like the voices of the long-dead Tolem. She wrenched at him with all her considerable strength, but he still sank into the wall.

Jelith tasted stone, mortar, dust, old death, horror, and then the blood-drenched bedrock of the underground. He staggered free, gasped for air, and found himself in a wide corridor of polished onyx, inlaid with bands of blood red quartz. There were no lamps, but light seeped from the stone. An instant later, something slammed into him from behind. He turned and found himself staring up at Kryranen.

She staggered, caught him by the shoulder to steady herself. "That was unexpected," she gasped. "Are we on the other side of the wall?"

Jelith turned, eyeing the strange corridor, the stranger light. "I fear not." He hadn't sensed this space from the other side. This was something of the otherworld, something the spirits had created.

"I suppose that was to be expected. I..." Her grip on his shoulder tightened, and she said, "We could ask them."

Jelith looked behind him, and his heart seized.

Figures moved down the corridor toward them. They seemed Human, though their faces and forms were too shadowy to discern. Their motion forward was measured and as inevitable as the tide. "This...is not good," Jelith said under his breath.

"Astute observation," Kryranen muttered. She raised her voice to say, "We mean no harm. We've told the householder to seal off the wall of your temple and leave it undisturbed—"

The figures morphed out of Human form and into looming, terrible shapes that Jelith's eyes couldn't define. In a mass, the shadow creatures rushed forward.

They didn't care for that, Jelith thought as he fell back with Kryranen, drawing his sword. Then the darkness swarmed them and there was no time to think.

The creatures were just solid enough to land blows, but not much affected by Jelith and Kryranen's swords. Jelith ducked, blocked, and swung, dodged attempts to seize his throat, his limbs, to claw at his eyes, all while trying to keep Kryranen in sight. If they were separated... well, he didn't want to contemplate it.

Then the diminutive Kin spotted living color and movement among the shadow-shapes. He caught two glimpses before he managed to duck another, a blow aimed at his head, and get a better look. Jelith boggled at the strange sight. It was a Human woman, dancing wildly among the shadows. She was light-skinned and light-haired, dressed in torn silk draped around her like a... *Shroud*, Jelith realized. *It's her.*

Acting on impulse, he darted forward and snatched her around the waist. She was as solid as the shadows, and struggled and pounded at him. He had lost his bearings in the melee and shouted desperately, "Kryranen, wall!" hoping she would understand.

A large warm body struck him like a runaway cart. It caught hold of his shoulders and slammed him into the onyx stone. Jelith drew on every ounce of his Element and pushed forward into the wall.

For an instant he thought it wouldn't work. The stone felt as impenetrable as wood. Then it melted around him. He felt the drag of Kryranen's body and of the fighting revenant, then Kryranen started to slip away. In panic, he gripped her hand where it rested on his shoulder and shoved forward.

A moment later he slammed into a floor. Kryranen landed on top of him with a loud "oof!" and rolled away. Dazed, Jelith sat up.

They were back in the underground storage chamber. On the wall before them was a roughly Jelith-sized scar, chunks of mortar and rock scattered around it. There was nothing on the other side of the wall except bedrock. Jelith looked for the revenant, then realized he sat in the middle of a pile of scattered bones and rotted cloth, all that was left of her. He looked at Kryranen, who was covered with rock dust, her clothes stained with sweat, but otherwise seemed none the worse for wear. Breathing hard, she said, "I think our work here is done."

"I concur. Let us wait for our employers outside."

They took a table cover from the pantry and used it to carefully and quickly collect every scrap of bone, then went outside to sit on a bench in the courtyard and wait for the stonemasons. Jelith chose a wooden bench, just for safety's sake, and they rested their feet on the sparse grass.

"I suppose the Taux spirits took advantage of her," Kryranen said. "I still would have liked to speak to her."

"I don't know. She looked as if she was enjoying herself. She might not have been forthcoming." It was disappointing, but Jelith was not willing to trade their lives for answers.

Kryranen hesitated. "So...that temple corridor. It was not behind the wall, was it?"

"No."

"If we went into that temple – Saints help us – and searched, we would find nothing like that."

"Yes."

"So where were we?" She frowned. "Did we imagine it, and actually only fought shadows in the cellar until you pulled the girl's bones from the wall?"

"If it makes you feel better."

"It does not," she said frankly.

He shook his head. "We search a dangerous place, for dangerous things. I think our future holds much worse, if we continue on our course." It was his turn to hesitate. "Was it perhaps... Do you wish to stop our work?"

She sighed. "No. Sometimes I wish I could, but...perhaps we are possessed, or influenced, like Vatel."

It was not a comforting thought, there in the dark. "Perhaps we are just mad," Jelith said hopefully.

Kryranen smiled at him. "At least we are good company."

Illustration by Jeff Laubenstein

WATER REMEMBERS

Julie E. Czerneda

*L*ife returned to Taux the way it had first come, from the sea. Those who'd cautiously, then eagerly, resettled the vacant city found themselves welcomed by a port of such cunning construction that fifty years without tending had done no appreciable damage. The great seawalls and the hand-forged islands they protected remained intact despite the waves and the wicked storms that raged down this coast at season's turn.

The bay so sheltered was kept fresh, not by the twice-daily rise and fall of the tides beyond its mouth, but by the Wizards at its heart. Their Star Tower thrust from the depths, its structure impossibly tall and narrow, with windows like slanted eyes that glowed with an uncanny blue light. The top was shrouded in mist not even the summer sun could disperse, the base circled by an implacable current that made it impossible for ship or swimmer to approach, preserving the isolation of those who'd withdrawn from the world.

Which suited everyone else.

The elegant stone quay ringing the city's edge was intact, but Taux's wharves were another matter. The outthrust piers swayed against one another like cheerful drunks, their barnacled bases rotten to the core, while unguarded planks were ripped up and whisked away to build shelters. Taux's captains took what timber remained to build sturdy berths for their ships, extorting any fees they chose from those who came after.

For in Taux, there was no new wood to be had, or stone.

But there was always... opportunity.

Wizard's Fog, they called it, when those in the Star Tower loosed their spite to bother honest folk. The thick, cloying mist writhed through streets and alleyways, dampening sound and encouraging the Nightmen's cutpurses. It coiled like a great, eyeless snake in the bay, trapping ships and hiding all but the tip of one's nose.

Raising his mask, Hunhau sniffed reluctantly. The reek of flowers to the left. A lingering stench of cold ash to the right. The bite of the open sea like a beacon ahead. He wasn't lost. Not yet, anyway.

Before the smells overwhelmed him, making his eyes fill with tears, he replaced the mask, its plugs snug in his nostrils. He shuffled along, feet bare to feel the stone, and squinted through the eye holes, for what good it could do. Lamplight couldn't penetrate a wizardly mist and the sun had yet to rise above the horizon. Without his nose, he'd walk off the quay into the bay or, more likely, into a wall.

Of course, without his nose, he'd be in the Black Gate District, home in bed like everyone else. *Everyone honest*, he amended.

Hunhau took firm hold of the straps that held the deep woven basket to his shoulders. He wasn't, he reminded himself, going to miss this chance. Yesterday's breeze had found him in his shop and trickled through the wads he habitually shoved up his nose while working. His weak affinity for air was usually a nuisance, bringing what he didn't want to his too-large and overly sensitive nose, but such a breeze, redolent of a distant shore, meant something worth the effort on today's tide ... if he got to it first.

His toe struck an unexpected edge and Hunhau stopped to pull up his mask again. No need to inhale. The fetid odor of damp wool climbed up his nose, coupled with bat urine. He'd reached the stone bridge from the mainland portion of Taux to the Moon's Arm, the east-most island that sheltered the bay. This was the Waynside Bridge, twin to the Baymourn on the far side of the bay. He hurriedly replaced the mask and went on as quickly as he dared. The Jai-Ruk dockworkers who chose to sleep in hammocks under the bridge were not the pleasant sort. Not at all.

Not far now. Hunhau's outstretched fingers found the rail, cold and slick with dew. Moving with renewed confidence, he followed its downward curve until another stubbed toe painfully marked the end of the bridge. He was on the island, meaning the gap in the rail should be ... here.

He made his way down the tilted rubble of what had once been steps, following the familiar path. Before he reached the bottom, the mist began to thin, pierced by the faintest light. Sunrise.

He was late. The tide would come in soon, to steal back what it had brought. Worse, with the failing of the mist, others would come. He jumped from stone to damp sand and caught his balance.

Hunhau had discovered where to look years ago. Clean breezes from the open sea pushed all manner of flotsam and jetsam shorewards, to be stranded by the receding tide along this stretch of sand.

The others, wasteful wretches, sought the driftwood to burn. He sought the smooth wood, those pieces with shapes and whorls carved deep and wild to become masks.

Masks were always in demand, though only the elite of Taux could afford those of glorious imported jadeite, with obsidian eyes and rare plumes. Fewer still had the price – or were willing to pay it – for a mask of magical potency, bespelled to lure or deflect a gaze, to make the wearer appear otherwise, or to call luck to one's side like a dog.

Hunhau chuckled to himself. He'd yet to see a mask do more than hide a face. Yum Caax, his old master, had taught him masks were works of art, not magic, insisting what mattered was the craft, not the tricks. The craft was hard enough. Truth be told, Hunhau wasn't a very good maskmaker. Upon the old man's passing, he'd dutifully made Yum Caax's death mask then set up his own, more modest, shop. His masks were of wood, and he served a clientele of servants, itinerants, and the like, those happy to afford any mask at all. Their needs were straightforward: masks for celebration, masks to honor their dead. So long as the sea gave him wood, he made a fair profit.

So long as he refused those seeking something more than a mask, he stayed out of trouble. For Yum Caax had been right. The only magic a Taux maskmaker possessed was the ability to convince a customer to believe what a mask could do. When results inevitably failed that belief, it was that foolish maskmaker who'd pay, unless he or she ran far and fast enough.

Hunhau preferred a safe and long life. He bet on the games, but not to excess, enjoyed women and wine, in moderation, and prudently collected bits of blue shell for his own death mask, having accepted that his meager skills wouldn't attract an apprentice. On mornings when the conditions were right, he'd trundle along the quay, as this morning, and descend to the sand to gather driftwood.

Wizard's Fog... Hunhau shivered in the lingering damp, glad to see it lift even if that brought others to the sand. Now to see if the little breeze had been tease or promise. He lifted his mask to better look around. The clean sea air was potent, but didn't vex his stomach the way bilge and sailor-stink and that fusty odor from the sails did.

"Saints Great and Lesser," he gasped.

The exposed beach was strewn with wood of all shapes and sizes. Treasure for the taking!

And he was here first.

He picked his way through a delicious agony of choices, mind awhirl. Had a distant storm tossed shipwreck this way? Or had one of the dreadful waves that followed a disturbance of the earth washed an entire village out to sea?

Perhaps the Saints, despite his neglect, chose to smile on him. "I'll pray," he promised. To all of them, just in case.

All too soon, despite raising his standards well beyond what ordinarily he'd have taken and been glad of, Hunhau staggered happily beneath his overfilled basket, arms laden as well.

He should go back. The light of the rising sun glittered like a sword across the water, the mist a memory. He should go back and would, he promised himself.

After one more...

The maskmaker followed the curling line of wet sand, bright red crabs scuttling out of his way, and there it was, kissing land's edge mere steps ahead, a piece of driftwood already bent to fit a face, with the finest grain he'd seen.

Hunhau tossed aside the armload he'd collected and hurried to claim his prize, though there was no one else in sight.

But it was no more wood than the swirl of silver and blue pushing it closer was wave.

What he'd thought driftwood lifted with rare grace to become a head, and what surely, – oh surely! – had been ocean an instant before, like the spray salty on his lips, sculpted itself into pale shoulders and arms, and shaped the curved form of a woman from the froth.

A woman who gasped and fell forward, outstretched hands holding her from the sand, face hidden behind a sodden fall of hair. Hair, Hunhau noticed with dismay, that became water where it touched the damp sand, as did the white and gold cloth of her garments. No shipwreck, this. No hapless victim tossed from the seawall by murderer or Moon Priest. Those bodies he'd seen, bloated and grotesque, half-eaten by crab and seabird. They'd not bothered him, other than the stench. When he could, when there was a face still, he'd fashion a death mask as best he could from a plank or scrap of cloth, for he was a kindly man at heart.

This creature was nothing so safe or simple. His eyes lifted reluctantly to where the Star Tower pierced the sky beyond the seawall. Wizards lived there. Only there. And never left.

Until, he feared, now.

Heart in his throat, Hunhau replaced his mask and eased a careful step back, then another.

"Tell me, good man. Am I dead?"

Masks could hide a face and its expression, as her strange hair did now; the voice was harder to disguise. Hers was melodic and low, free of fear, as gentle as the lap of wave over his sandaled feet. It held him when he would have fled.

"I don't know," Hunhau answered honestly. "I'm but a maskmaker."

"Maskmaker?" She made an odd sound, like a seabird, her shoulders shaking. "Well met. I've need of your services." With that, the woman of the sea lifted her head, hair flowing aside, to show him her face.

Hunhau shrugged off his basket, precious driftwood spilling on the sand, and put an arm around her shoulders. "It's a healer you need. Come. Easy now," he said as he helped her stand. At his urging, she took a step on feet – he noticed numbly – she hadn't had before. He swallowed. "How could this…?"

"It doesn't matter," she said quietly. "Will you help me?"

Knowing what she asked, the maskmaker bent his head and sighed with true regret. "If I could, I would. I'm sorry. My masks have no magic."

"From now on, they will," she told him, and he heard the sea.

"I've worked with worse," Ghanan said firmly. He hadn't, ever. Couldn't imagine worse. But to be a stonemason in Taux, where every stone was blood-soaked and soul-stained, meant facing the unthinkable or not be paid. "Might take an extra few days," he added in a thoughtful mumble, making a show of leaning close to examine the wall in question.

Little faces stared back. Whatever the use of this subterranean corridor before the curse, it hadn't been anything sane. The stones, well-dressed and true to his knowing eye, were separated by rows of hand-sized figurines, crammed together like obscene mortar. Those at head-height stared out from hollow eyes, their noses cut away, mouths set in sorrowful lines or agape in agony. Those above were carved with death's heads, each skull given a smile. He didn't look down. The lower rows were jammed with limp little corpses, each tortured pose too realistic for comfort.

Zotz didn't appear to mind. The child sat on her stool, where he'd asked her to wait during this adult business of claims and contracts. Her hands lay limp, palm-up, in her lap; her dull gaze trailed along the rows of figurines, back and forth, her face empty of expression.

"It must be done quickly." Gamesmaster Ixchel kept her eyes on the plaster-strewn floor, though that view was hardly more reassuring, the plaster being blood red. Someone – or several someones – had chiselled that covering from the walls. If they'd hoped to make the space more palatable, Ghanan thought, they'd failed. The stone voices were louder than ever, whispers rattling hoarse and wordless at the edge of torchlight, assiduously ignored by the living. "Those coming after you will need their time to work," she continued. "All must be ready well before the games. You've seen our plans."

Before the discovery of this corridor running beneath the Black Gate's Ullamalitzli Tournament Field became general knowledge, the Gamemaster of the Golden Jaguar District had swept in to claim it. Ghanan had indeed seen her plans, laid out in an opulent, scale model kept locked away and well-guarded. They called for luxurious private and common rooms for players, with connected baths and saunas, storage for gear, and a large space for hosting what Ghanan guessed Ixchel hoped would be intimate victory celebrations. For one team. Hers. Visitors would have to make do with accommodations elsewhere in the Black Gate, or beyond, and so be at disadvantage.

"Remarkable," Ghanan acknowledged with a courteous nod. Ridiculous and sure to be untenable for the athletes once seepage from below exceeded the pumps, and damp rot set in, but such people didn't want his honest opinion, only his sweat. Their plans weren't his problem; cleansing the place so plumbers and other tradesfolk didn't run screaming in horror was.

No matter how.

The stonemason stepped gingerly through the fragments and dust. "Once this is cleared away, I'll start work."

"The stones stay," insisted Tlacolotl Vash. By his build and manner, the man could have been a fishmonger straight from the docks; certainly his rough clothing and scuffed boots said no different. But around his neck was the scarf that marked him a Red Pillar, one of the city's ruling merchant elite, and a pair of heavily-armed, blue-cloaked Sturgeons waited by the stairs leading up, their hard gaze never leaving the stonemason. Tlacolotl gave the walls an impatient look. "Replacing any is out of the question."

It always was, but Ghanan couldn't argue with what gave him a living. Generations of the Tolem had spent their fortunes to bring stone across the sea, building their city here where none belonged. Maybe they'd liked the view. He shrugged. To those now living in Taux, the stones were priceless.

Once they stopped screaming.

"I've worked with worse," he repeated. Though not, until now, within the Black Gate District. The reason most people had settled – and still lived – within the original massive stadium had been the relative quiet of its stone. Fewer had died there on the grim day that ended the great city's prior life a half-century earlier.

Too many had died down here.

Ixchel looked up. "Stonemason Ghanan comes with the highest recommendation, Tlacolotl," she said stiffly, eyes aglitter. "Our Jaguars will prepare and recuperate in magnificent, private splendor. They'll be victorious. We begin a dynasty!"

Tlacolotl looked unimpressed. "Secrecy," he growled. "That above all. If our competitors get wind of what we intend here…"

"You work alone. Isn't that right, Ghanan?"

"My daughter assists me," he replied. His hand found itself on Zotz's shoulder and his mouth smiled of its own accord. She didn't look up and Ghanan, freed, lifted away his hand. "Your secrets are safe," he said wearily. "Zotz is mute."

In the pause that followed, the stones whispered and gibbered. The Sturgeons shifted uneasily and the Gamesmaster's skin paled beneath its paint.

"You'd make your own child endure what's here." The Red Pillar's voice was cold. "A child like this."

Escape beckoned, as it always did, as if it were possible.

But it wasn't. Words spilled through unwilling lips. "Zotz has talent for the work," Ghanan heard himself reply. "It's both of us or none. Her mother's passed and I won't leave her alone."

Alone was how he'd found her. Two years ago, he'd stepped in an alley for a leak and there she'd been, naked but for mud, her hair a filthy mat. No street waif, disputing with rats for kitchen leavings; such he'd have taken to the priestesses of Shera, the Saint who cared for hearth and home, and those who had neither. This child picked at the stone wall, what remained of her fingernails leaving trails of blood behind.

She'd stopped when he touched her shoulder, stopped and looked up with eyes like charnel pits, brimming with the faces of the dead.

He'd have run, had he been able, but his cursed knee had locked and he'd staggered in place, bile rising in his throat.

Her lids had closed, then reopened over dull, ordinary eyes that dismissed him before the child – or whatever it was – went back to pawing at the stone.

He'd have run– and should have. Saints knew now he wished he had. But without the witness of those impossible eyes, curiosity had trapped him. She didn't scrabble at random. Her bloody fingers pried at subtle flaws in the stone, flaws he'd recognized.

They were those he sought when trying to muffle the voices in the stones for his clients.

Ignoring the sick lurch under his heart, Ghanan had put an ear to the cold stone, braced for the screams and madness.

Silence.

He'd pulled back to stare at the child. His clumsy attempts to chip and patch achieved nothing like this. What she did, however and to what purpose, cleansed the stone for good.

She'd lifted a foot and crabbed sideways to reach the next in the row.

To this day, Ghanan didn't know why he'd taken hammer and chisel from his belt, why he'd gently pushed aside her bleeding fingers to carefully chip the next spot of fracture.

Why he'd stood watching as she pressed her mouth to the exposed surface, sucking and swallowing like a babe at breast.

Why he'd ever thought to take her home...

"Of course you mustn't leave your daughter," Ixchel said graciously, her eyes fixed longingly on the stairs to the surface. "This space will be ready for you by midday tomorrow. Do what you must, stonemason. All that matters is having these rooms finished and ready before the games."

Ghanan bowed, trapped once more.

"Should be interesting games this season," Tohil commented. The big Sturgeon leaned against the wall; though in the shade, sweat beaded along the raised tattoos on his black skin and dripped from his earrings. The quilted cotton armor and blue overrobe of his station weren't gifts in midsummer, not in Taux, but no Sturgeon patrolled the streets without them. "Bet on it, my friend. Our Snakes can't lose."

Hunhau handed Tohil a flask. "I'm confused," he said, amused. "Or you are. What happened to "Drop every gutless player in the swamp?""

They'd spent many a night in the Emerald Serpent contemplating suitable fates for their once-beloved team. The Black Gate's Snakes' pathetic showing last year still rankled.

"Things'll be different." Tohil took a deep swig, drawing the back of his hand across his full lips, then stared at the flask in mock amazement. "Sigfried's Saintly Beard. I know it's water but how can it taste better than beer?"

The maskmaker reclaimed his flask. "Because you're hot. Now what's this about 'our' Snakes?"

"Not that you heard it from me," Tohil began, meaning he'd heard whatever it was from another who wished to stay anonymous, and likely several others before that. Rumor, in Taux, was a many-legged beast. "But there's been some rooms found – beneath the main field itself. The Gamesmaster plans to house her oh-so-mighty Jaguars there. Rooms of cursed stone," he added sagely, as if his wide shoulders weren't resting on the very same substance. "They'll get no rest there."

"Stone can be cleansed," the maskmaker pointed out. Sunlight silenced the voices of Taux's former, unfortunate inhabitants; various measures could mute them. The Raised Market was full of those claiming to remove them entirely, as well as bunions and the evil eye for an extra fee.

"As to…" Tohil straightened, his slouch gone.

Hunhau glanced down the row of litters. Which had caught his friend's professional interest? There were several of the vehicles parked, their sturdy bearers lounging nearby, kicking a sepak ball back and forth, or dozing, but it would be more surprising to find the laneway empty, given this was the side entrance to The Silk Purse, the most infamous brothel in Taux.

Two years past he'd brought the woman from the sea here, aware that the Purse's house physician was, if not the best in Taux, then by far the most practiced and discrete. Two years, her wounds fully healed, yet still she came, each 7th day morning. Hunhau asked for no explanation, nor did she offer one.

For like the sea, Cenoté brimmed with secrets.

Like the sea, her gifts were extraordinary and unexpected. The flask at his hip, ever full of sweet, cool water. The mask he now wore. The outer surface resembled the one his old master had made for him, but inside? No plugs crammed his nostrils or constricted his breathing. The air that passed through the holes at eyes, nose, and mouth was fresh and free of odor, no matter where he was. Cenoté had poured water from her cupped hands onto the wood, that was all.

Magic of the purest sort. Hunhau breathed it, drank it, and counted himself fortunate by every measure to have befriended it.

It hadn't been a litter that caught Tohil's eye. The side door had opened and a servant bowed as she ushered a tall woman into the brighter light. Plumes fluttered along the street as litter bearers quickly found somewhere else to stare.

Cenoté.

Her height was remarkable, despite the scholarly stoop of years spent hunched over worktable and book, and now in their shop. Painstaking and attentive, gifted with strong, delicate hands, she'd been a brilliant apprentice for less than a month.

From then on, Hunhau had been the one striving to learn.

"You can tell me more about the Snakes' chances the next time we meet," he told his friend, snapping fingers to rouse their litter bearers. The four young men pulled on their masks, their heads transformed to those of sea eagles, white feathers trailing over their bare shoulders, and took their places.

Cenoté moved with unconscious grace, the cane an extension of her slender arm. When required to venture from the shop, she wound strips of cloth around her head to cover her blue-green hair and donned a shapeless robe. Though she cared nothing for her appearance, Hunhau understood its importance in Taux's busy streets, where everyone watched and judged. He nodded to himself, satisfied by the rich fabric that flowed around her well-sandaled feet.

If not by her mask.

She wore the grotesque thing with such sure dignity, it might have been crusted in diamonds. The ugly chunk of grey seasoned wood was secured to her face by paired leather straps; uneven holes, wave-worn rather than carved, gaped like dark wounds over her mouth and eyes. Taux being what it was, at first there'd been a flurry of copies, gossipmongers having claimed the mask must hide a beauty so rare and exquisite it would drive men mad if revealed. Young ladies had demanded crude masks of their own, to imply the same.

The fad, not surprisingly, passed quicker than most. The curiosity about what lay beneath her mask had taken longer to fade. Hunhau preferred it not be awakened again.

Tohil saluted Cenoté as she neared. "Greetings, good lady."

The mask tilted a shy acknowledgement.

"We'd best be going." Hunhau took Cenoté's elbow to urge her to the litter.

With a quickness belied by his bulk, the Sturgeon was there first. "Was she there?" he asked in a low voice. "Did you get an answer?"

Safe behind his own mask, Hunhau rolled his eyes. This game was getting old. "Cenoté's not your messenger, Tohil," he scolded. "And no courtesan's going to give you so much as a 'good morning' without coin. Leave be."

"It's all right, Hunhau." Cenoté's soft voice interposed. "Plums-By-Moonlight did indeed reply. 'Jugglers, cheese, and peacocks.' Does that make sense to you, Tohil?"

She spoke to empty air as the Sturgeon took off down the lane as if pursuing an unlicensed tax collector, the bearers staring after him in astonishment.

"It must have," Hunhau commented dryly. "Let's get you home." Whenever they went out, there was a vulnerability about her, as if the very walls of Taux seethed with what she was and made ready to shout it. Nothing ever happened, but he worried, that was the truth.

The litter was plain but well made, with a roof for rain and thick privacy curtains. As Hunhau made to draw those, the bearers knowing full well the route they preferred, Cenoté delayed him with a touch of her hand. "The shop, Hunhau, briefly. Then the Raised Market."

Four eagle masks turned as one.

"The market," she insisted.

Where she'd never gone before. Where they'd be in crowds. Uncontrollable, dangerous crowds.

"Of course." Curtains snugged tight, Hunhau settled into his seat, fighting his unease as the bearers lifted the litter and stepped out at their smooth steady pace. "May I ask why?" he said, after a moment.

The mask of wood turned to him and something stirred in the dark where eyes should have been. When she spoke, for an instant he thought he heard the howl of storm-driven waves. "I've found her."

A chill fingered the maskmaker's bones despite the heat. He opened his mouth, shut it, then tried again. "Found w-who?"

"The one I tried to stop that night. My enemy." To his dismay, Cenoté added calmly, "now yours. She drinks the dead. Left unchallenged, she'll turn on the living next. There's no time to waste." Her fingers found his hand. She laid hers, callused and cool, atop it. "The Shining Sea tossed me at your feet, good Hunhau. This is why. So I would have your help."

"Mine?" he echoed, feeling as though the litter had tipped. "What can I do? I've no magic. You're the Wizard!" Hunhau shut his mouth, too late. It was out. What he'd never dared say to her.

Wizard.

"No more." Her mask turned in the direction of the bay for a moment, then aimed forward. "One does not question the Sea. This evil can no longer be fought from the tower. It must be fought here, now. I can't do it without you. Will you help me?"

Involve himself in the battles of Wizards? Risk himself for the people of Taux, which meant the nasty Jai-Ruk under the bridge as much as his friend Tohil, neither of whom would believe this?

The Saints knew he wasn't a hero.

Instead of answering, Hunhau poked his masked face through the curtains. "Pick up the pace, lads," he ordered, pleased his voice sounded normal. "We're in a hurry today."

The saints knew he'd made his choice, two years ago on the sand.

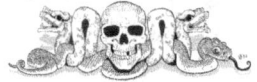

Food cooling in his bowl, Ghanan sat at the wooden table, watching his wife. Ah Peku washed the child with care and dried her with their softest towel, then dressed her as she would a doll. Zotz endured these ministrations with limp uncaring patience, moving only when prompted. It was their ritual, now.

He dropped his face into his hands.

"Husband." Softly. "You must eat."

Last night, every night, had been the same. Come home from work at sunset, strip and wash stone dust from his skin, pull on a clean robe. There'd been a time when evening's delicious cool drew them out for wine and dancing in the streets, or a moonlit walk along the quay. A time when he'd lifted the love of his life in his arms and known himself the wealthiest man in the world.

A time before Zotz.

Now sunset was when he brought the loathsome creature to the alley behind their home, so she could go on hands and knees to vomit forth the day's darkness. Now nights were to hide behind locked doors. For he'd watched, that first time, and seen the darkness hump itself to the drain. It had clung to the edge and stared back at him, eyes aglow with hate, before slithering out of sight. One for each day worked.

And each day worked, word spread of the stonemason who could silence the stones. Offers poured in and Zotz made him take every one.

Two years. Ghanan imagined hordes beneath their feet, imagined them meeting and becoming one monstrous thing, imagined ... but what could he guess of her purpose? He was her hands and voice, that was all.

How Ah Peku forgave him for bringing Zotz into their lives, how she endured it, Ghanan couldn't begin to guess. Trembling, the stonemason took up his spoon and made himself eat while his wife led the child, who didn't eat or drink, to the little chair they'd made for her. Having sat Zotz down to wait, Ah Peku turned away, wiping her hands on her apron.

Their eyes met, the compassion in hers more than he deserved. Ghanan opened his mouth to say so, but nothing came out. Zotz wouldn't let him speak at home. Not while she – while it – watched.

Instead, he lifted his arm and Ah Peku came to sit by him on the bench. He pulled her close, burying his face in her hair.

It smelled of life.

Once inside the shop, Cenoté asked Hunhau to bar the door, then help her from her raiment. The strips around her hair she left, as she was wont to do when ready to work.

Skin like the inside of a shell, hair like a waterfall, lips pale and perfect. Beautiful, she was, in the way a wave crashing against rock or the reflection of stars in the utter calm of a summer sea could steal a man's breath or call poetry from a dolt. Was she beautiful as a woman? Though she stood clad only in her breechclout, Hunhau couldn't say. His tastes ran to women of soft flesh, after all, and Cenoté was almost gaunt.

Then there was her face. Scars, deep and rippled, sealed the gaps where her eyes had been brutally torn out. By some mercy, she didn't remember what had happened; Hunhau couldn't forget his first glimpse of those dreadful wounds, the white glint of bone. That she'd survived – it had taken more than a skilled physician. It had taken terrifying will.

Now, though blind, she moved around the shop with brisk confidence, choosing a piece of driftwood from the bin to take to her worktable. Hunhau clamped it to the stand, itself turned or tilted by foot petals beneath the table.

Masks lined the upper shelves, masks no one could mistake as being made by anyone else. They were breathtaking, with great eyes and vivid colors. Cenoté made them for the neighbourhood children, to play as turtle, dolphin, or shark; they were not for sale. The idea of taking coin for the work of her hands offended her; she didn't say it, but Hunhau could tell.

Cenoté helped him instead. The masks she began and he finished were the best he'd ever done. As months went by, even those he did on his own – for Cenoté would have nothing to do with death masks – improved. His old master would have been amazed.

What she loved to make were cups. Cups. Bowls. Ewers. Jars. Anything to hold water and everything did, without a leak. They sat on every shelf and lined the walls. Hunhau had grown used to the way rain bent itself to enter the open windows of the shop, flowing and splashing only where Cenoté wished.

Though once in a while, it splashed on him. He'd sputter and protest, secretly pleased to catch a rare dimple at the corner of her mouth.

Once a month, at the highest tide, Cenoté would send him back to where he'd found her, to fill a special cup. With reverent movements, she'd put it to her lips and drink as if the saltwater were wine. When she'd had her fill, she'd soak what remained with a sponge and lave the ruin where her eyes had been.

On those nights, she'd go to her bed early and cry, very softly. He'd listen, heartsick and helpless. There was no cure for such pain. There was no imagining it.

He'd come to love her as any sailor loved the sea: lost apart, knowing better than to seek that perilous embrace. And now it was over. What hope did a blind ex-wizard and a maskmaker have against a creature that could drink the dead?

"Water, please, Hunhau. We must hurry. Any bowl will do."

He brought the largest, careful not to spill a drop, and set it on the table. Her face turned and tilted as she lifted a hand towards him. Understanding, he removed his mask and came in reach. Like raindrops, her fingertips played over his face, tracing his forehead, his cheeks, and, though he winced inwardly, his great nose. Or maybe not so inwardly, for her lips curved and she tapped the tip of his nose lightly before taking back her hand.

Whatever Cenoté had read of his face must have satisfied her, for without delay she sat on her stool and crooked an imperious finger at the bowl. Water rose in a thin twisting rope and leaned towards her.

No matter how many times he'd witnessed her magic, his heart still pounded in his chest.

The finger flicked at the wood and water followed, striking like a snake. A chunk broke away with a snap, then another and another, as Cenoté shaped the mask, her fingers now dancing, more twists of water flying through the air in response.

Slivers followed as she began a finer shaping. Hunhau leaned close. This was no sea creature or bird. What grew from driftwood was a face of astonishing realism. A woman's, serene and strong, with flawless, almond-shaped eyes.

Had it been hers?

Cenoté twirled her forefinger and the water returned to the bowl. Without waiting to be asked, Hunhau moved that bowl aside. Such water retained some hint of her magic. Later, if there was a later, he'd take it to the common garden and pour it on the roots of his neighbor's olive tree. He'd been anxious at first, but the tree seemed unaffected, other than a welcome increase in fruit.

"Thank you," she murmured. "The tray next, good Hunhau. Fill it from one of the covered jars, please. And bring your paints."

Rare, that Cenoté would call for more water. As for paints? The maskmaker hesitated. They'd take hours to dry. It was blisteringly hot in the courtyard, even in the shade. "I should send the bearers away then."

The hint of a dimple on her otherwise serious face. "This won't take long."

"But the paint ..."

"Trust me."

He shut his mouth and grabbed a jug, going to the back of the shop. The covered jars were his height and stood in a row. After months of squeezing by them, Hunhau had taken to using the tops as shelves. Cheeks rosy with embarrassment, he dragged a step to the first in line and climbed up, hastily removing a set of stacked baskets and, yes, that box of tile pieces he'd thought might be useful.

Fight evil? He couldn't even keep his shop tidy.

The woven sisal lid pricked his fingers as he pried it off. He held his breath, sure the stuff would have rotted in the damp, but the underside appeared newly made. As for the water inside?

Hunhau dared a little sniff.

A silly smile broke over his face. He inhaled deeply, filling his lungs. This was rain after a drought. Air after lightning. A newborn's sweet breath. All at once and ...

"Hunhau?"

He was taking too long. "Coming." Blushing more hotly, the maskmaker quickly dipped the jug, filling it to the brim. Holding it in the crook of his arm, he fumbled the lid back on the jar and began to climb down.

"Don't touch it," Cenoté said absently.

Freezing midstep, Hunhau stared into the jug as water sloshed perilously near its rim – and his bare arm – before settling. "W-why?"

"It will remember you."

He shouldn't have expected a comprehensible answer. Moving with greater care, Hunhau brought the jug to the table. Pouring the water into the shallow tray, he couldn't help but sniff again. If the world could smell like this, he'd never need a mask.

Had there been anything different about the water or the jars, any sign of exceptional magic? He thought, now that he made the effort, that Cenoté had reached her hand into each; he'd assumed to make sure the jar was full, as she would by keeping a fingertip inside her cup when pouring wine.

Unclamping the mask, she slipped it gently into the filled tray. It sank to the bottom, looking up.

"What colors should it have?" Cenoté asked him, as if she'd forgotten.

If this had been her face...

"A moment," Hunhau replied. Hurrying to a cabinet, he threw open its door and shoved aside bags of pigment. Nothing he had would do.

Reaching to the very back of the shelf, the maskmaker pulled free a long, low box. He brushed the worn carving of its lid, then nodded to himself. These were the paints Yum Caax had reserved for his finest works, blends of the rarest, most exotic materials. His former apprentice hadn't dared touch them.

He brought the box to the table, unlatched the sides, and lifted the lid. The tiny crystal vials were as he remembered; the colors inside vivid and alive. "These," Hunhau said without doubt, choosing four to press into her waiting hands.

Her fingers closed. Cenoté's head tilted, listening to what he couldn't hear, then she almost smiled. "And you say you've no magic, my friend. Watch."

Before he could think to stop her, she dropped the unopened vials into the tray.

They didn't sink, as crystal should and wood shouldn't, but floated to the four corners like sparkling boats. At Cenoté's bent finger, they began to spin until each vial was centred within its own tiny whirlpool, though the water over the mask's face was undisturbed.

The seals cracked, spilling priceless pigment. Hunhau's cry died in his throat as he saw the vials themselves remained dry and almost full. Color spread in hazy clouds and narrow, intense bands: twilight rose, storm black, pearl white, and a blue so achingly pure it might have been carved from ancient ice.

The colors found the mask.

Suddenly, both wood and water vanished. Hunhau found himself staring not at a mask, but a face. Skin of pearl, lips and cheeks of soft rose, brows black and upswept like wings.

Without warning, the long black lashes parted, revealing eyes like the wild, open ocean. He staggered back. "It moves!"

"It remembers me," Cenoté said matter-of-factly, but he thought her hands trembled as she lifted the mask from the tray. She held it before her face. "Will it pass, good Hunhau?"

A Wizard's face gazed down at him, cold and aloof. Beautiful, the way elegant and deadly things could be, but this wasn't Cenoté. This wasn't the person closer to him than any family or friend. "I don't know what to say," he managed. "I don't know who this is. Who you want to be."

"How not?" She moved the mask aside, showing him the familiar ruin above a mouth downturned in distress. Her fingertips traced the tension in his jaw and found his frown. Cenoté nodded. "I understand. What we've crafted is a memory, nothing more. I can't go back to that life," she said gently. "I thought you knew I don't want to. I'm happy here, Hunhau, and free as I've ever been." She raised the mask again, with its disconcerting eyes. "To fight, however, I must see our enemy. This is the means."

That she was happy and wanted to stay was something to warm the heart and treasure, but the rest? "You could have made such a mask before," Hunhau accused. "You've let yourself be blind!"

"I am blind, my friend, and always will be." Cenoté laid the mask on the table. "Without eyes, a Wizard cannot perform the greater magics. Without eyes, the Afterglow Sea is beyond my reach." She seemed to come to some decision. "Understand me, Hunhau. This," her fingers touched the scarred and empty sockets, "was no accident. The last thing I remember is being in a scrying room, searching for this creature. Someone in the tower stole my eyes. A traitor." Beneath her voice, the fury of a breaking wave. "Whoever it was meant to cripple me and has." Her fingers rested cool on his face, then brushed like mist across his eyes. "But for a little while, this mask will let me borrow your sight. If you're willing?"

He squinted at her. "Ten coins says it's going to hurt."

"Twenty," that was surely a dimple, "says we'll die horribly in the attempt."

"I should never have taught you to gamble," he complained.

"All life's a gamble." Cenoté actually smiled. "Now help me dress. We've a distance to travel."

By the play of torchlight, the empty eyes moved, the little corpses writhed. The stones appeared to rest on the figurines, but it was a clever illusion. The stonecraft of those who'd built the original city was without equal.

But why this?

Resolutely, Ghanan looked away to the good stone, born of the earth and not the whim of evil minds. He'd come to believe in evil.

Evil squatted impatiently before the wall, waiting for him to feed it.

Which was a problem. The pair of Sturgeons stood on guard at the base of the stairs and Zotz didn't allow witnesses, normally using Ghanan to drive them away. She'd made him deny friendship and scorn goodwill, until these days others in the trade gave him foul looks and a wide berth. She'd put such vile words in his mouth he'd offended the gentle old priest who'd stood by to watch him work and made him strike at a too-curious boy. With the priest had gone his hope that such a man, surely knowledgeable in the ways of good and evil, would see Zotz for what she was and free him. With the boy – with the boy, wide-eyed and scared, had risen a sick dread of what she could make him do, if not given her way.

But he could do nothing against these men. Offended Sturgeons were more likely to use their staffs on his head than leave. Did Zotz understand that? Ghanan delayed, pretending to search for a tool in his kit as he gave the men assessing looks. Saints, they were huge, with arms like tree limbs, and had the easy confidence – or single-mindedness– of those to whom a dank cellar rife with the whispers of the dead was simply another place to guard.

Suddenly, Zotz began to rock back and forth, her arms clasped around her middle. The stonemason froze in place, afraid what might come next. Sure enough, her mouth opened and she let out a shrill, keening cry.

It was a sound no child should have been able to make. Hairs rose on Ghanan's arms and neck.

The Sturgeons exchanged annoyed looks. "What's wrong with her?" one demanded.

"She doesn't like strangers." He had to raise his voice as the dreadful screech grew louder, threatening his sanity. "Please, good Sirs. If you would wait at the top of the stairs, just out of sight, I'm sure she'll stop."

They didn't suspect a child – no one ever did, Ghanan thought. With disgusted shakes of their heads, the two guardsmen turned and went up the wide steps.

Zotz closed her mouth and looked at him.

"To work. I know." The sooner it was done, he told himself, the sooner the creature would let him return home. The stonemason stripped off his jerkin and took up his chisel and hammer, only then checking to see where to start. Zotz knew where the voices were loudest and would insist he open the stone there first.

Her small fingers stroked the figures along the lower row, the ones shown in torment.

He hesitated. The voices came from the stones. Yes, there'd been a time when their whispered almost-words and distant screams had made him break into a cold sweat, when it had been a matter of pride to stand and work, to do what he could to bring peace to a wall or building. To make Taux a better place for the living.

But now he pitied the dead and grieved when they fell silent. Zotz stole something from them, something precious. He no longer doubted it. To rob those already condemned…

A crooked finger tapped impatiently.

Ghanan sank to his haunches before the wall. He made the mistake of glancing at the creature. Her eyes were hollow pits and her mouth gaped, the tongue lolling like a dog's. Instead of honest spit, something black and loathsome dribbled from the corners of her child's lips. She pointed again, with unfamiliar urgency.

There was something here, he realized abruptly. Something she'd been looking for and finally found.

It wouldn't be anything good.

Ghanan fought to resist the creature's will. Drop the chisel, he begged his fingers. Just that, or cry out and draw the Sturgeons down to investigate.

Sweat poured into his eyes and stung, but his fingers stayed locked to the tool, fitting it to the heart of a small tortured shape. His lips moved, but nothing came out as his other hand lifted the hammer.

Voices wailed and gibbered in terror. The torches guttered as the hammer fell and the first figure split open, spilling tiny organs and blood.

Zotz shoved him aside, eager to feast.

If Taux's builders had intended the Black Gate to overawe those entering their great stadium, they'd succeeded. The massive obsidian gate stood before its bridge to the city as it always had, its ferocious carved visages glaring out in threat. The Ullamalitzli Stadium beyond it, however, had become something else: a city within a city. Every scrap of its defensible, blissfully quiet stone had been squatted on, settled, and, in some cases, rebuilt entirely by those who came after. What had been broad bleachers now supported rows of wooden tenements, answering to the fate of the city's docks. The once-magnificent Raised Celebration platform, girded by the gate and its twin guard towers, was home to the ramshackle booths and colorful awnings of the Raised Market, a disorderly mass that had spilled out across what had been a sunken practice court and now reached greedily for the precious space of the main Tournament Field.

On the other side of the field, where the rich and mighty had sat in three-storey stone boxes at the centre of the stadium, the Emerald Serpent and Silk Purse nestled back-to-back, like guilty lovers unable to face one another by day. Beyond those dens of profitable iniquity was, by no accident, a practice court that echoed with the ring of swordplay, being used by athletes of every ilk, including assassins.

The former Royal Raised Gardens remained beyond at the rear for the great stadium, but its beds now grew fruits and vegetables, and to either side stood the Wizards' Gifts, inexhaustible fountains of sweet water. Furthest from the gate and presumed safest, was the area claimed by the second class nobility – though some would argue buying a title or being a crime lord didn't count – of those who called the Black Gate home.

Hunhau's little shop sat much closer to the gate, tucked in a blind corner on the lowermost floor of a building on the first bleacher. It wasn't much, but possessed something rare: privacy. The shop's door opened to the outside and a shared courtyard, with no inner neighbors using it for a corridor.

It was too much to hope they were unobserved. Windows and balconies overlooked the courtyard, and the Black Gate's inhabitants were insatiably curious. Hunhau tried not to glance up as he helped Cenoté into the litter, but he couldn't help it. In the distance the Star Tower rose beyond the stadium walls. Did Wizards watch?

Did the traitor?

They left the litter at the edge of the market. He gave the bearers coin for a meal and extra for a drink or two, having imposed on them to wait yet again. The men were cheerful. Hunhau wasn't.

Anything could be had, for a price, in the Raised Market. Its overlapping awnings and flags made a chaotic display that would shrink like magic the night before a game, replaced, of course, by seats and benches of varying luxury and price, as well as refreshment dealers and those waiting to take bets. Today, though, the usual uproar of yells, chants, yips, chimes, and bells – among less identifiable noises – bounced from wall to wall, making it unlikely any single one could be heard, let alone attract a customer.

Then there was the smell. Hunhau loathed coming here, even in his mask, all too easily imagining the reek. But here he was, in the thick of it.

"A large tent beside a snake merchant," Cenoté whispered. "Near the Tournament Field." She rested her hand on his shoulder, having left her cane behind, and he felt that responsibility keenly as he guided them through the jostling crowd. They'd passed three stalls with snakes hissing in their baskets already.

Hunhau slapped at a pickpocket's hand, receiving an unrepentant grin as the waif ducked away. "Are you sure we should…" he began, then looked past the would-be thief. "I think I found it."

No ordinary booth this. The thick poles holding up the awning were carved into twisting serpents with jade eyes and a carpet done to look like silver scales beckoned customers through velvet curtains. Only the wealthy need enter, they said.

"And the tent, Hunhau?"

As tents went, the dull brown one leaning next to the snake merchant's fine establishment looked more suited to covering a dung heap. A very large dung heap. Hunhau looked for another, but saw only more booths with awnings. And people. Half of Taux was here, and not the better half either. Criers ran through, some waving staffs with flags, others tossing samples and causing fights. Forced aside by a grim pair of Jai-Ruk, the maskmaker lost his courage and simply kept moving, leading Cenoté to the open space beside one of the snake poles. "I see it," he admitted glumly.

"What's wrong?" She'd unbound her remarkable hair, though it remained beneath the hood of her silk cloak. Her face...

Once she'd pressed the mask to her face, it had become her face. The real and created had merged, blurring one into the other. No scars remained, but the blue eyes were hazed over and milky. Stern lines had drawn themselves at the corners of the mouth, taking away the half-seen dimple he loved.

"Everything," he fussed. "Who sent us here? How do we know this isn't a trap?"

An eyebrow, once wood and paint, lifted. "It may be," Cenoté agreed easily and Hunhau's heart sank. "Nothing's changed. The eater is here and must be fought."

"Here?" A less likely spot for a magical confrontation couldn't be imagined.

"The tent," she reminded him.

Hunhau sighed but argued no more.

The tent's entry was tied shut. From the litter on the ground before it, it hadn't been used in days. Rather than be caught fumbling with knots or a knife – not that he'd thought to bring one – Hunhau waited for the next crier to distract the crowd, then drew Cenoté into the narrow space beside the tent, hoping to find another way.

What he found, after some too-noisy stumbles over ropes, was that the market side of the tent was a clever ruse. The real entrance faced the Tournament Field. There was a much larger door on that side, held open by rings on golden hooks. As he hesitated, Cenoté's fingers pressed his shoulder encouragingly. Courage, that meant.

Hunhau went on hands and knees, poking his masked face around the edge of the door. The interior of the tent was a revelation. Another door opened across from him, while within, no expense had been spared. The fabric lining was cotton, died pale gold, and woven carpets covered the floor. Jaguar masks stood on poles along the wall; masks he recognized. Those belonged to the team itself as, he guessed, would the chests beneath them. But why store them here?

What had Tohil said? That the Gamesmaster planned to house her team in rooms – rooms beneath the playing field. Moving very slowly, he turned to look the other way.

Where the front door of the tent would open was a gaping hole in the floor, flanked by guards. Big ones.

They were staring into the hole. That was all that saved him from discovery. Shaking at his luck, and their lack of it, Hunhau pulled back hastily and rose to his feet. He took Cenoté's hand and began leading her away. She resisted.

Which was when the new, even bigger guard showed up, striding towards them.

Chip, chip, chip. The bodies were tiny – their anguish wasn't. As Zotz sucked each dry, her thin child's frame expanded, like some spider filling with the juice of prey.

With each desecration, the underground corridor grew darker, as if the light from the torches failed, though the flames were unchanged.

This was his fault, Ghanan told himself, half-mad with shame. He'd fallen into the creature's trap, for he no longer believed their meeting an accident. He'd let her enthral him and this was the result. Tears streamed down his face, mingling with sweat and dust, but he could no more stop his hands than the ending of the world.

From Tohil's smug look and wink, Plums-By-Moonlight had done more than give him Cenoté's instructions. He'd walked right by Hunhau and

into the tent, exhorting his fellow Sturgeons to their duty. A riot at The Silk Purse! The street filled with naked courtesans of both sexes –Tohil clearly knew his audience –needing rescue! Compared with make-work guarding a hole in the ground, there'd been no doubt which they'd choose. The three had run out with a clatter of weapons at the ready.

A worried Hunhau led Cenoté inside the tent. "Won't he get in trouble?"

"There is a riot," Cenoté said absently. "A small one."

Another secret. Another time, he might have wondered, but not now. The closer they came to the hole, the more his fear of it grew. It was as if that opening, now revealed to be an ornate stair leading down, went to his grave.

No wonder the guards had been willing to abandon their post. If it weren't for Cenoté's hand, firm and steady on his shoulder, he'd have run too.

Her other hand lifted, palm up. "It's time, my friend."

Bracing himself, Hunhau took off his mask and secured it to his belt. His face felt naked, the skin itchy. When he could hold off no longer, he gasped out the air he'd held in his lungs, then inhaled through his nose.

"Agh!" The stench of death and rot and worse burned his nostrils. Nothing should smell like this, he wailed to himself, doubling over. Nothing could! What was down there?

"Hunhau? Are you all right?"

He waved a hand to beg a moment, eyes watering, forgetting she was blind.

"I'm so sorry. Thank you for this." Cenoté's fingers found his face. They stroked his nose and the stench vanished. As he straightened with astonished relief, she caught his tears on her cool fingers and touched them to her clouded eyes.

She blinked and her eyes cleared.

Hunhau blinked too. The floor had moved further away. No, he now saw from a greater height! "I see through your eyes!"

"I see through yours. Stay with me," Cenoté ordered. Tossing her cloak to the floor, she gathered up her robe in two hands and started nimbly down the stairs, hair streaming like a waterfall over her back. "Mind your feet."

Good advice. Unable to trust depth or distance, the maskmaker felt his way down beside her.

Cold. Cold and damp and, though he was grateful not to smell it, something inside Hunhau knew the air wasn't right. It wasn't right at all.

Down they went. The stairs were broad and well made, worn in the centre. What the place had been the maskmaker didn't dare guess, but it had seen use and not a kind one. The Gamesmaster was mad to think she could house anyone or anything in here, even were the stones silenced.

"Stay close," Cenoté whispered, taking his hand as they took the final step together.

There were torches. Why was it so dark? The corridor beyond stretched like a gaping mouth while just in front of them…

Having readied himself for a monster, Hunhau sagged with relief. "Don't be concerned," he assured the obviously startled stonemason, crouched with his hammer and chisel poised in midair. The plump child, doubtless his daughter, stared at Cenoté. "We're not here to disturb you."

"Oh, but we are." Cenoté's fingers tightened on his. "Look at their water, Hunhau. See them as they truly are."

And he could, Hunhau realized. The stonemason, rising slowly, was a cresting wave, tense and constrained, yet full of color and grace. While the child … the child was dust and ash and every regret he'd ever felt.

It spoke, using the man's lips. "You are blind, Wizard, and powerless."

"You are found, soul-eater," Cenoté said, and in her voice was a hurricane's wrath. "And I'm not alone." Her hand lifted from Hunhau's, joined the other in a sweeping summons.

Water burst from the walls, rose from the floor, water that formed itself into nightmare shapes. Hands with shattered fingers reached. Legs that were stumps walked. Faces, ruined and rotted, opened what remained of their mouths to shout curses without sound. All aimed for the child.

The stonemason leapt forward, tools raised. "Stop me!" he pleaded as he splashed through the watershapes. They reformed at once, oblivious to all but their tormentor. "Stop me, please!"

Time didn't pass as it should. The maskmaker saw every step the man took, felt, as if it were his own, the sick horror filling the poor man's eyes.

Stepping forward, Hunhau pulled his beloved mask from his belt and smashed it over the stonemason's head.

The thick wood cracked and split. Staggered, the man fell to his knees, pieces of mask dropping beside him.

Hunhau quickly grabbed the tools from the man's hands and tossed them as far as he could. They disappeared within the rising flood.

"You haven't won," the stonemason's mouth said. "What I've birthed will burrow under this city and find the Afterglow. We shall have its power!"

Water surged to lift the child and pin her against the wall, thin legs and arms at awkward angles. "'We,' small one?" Cenoté mocked gently.

"Your masters share nothing with the likes of you. If I thought you knew anything of their true intent I'd grant you safe passage from this city in return, but you are a thing shaped from lies and ill intent."

Black ooze drooled from the child's mouth. Her puppet's lips twisted and spat. "And the name of he who betrayed you, Wizard? What will you grant for that? I know it, I do. I know all the dark secrets. Even yours!"

The watershapes faltered, then straightened. "By the Shining Sea, take them to Castaway Hells with you!" Cenoté stepped forward, or did she flow with the water, become one of the shapes?

The child's mouth gaped impossibly wide and she vomited a vile black dust. Hunhau shielded his face as it struck, coughing and gasping for breath.

"See her!" Cenoté commanded.

He dropped his hands to stare at the soul-eater as it dropped all pretence.

No longer a child. No longer small. It spread itself over the stones like a foul stain, black hooked edges digging into cracks and crevices, pulling.

It wasn't trying to escape. It scrabbled at the stone, making a dreadful sucking sound. It was feeding! Growing larger!

"This ends," Cenoté said, ice calm, and raised both hands. The watershapes flew through the air to crash against the wall!

A wave would have receded at once, but this wasn't a wave. Tortured hands gripped. Broken mouths chewed. Given form, the dead fought for themselves and for Taux. The now-desperate soul-eater tried to consume them, but these had already lost their souls and could not be touched.

The stonemason wailed, then fell silent.

When at last the wave did recede, draining down through the tile floor, the black stain was gone and the wall, new and white, glittered in the torchlight.

Hunhau noticed the figurines between the stones for the first time. Little faces gazed back. Those at head-height laughed. Those above seemed to sleep. The lower rows held lovers, their limbs intertwined.

He took a cautious sniff, then a deeper one. The air was as fresh as any he'd smelled.

"Zotz…" The stonemason sat on the floor, his eyes dazed. Not, Hunhau thought, from the blow. "Is she gone?"

"This one, yes," Cenoté said disconcertingly. "The prize is too great. They will make more. They will try again. Whoever they are."

Hearing the weariness in her voice, Hunhau turned. With one hand, she held a mask of crude wood over her face, its colors run into lines and splotches of black, blue, and grey. As he watched, the floor beneath her dried; slender toes peeked from under her hem. "You're free," she told the man. "Hunhau?"

The maskmaker helped the stonemason to his feet. "Sorry…"

"For this?" The man touched his head. "I thank you for it." He had a strong and pleasant face, now that the horror had left it. "My name's Ghanan. I'm forever in your debt, good lady." He gave the wall a look of wonder. "I believe I'm not the only one."

"Speak not of debt, Ghanan. You fought her will all this time. That kept her small. That gave us this chance."

Hunhau could hear the dimple. Collecting Cenoté's hand, he led it to his shoulder. "It's time we left. I don't think the riot will last much longer."

Ghanan chuckled, a warm rich sound unlikely to have been heard in this place before. "I don't think I'll ask." He nodded at the stairs. "Shall we? I need to see my wife." He made no move to collect his tools.

For some reason, perhaps the same one, Hunhau didn't want the pieces of his mask. He tapped the side of his great nose instead. "I'll lead the way."

And he did.

There are those who come to Taux to steal and prey on the weak. There are those who seek a hiding place or new victims for their play. And there are those who sense a hidden power and would claim it for their own.

But there are those who live within Taux's walls, who stand in her great Tower who will deny evil with their last breath.

Given a chance.

Illustration by Jeff Laubenstein

CHARLATAN

Scott Taylor

The stones were slick with sea mist as Savino crept down another stair. Behind, the silver light of the Ghost Moon bled away into amber as the Blood Moon replaced it in their nightly dance.

"This is just another example of how you are a fool," he whispered to himself.

His torch guttered, a foul breeze blowing up from the depths at the words. Below, the slithering sound of scales being pulled over stone was followed by a splash, and his stomach churned.

Crouching low, he slipped the torch into a fracture of the stair, took a long breath, and then removed his pack.

"Three days ago I was a man without a care, and now I face a serpent like some damnable knight of Gariny…"

He reached into his pack, brought forth his ice-shoes and unbuckled the leather straps. His boots were wet, the leather dark with sea water, but he placed the whale-bone runners beneath his soles and wrenched the tethers tight before clasping the buckles. With a hard slam, he tested each blade, both staying in place as a deep hiss rose up the stair.

"You've no fire, serpent, and are far too big to fit in this old priest's entry," so keep your threats to yourself," he said.

Withdrawing a vial from his pack, he undid the stopper and applied another touch of liquid to his palms, the smell of undiluted jasmine filling the stair.

Finally, he leaned his head back against the cool stone, closed his eyes, and sighed.

"Three days ago… Saints, it seems like a year…"

"How many men have you killed?" Esmeralda Serata asked.

Savino's voice was bored, "I'm not into record keeping…"

The sanguine young woman rose naked from the bed, swooned, and then grabbed the windowsill. Her left hand, bandaged at the knuckles, rose to push aside golden curls and rub her head just above the right temple.

"You've not recovered, Esmer, come back to bed before you fall over."

A curse slipped her lips, a harbor breeze swishing the palm fronds outside the window and tightening her nipples. She turned on him, the lines of her body drawing his eyes away from her face. Leaning back into the sill, she crossed her long legs.

"I've got to know, Savino, you have to teach me your secrets," she said.

"Your tutors are already fine blades, you wear the silver badge, and even a master duelist has taken you under his wing, so why do you need me?" he asked.

She smiled, all things innocent pouring into her lovely face. "You mistake me, Savino, I've had practice, certainly, but not with a master."

"Thrice a week you come to me with jasmine on your skin, love, and only one man in the city could have put it on you," he replied.

Her eyes narrowed, the angelic countenance sliding away into the veneer of a viper.

"Teach me, I've earned it," she whispered.

A smile crossed his lips but she didn't return it. They stared at each other, doves taking wing outside as a city bell sounded the changing of the watch from the Gold Jaguar's beacon hill at a quarter of noon.

Finally, he shook his head, "What you seek is folly, and I don't share secrets for revenge, even for one who shares my bed."

Light faded from her face, eyes darkening before she pushed away from the window and walked from the room. He could smell the heat of her fury, the chatter of the beaded door hangings mocking her retreat.

Sighing, he got to his feet and stretched, a breeze forming around him as he took a deep breath. Outside the window, a Jai-Ruk was arguing with his wife across the alley, and he laughed at a particularly fine retort from the female.

Below, a knock sounded.

"Are you expecting someone?" he called into the far room.

Esmer didn't reply, but a dog had begun barking, and the arguing neighbor slammed his shutter closed.

Throwing on his breeches, boots, and shirt, Savino heard the knocks sound again, this time more forcefully. At the stair he grabbed his rapier, slid if from its sheath, and made his way down to the door.

"We know you're in there, Savino," a deep voice echoed through the door.

He turned, made it up two steps, when the voice continued, "And we have a crossbow on the window."

Stopping, he closed his eyes and shook his head. Above, Esmer's voice trailed down the stairs, "If you'd have taught me, I could have warned you, but you know better than most that nothing in Taux is free."

"May Saint Amanda bless you!" he yelled up to her.

A laugh followed, but he turned back to the door and threw the heavy bolt. The wood frame slowly swung inward, Savino sheathing his blade as the morning sun forced him to raise his elbow to shield his eyes.

Outside, three dark figures stood. One was Tohil, his Sturgeon blue standing out. The other two wore dueling leathers, and gilded rapiers at their hips.

"What can I do for you gentlemen?" he asked.

One of the two reached inside his half-laced doublet and produced a folded piece of parchment set with a wax seal.

Savino dropped his arm, took the letter, and asked, "Razor couriers… is the dueling business so downtrodden these past weeks you've taken extra work?"

The younger of the two Razors reached for his rapier, but a wary eye from Tohil – the man stood a head taller than the rakish duelist – backed him down.

Sliding his thumb into a flap, Savino broke the wax, marked with the standard of House Vash, and unfolded the letter.

> For acts perpetrated against House Vash, you are formerly challenged for a midnight council upon the Baymourn Bridge three days hence.

Savino looked up, a smile crossing his lips. "Who is the sender?" he asked.

"Yoatl Vash", the Razor replied.

Inside, Savino felt his stomach fall, bile rising in his nostrils, but his face was implacable and the smile remained.

"Tell Master Vash he shall see me at the appointed hour," he replied.

Tohil was absently watching a litter on the street, the tattoos on his face playing like dark snakes in the light. Sturgeons were under strict orders to disallow death duels, but upper class Razors needed an escort when entering the Black Gate, and the large Sturgeon was known for his discretion.

The two duelists nodded, turned, and Tohil snapped back to attention.

"Keep out of trouble," Tohil said.

The Sturgeon raised a hand and waved down the street, and Savino saw a shadowed form lower a crossbow and retreat into an alley.

"You too Tohil," Savino replied.

Laughing, his white teeth gleaming, Tohil marched after the Razors, his blue raiment cutting a swath through the crowds now swelling the street as the city rose from its slumber.

Savino leaned against the frame of the door, closed his eyes and let his head fall back. Above, he heard Esmer moving about the bedroom before the remainder of his clothes and a hat came tumbling down the stair.

"You are a kind woman!" he called.

There was no answer, and he collected his things before turning into the light of the street.

The stink of sweat was heavy in Savino's nose as he slammed the ball home, two smaller men cursing and falling away beneath him before his feet returned to the dirt of the Ullamalitzli court. A dozen scattered claps and a single curse were all that marked the valor of his effort.

Dethocrates came forward and drew him into a hearty embrace, the Jai-Ruk's arms twice the size of his own.

"Well done, my friend, the air is with you today!"

Savino disengaged from the large man, Borowl and Talb coming up from the far side of the court to shake his hand before they went to brag to some off-shift ladies of the Purse watching from the stands.

"I'd better enjoy the wins while I can," Savino said.

Dethocrates laughed, "That sounds ominous, is it worth talking about?"

"Sure, if you enjoy hearing a requiem."

The two walked toward a ladder dropped into the field pit by youths, the other team having already used it to escape the field in dejection.

"I've heard my fair share of mournful tales, so let me have it."

"You know Ayleen Vash?" Savino asked, climbing.

"The Silver Charm of the Jagaur, how could I not?"

"Evidently I've tarnished her luster…"

"Impossible, the girl never leaves the cloister of her father's keepers," Deth replied.

Savino, stepping away from the top of the ladder after his climb, put his hands in a water barrel and splashed his body with the cool liquid. He rinsed his face, neck, and armpits before a boy offered him his shirt.

"You won me a coin today, Master Emantra," the boy said.

Savino looked down, smiled, and tousled the boy's hair.

"Gambling is the quickest way to the grave," he said, and the boy frowned, before adding, "And to untold riches if you are wise."

The boy brightened, and Savino turned back to Deth as he rinsed his hulking, grey-skinned body.

"You are right, of course," Savino began, "Yoatl Vash would never let his niece wander without a well-seasoned bodyguard at her side."

Deth turned, frowning, "You didn't?"

Savino threw his hand up in mock defense, "She was no conquest, the girl had already found experience before I laid any claim, but something must have happened to put her virtue in question and I'm the one to take the fall. Or so it seems."

"You may as well have stolen gold from the fabled Emerald Serpent of the Sun Isle; you'd live no longer and there would surely be less pain involved in your death," Dethocrates observed.

"The Emerald Serpent is no fable, and those that know say it's not stealing the gold, it's keeping it that is the trouble," Savino replied.

Dethocrates lifted a dark bushy eyebrow, "You know too much on this subject for my tastes, old friend, but it does give weight to Torrent's words to watch out for you and your schemes."

Savino sighed, pulled on his shirt, and watched children descend the ladder with giggling glee as they prepared for a less intense game.

"Ah Torrent, now there is a name I've not heard in several a moon. If only she hadn't left the city I might still have a chance in all this mess."

Deth harrumphed, "Then I guess you hadn't heard that she's back and staying at the Serpent."

Air swirled around the two of them, a breeze so fresh it could have come from a hundred miles outside the city.

"What did you say?" Savino asked.

Frowning, Deth walked away from the field, calling over his shoulder, "I said Torrent was back."

"I'm going to need you!" Savino shouted.

Deth waived, held a thumb up in the air, and then disappeared into the Silver Circle. Savino smiled, grabbed his hat and blade, and then ran in the opposite direction toward the front doors of the Emerald Serpent.

The eastern side of the Silver Circle, the street that ringed the inner grounds of the Black Gate, was no less crowded than the west, and Savino slipped into the throng of workers shuffling out of the tenement houses to their daily labors outside the Gate. The mass of them took the grand canal ferry to the Smoke Dragon District and then back again at dusk, their days spent in the sweat shops of the Red Pillars.

Intermingled with them were the outsiders, those not of the Gate. Tonight the local Snakes went against the wealthy district's Jaguars in a grand tournament game, and the Black Gate was open for business, the population of the old stadium swelling to twice its normal size.

The journey to the Serpent's door was no more than fifty feet, but it took him a full minute to touch the steps through the traffic. Doors of iron-wrapped oak stood open, smoke and the smell of a morning's fixings spilling out the stained keystone at the top of the entry arch.

He moved inside, light shining down in great colored pillars from the windowed terraces above, their heavy curtains drawn back in the morning to bring some cheer to the hard interior. To the left of the entry were curtained booths, three of the six drawn closed and green-flamed candles burning to signal business being dealt. On the right, running into the belly of the hall, were three dozen tables, half stacked with chairs near the door and those closer in occupied by those seeking to break their fast.

Above, a gallery wrapped around the main floor, a single twisting stair leading up to a shadowed alcove where it was said Saint Shera once counted coin when she'd owned the tavern in the troubled times of the Five Year War. Further back, beyond the crescent bar were private rooms. In one of those, marked with a heavy bolt, the entrance to the catacombs was known to those foolhardy treasure seekers who sometimes paid the tavernkeep, Quilan, precious Coatls for access as they sought riches better left undisturbed in the bowels of the ancient city.

Savino noted all this in passing, his gait moving him through the maze of tables, past the morning diners, and toward a smaller section of booths tucked to the right of the bar. There, seated on two cushions in the furthest booth, sat Lareo.

The Eldaryn was small, half the size of a full-grown Human, with spiked hair like burnished platinum tipped with faded tendrils of blue.

He had a mustache resembling curled copper wire, and his red eyes were surrounded by tortoise-shell glasses. A trinket of silver caught the morning light in his small fingers as he inspected it, a box with many drawers and expanding shelves next to him on the top of the table.

"Lareo," Savino called in greeting.

Looking away from his prize, the trader smiled and a wave of heat blew past Savino as he stepped to the far side of the booth.

"May I?" Savino asked.

Lareo nodded, saying, "It's early for a scheme this morning, even for you."

"What makes you think I've a scheme in mind?" Savino asked.

Lareo raised a coppery eyebrow, laughed, and then put his silver away. With a deft flick of fingers too quick to follow, he closed the box and pushed it aside.

"I'd heard Yoatl had challenged you, but I figured you would skip town instead of seek my service, unless of course it's my service you need in getting out," Lareo said.

Savino smiled, "Actually, I need a pair of ice blades."

Lareo's eyes grew large behind his lenses before he squinted until his crimson irises burned like embers.

"What game are you playing?" the trader asked.

"It's best you don't know," Savino replied.

"That may set well with your girls, wind-born, but to me it sounds hollow as an abandoned cave," Lareo answered.

"If you must know, I want to go skating," Savino said.

The air bloomed with heat, sweat beading on Savino's forehead and he brushed it away with the back of his hand.

"Skating? In Taux?" Lareo asked.

"Yes, it's the perfect time of year, don't you think?" Savino asked.

Lareo laughed, "You've lost what little sense I've credited you with. Even in the Lupin Hills there can't be ice this time of year, and yet you want to skate in a city that's never seen a single snowflake?"

"Does it really matter what I want to waste my coin on? I was raised in Mistfin, and could skate before I could walk, so perhaps I simply want to remember my youth before I pass from this world." Savino said.

Sitting back, Lareo crossed his arms over the silk shirt at his breast, one corner of his mouth coming up in a curl.

"I may be able to acquire what you're after," he said.

"May?" Savino asked.

"Well, that sort of cargo can sometimes be found on the craft barges coming out of Findalynn in the winter season. There are a few ships from Dragmarsh in the harbor, but it won't be easy."

"Nothing worthwhile ever is," Savino said.

"Is that what you told young Ayleen Vash?"

Savino laughed, his face a mask of well-practiced charm. "Whatever happens, Lareo, I want you to understand one thing, and make sure all that ask know what I proclaim as well."

Lareo waited, the heat from his little body swelling with each second of anticipation.

"She was worth it," Savino said.

A smile that nearly burst into flame spread beneath the Eldaryn's copper mustache, and he then spit in his hand with a hiss as the liquid turned to vapor before he offered it up. Savino looked at the trader's hand, bit the inside of his cheek, and shook. The pain was intense, like grabbing the handle of an iron pan from the fire, but he held firm.

"With a statement like that, Savino, you know I'm bound by love of a life well-lived to get you those ice shoes, but I'll have a heavy purse of 5 Gold Jaguars for my trouble," Lareo stated.

Savino nodded, shook hard, and then pulled his hand back with a hiss escaping his lips. The skin was intact, but it pulsed with crimson and stung like a lash had been laid to it.

"I'll need them yesterday," Savino said.

Lareo nodded, "With your duel in less than two days, I'm sure you do. Be here at sun setting and I'll have what you seek."

Rising, Savino tipped his hat and then headed for the bar, the Eldaryn's laughter following him like the baying of a Sturgeon's hound.

The Serpent was packed, almost overwhelmed, the throng of patrons drowning their sorrows at yet another defeat of their beloved Snakes. Outside, the reverie of the Vash carnival had died away, the coming of the tome mage and his three-headed serpent, and the death of Vash's talismonger, Pelantus, still lingering on the fringes of almost all conversation.

Savino drummed his fingers on the top of a table, the booth he'd secured hours before was eyed by more than one group of men still standing in the packed house and deep into their cups. He made sure his blade hung free, the amethyst falcon upon the pommel letting everyone know who and what he was.

In this town reputation was everything, even if it was a lie.

A large hand touched his shoulder and he gave a start, Deth laughing as he slid into the far side of the table. When the Jai-Ruk took a seat, those eyes brave enough to covet the booth turned away. Savino reached up and grabbed the curtain, drew it, and the single candle on the table left both of them in shadow.

"Did you get it?" Savino whispered.

The smell of tilled earth washed across the enclosed space, Deth's tiny white tusks showing in the light.

"Would I be here if I didn't?" Deth asked.

The Ruk produced a pouch and dropped it into Savino's hand, the ties unbound and open before he could speak further. The ruby, set in gold and hung from a thin chain with smaller versions about it, danced in the light, and both rogues stared at it.

"Do you know how much it's worth?" Deth asked.

"It's worthless to anyone in Taux. The Vash family will have a bounty as soon as they discover it wasn't destroyed," Savino replied.

"A stroke of luck for us, but it won't last long, I've heard Whitey has been called from the Tortoise to investigate," Deth said.

"Then it's a good thing I'm in a hurry," Savino said.

He slipped the gem back in the bag and then placed it inside a pocket hidden in his doublet.

"What of Andril?" Savino asked.

"He has no idea, but he'll get his share nonetheless, I don't short my partners," Deth said.

Savino smiled, "A good thing that, as well as you making good on debts."

"Well after this, we're even, understood?" Deth said.

"Agreed, assuming you can second me tomorrow night in my duel on the Baymourn Bridge."

Deth frowned, his tusks growing at the action, "I suppose I'll have to if I'm collecting bets."

"Good, and be sure to bring my sword and a bucket of vinegar," Savino said.

"What?"

Savino unbuckled his blade, placed it on the tabletop, and drew the curtain back.

"Just do it, now I've got to find Torrent."

Deth tried to say something else, but Savino closed the curtain on him, the sound of laughter exploding on the far side of the bar.

There, a raven-haired beauty in dueling leathers rose, lifted a tankard, and slid back toward the rear tables behind the bar.

Torrent… just in time…

The bell chimed once, the hollow sound drifting into the harbor and down the twisting stair to where Savino sat. He jerked his head away from the wall, grabbed his torch, and clattered down the stair.

Thirty feet below a wave of cold air blew past him, the stone walls spider-webbed with frost as he entered the vault of a large subterranean cave. He hurled the torch into the air, its light illuminating the chamber as it spun.

Halfway across, it fell with a clatter onto a smooth surface of ice. A thousand glimmering reflections danced orange around it, and beyond them, a pile of treasure from the dreams of another age lay atop a small landmass, forming their own, smaller, island of gold.

In a single leap, he jumped from the steps to the ice, the bone-blades catching as he waved his arms. Wind caught him, buffeted him, and he gained speed and balance as he slid across the frozen surface to the waiting horde.

He pulled up short, a spray of ice shavings cast in the air as he righted himself and drew a mask about his lower face. A shadow slipped below the surface of the ice, the shape illuminated by the guttering torch as he leaned down and removed a single gold coin from the mountainous pile.

Flipping it over, he slid two steps back and knelt before placing it against the surface of the ice.

"Here you go, big fella, get a good look…" he whispered.

A yellow eye slit with a black pupil pressed against the ice, the orb the size of an Ullamalitzli ball as it spun and blinked beneath the surface.

Smiling, his picked the coin up, flipped it, caught it, and then placed it inside his cloak. Beneath him the ice strained, cracking noises echoing about the room.

"Not yet you don't," he said.

Forcing a skate to the right, he picked up speed and fled the vault, a distant roar following him out the tidal caves as he raced into the light of the Blood Moon. Around him the bay of Taux stood frozen, waves caught like amber amid the bloody moon's glare as he sped over and around the largest.

He had to round the far island, the ruins of the old Sun Temple playing in the night as the lights of Taux spread out before him.

A tremor shook the ice. His blades held, but he adjusted his course, zigzagging this way and that as he sped toward the far shore. Somewhere over the ice a howl sounded, its echo drifting to him as the wind sped past in his dead heat toward the shore.

He kept moving. A bell sounded from the city and he cursed, the docks still a good distance away.

Pushing his legs hard, he raced on. Behind him a thunderous sound split the night, and he glanced back to see a rolling wave of water moving up in a circle from some distant point in the bay.

"Torrent!" he called.

The water moved ever closer as his straining legs burned until he could hear the sucking spray of it at his back. He leaned down and closed his eyes as the remaining ice at his back exploded, the dark shape of a serpent snapping at the opening provided by the melting ice.

The beast's attack was too soon, the ice staying its massive jaws and the impact of its upward strike sent Savino tumbling into the air. The world spun, and he summoned all the air he could. He was no full-blood Aspara, so flight was denied him, but his Element did buy him a few extra seconds in his vault.

Savino tumbled, eyes watching the dark water below as it called his doom, but as quickly as the explosive thaw had come, the ever extending circle of it refroze and at the last moment he struck hard against ice once more.

Pain ripped though his side, his descent stopped hard as he struck and then spun away across the newly minted surface. Beneath him another tremor sounded, but he shook his head, cursed and scrambled to his feet.

"I'll not forget this Torrent, you can be sure of that..."

His blades caught again, and he pressed on, the pain and adrenaline mixing as the bells continued to call out the midnight hour. Ahead, yellow lanterns were lit, the Baymourn Bridge spanning the distance between the city proper and the Arm of the Sun. Dark shapes milled there, those brave enough to come out at this hour prepared for a fight.

He drew close as the reverb of the final bell went silent. He came to an abrupt stop beneath the city side of the bridge. Drawing a knife, he slashed the ties on his boots, the blades falling away as he ascended the water stair two by two toward a small throng of souls at the bridge's entry.

"He's craven, and you can all see that!" A voice shouted.

"No, just a bit delayed," he yelled.

People parted and he threw off his cloak and scarf, sweat running into his eyes as he moved toward where Dethocrates stood at the bridge's bayside rail.

"You look spent," Vash proclaimed from beneath the lamps.

"Nothing a good dash of water won't cure," Savino said, driving his hands into the bucket held in one of Deth's hands.

The stink of vinegar was powerful, but he splashed his face, and provided a good show of enjoying the liquid as Deth shook his head in disbelief.

"There, much better!" Savino exclaimed.

He drew his falcon rapier from Deth's hip, took two steps forward and heard the onrush of water thundering toward them from somewhere in the bay.

"You've chosen an auspicious night, Master Vash, as it seems magic has been at work in the harbor," Savino saluted.

Vash raised his rapier, the smell of the man's jasmine perfume mixing with the acidic tang of vinegar from Savino's dripping hands.

"Oh," Savino interrupted before reaching into his doublet, "I thought I should provide your payment for the ferryman."

With a quick flip, he tossed a gold coin through the air. Vash caught it with a deft flurry, the shine sparkling between his fingers.

"A nice gesture, Savino, but you'll be the one needing…"

Before the words could be delivered a tower of water burst from beneath the bridge. The onlookers fell back with screams and pale faces as a giant serpent with scales glowing emerald shot from the water and snatched Vash from the bridge in one great gulp. The clatter of the man's rapier sounded on the flagstone and then serpent was gone, those gathered staring in stunned silence as Savino moved forward.

"It seems the Saints and even the Old Gods favor me in this duel," Savino said.

With a flick of his boot, he lifted Vash's bejeweled rapier into the air and caught it. Deth was beside him with his cloak, and the two exchanged their burdens, Deth securing Vash's rapier in his coat.

"I guess that's all there is to see, so let money change hands and for those of you who bet on me tonight, there is free drink at the Emerald Serpent," he said.

Many an eye looked to the dark waters of the bay at this final word, but eventually they nodded, and the collection of folk broke up after a flurry of whispers and transactions.

Deth leaned in, whispering, "It's much too far to the Serpent this night, Savino."

"Then I guess I'll not be buying strangers' drinks," Savino smiled.

The two walked from the bridge together, both drawing dark cloaks over their heads. Savino cast an eye out into the bay, a smile on his lips as he watched the recently-thawed water lap at the quay.

Such was life in Taux, where those who lived by their wits could attain wealth and glory, all the while skating on thin ice…

Illustration by Jeff Laubenstein

FOOTSTEPS OF BLOOD

Rob Mancebo

*T*ohil ran the tip of his tongue across dry lips as he crouched in a shadowed alcove where the sky-blue cloak of his office wouldn't give him away. The crooked streets of Taux's Haunted Temple District were peppered with a thousand-and-one such nooks, shrines to both old gods and usurping saints. He loved a hunt and felt his heart beating like the deep thrum of a war drum in his veins. *Quietly,* he cautioned himself, *Quietly. Don't spook the quarry.* He supported his sword sheath in his left hand lest it scrape across moving thigh or bang against a wall. He was hunting this moonlit night to observe, not to fight– at least, not yet.

"Are you sure this is all you require, Master?"

The stone alleyway enhanced a low, wheedling voice as a saffron-clad merchant drew open the corners of a velvet bag to display its contents to his shadowed patron. Tohil glimpsed the frosty shine of polished metal in the rusty moonlight before the seller re-covered the item.

"Yes, that is all," a black-cloaked man assured him.

Tohil saw the dark figure press a weighty purse, bigger than a man's fist, into the merchant's grasping fingers. He was rewarded by the merchant dropping the velvet bag into his outstretched hand. The dark man clutched at the item as though it was very precious, before drawing it under his sable cloak and heading away down one of the many alleys. The merchant left in the other direction, and Tohil stepped out of the shadows. He hesitated a mere moment before rushing after his quarry in a crouching jog. He had no interest in the merchant, Kine, who kept a jewelry booth in the raised market. The fellow was always digging in and about the ruined areas of the city for old trinkets and talismans to sell. There was never any knowing what the scavenger might unearth. Tohil was after bigger game in his predawn hunt. He'd arrived too late to interrogate the merchant quietly before the transaction, so he was left to glean information from the stranger.

That the shadowy man he followed had no skill in the darkened maze of streets was immediately apparent. Tohil heard banging and, an occasional clatter, as his quarry stumbled through the darkness. After some minutes of blundering, the stranger mumbled an inarticulate prayer to summon a spark of fire to a small lamp. Thereafter it was even easier for the burly Sturgeon to follow him.

Tohil smiled to himself.

What sort of a fool would light a lamp in such a place?

Even a Razor Duelist with a death-wish wouldn't be so brazen. Skulking street gangs and the cutpurses of the Nightmen Guild were always on the look-out for easy targets. A night-blind buffoon skulking among the city's Haunted Towers would certainly be a tempting morsel in the wee hours of the morning. Tohil hefted his sheathed sword in his left hand and closed in upon his prey.

The lantern bearer was obvious, but the waiting ambushers were not. Tohil was almost upon his prey when the man lifted his lantern high and called out, "Who's there?"

The answering chorus of laughter made the big Sturgeon breathe a quick thanks to St. Siegfried for the warning. Wraith-like, he sidestepped and crouched down behind a refuse pile in a stinking alleyway to observe the coming fight.

Five men were revealed as they stepped into the glowing halo of the stranger's lamp. They were dressed in baggy, black clothing slimmed about their torsos by snug, sable surcoats. The only sign of color about any of them was a pale circle each bore upon his left breast. Tohil recognized the emblem as that of the 'Sons of the Moon,' a local gang of growing power.

The man did not show the good sense to flee, but instead flung the lamp down to smash against the cobbles so the licking flames gave illumination to the area. He hunched a shoulder to swing free a blackened buckler slung across his back, and withdrew a *macuahuitl* – an old style, obsidian-edged warclub – from under his robes.

"An obstinate fool, aren't you?" One of the young street thugs said with a laugh. He whipped out a fine steel rapier as he advanced boldly to meet the stranger. While approaching, the young man tried to circle to get the stranger to turn his back to the rest of the gang, but his opponent mirrored the youth's line of movement until the pair of them were blocked from side-stepping further by a building wall that lined the lane. The Son of the Moon executed a forthright lunge to plant his point through the stranger, but the man deflected the tip of the blade with his buckler and snapped a word. There was a sharp noise. It was strangely like an echo, but with no discernable source, and Tohil saw the swordsman flinch. The alleyway became rife with the smell and tingle of magic as the stranger thrust his weapon under his attacker's outstretched arm. The line of the weapon's obsidian blades ripped a ragged wound across the youth's arm and as the swordsman flinched back at the pain, the stranger recovered his position in such a manner as to rip the *macaqhuitl* across the young man's thigh as well. Blood ran black in the firelight and the thug staggered away.

From his vantage point, Tohil nodded in respect. The stranger had completely incapacitated his foe, arm and leg, with that single attack.

The youth's compatriots drew blades and rushed as a pack. As they closed, the stranger gave an early sweep of his weapon while snapping a command. A boom of thunder rocked the alleyway. The attackers hesitated while the lone man used his club to dash aside a sword tip and slash another punk's face deeply as he recovered his stance.

"Have at him lads," one of the gang members shouted. "He's no Wizard. It's only tricks!"

The gang pressed in and the man did a masterful job of shifting position to work at close-quarters and yet keep one thug between him and the other two. Tohil had only been sent to follow and learn about the mysterious artifact that Kine had bragged of finding. Still, three-to-one odds were just too much for a single man to handle. Watching the stranger's valiant defense made the Sturgeon's blood course and his spark kindle hot in his chest.

"City Watch, at your back!" Tohil bellowed as he rushed into the fray. The city Captain may have ordered him out as an observer, but never had he been a laggard when blades sang and hot blood splattered upon the streets.

One of the Sons of the Moon flinched back at the Sturgeon's bellow and received a crippling slash to his leg as a reward for his momentary distraction. Then Tohil was standing shoulder-to-shoulder with the stranger and giving the remnants of the street gang no chance to escape. Tohil ran his blade through an opponent's throat in an expert lunge but the stranger continued to use his cruder weapon to only wound. The man slashed his opponent's arm then struck with three flashing blows that left the young man to writhe upon the ground as a cringing, bleeding wreck. The wounds inflicted by the *macaqhuitl's* jagged edges of volcanic glass were ragged and gaping.

And the fight was over. Tohil and the stranger scanned the alleyway for other combatants, but it was empty save for themselves and those of the fallen who had been killed or were too injured to flee.

"We'll see you again!" A youth threatened from the ground as he held a hand to staunch the blood flowing from his leg. "The Sons of the Moon will hunt you down—"

Tohil closed the space between them with a bound, ramming his sword full-force through the young man's open mouth. A crunching twist freed his blade from the body and he looked to the rest of the wounded and demanded, "Anyone else wish to continue this game?"

"But— but you're a Sturgeon, you can't just murder wounded people in the streets," one of the fallen whined.

"Oh, I must follow rules of chivalry while you pack of swine ignore them? Ha! My city – *my* rules. That your friend dropped his sword before threatening me was just foolishness on his part." Tohil stepped over and wiped his blade clean on the cringing man's tunic. "Now I will ask again, does anyone else wish to continue this game?"

The wounded thugs groaned that they did not, and pleaded for their lives. Tohil turned his back upon them with scorn. The stranger still held his weapon ready until Tohil sheathed his blade. Only then did the dark-swathed figure re-sling his buckler to guard against a knife in the back and hang his *macaqhuitl* upon a hook under his cloak.

"I am Tohil, a Sturgeon of Taux," the guardsman introduced himself while holding out a hand.

The stranger looked at Tohil's dark, tattooed face for several heartbeats before sliding his right hand out from under his cloak and taking the Sturgeon's in a hearty grip. "I am Matlal, a simple traveler to this city. I thank you for your help, though I fancy I could have finished off these clumsy dogs myself."

The left hand remained beneath his hanging cloak and Tohil smiled at the stranger's caution. He had no doubt that there was a knife in that left hand in case of treachery. He laughed as he shook Matlal's hand. "Not so simple a traveler as you might claim," he said and waved at the scattering of rogues trying to bind up wounds. "That was as clever a use of magic as I've seen. Just a little distraction at the right moment. If every traveler could defend himself as well as you do, there'd be a deal less of these pitiful thieves about.

The man gave a nod of acknowledgement, but did not reply to the praise.

"Come," Tohil told him. "Fighting's thirsty work and this is my city. I know just the place to take care of anything you need."

"What do you know of what I need?" the man asked quietly.

"Me? I'm only a mercenary Sturgeon. I don't pretend to know anything more than fighting, but come with me to the Emerald Serpent and I will introduce you to a good friend of mine, Quilan. Now he's an innkeeper with his ear to the ground. He can find a fellow anything his heart might desire: whether it's a ship to far away lands, an assassin to quiet a feud, or a meal and a cup of good wine."

"What about a room for the night?"

"He has several, but the cut and fabric of your cloak shows you to be a man of taste and means. For such a simple necessity let me tempt you with the comforts of the Silk Purse. The two establishments stand conveniently back-to-back. At the Purse, the rooms are finer and their drinks somewhat more expensive, but the company there is infinitely more entertaining."

"Entertaining?" Matlal seemed interested.

"*Infinitely* more entertaining," Tohil repeated. "Come, I'll take you there. The pair of us together are less likely to draw any more of these annoying parasites. He kicked one of the crawling wounded out of his path, and led off down the street.

"This is the famous Black Gate of Taux." Matlal hesitated before following Tohil through the ancient, stone archway. The man brushed his fingertips across the dark, groaning stone of the structure and recoiled.

"Unsettling, isn't it?" Tohil observed. "They moan like that throughout the nights. Daylight calms them somewhat."

"It's said that the stones wail with the voices of the city's former inhabitants," Matlal mused.

"Yes, and they're even louder at certain times of the year," the Sturgeon replied. "It's damned creepy to be in this city on those nights, I can tell you. More than a half a century ago the city was emptied as every soul was sucked into the stones. Only their dark, old gods know why. When we hear the voices whisper, no one knows if the spirits are intoning spells to escape their stony prison– or casting curses to draw the rest of us in with them. The old ones were a black-hearted race steeped in blood and sorcery. Best to disturb them as little as may be."

"Better to let the dead rest, eh?" Matlal asked.

"It is that," Tohil told him with a wave to follow along. "Beyond the Black Gate is the old *Ullamalitzli* Stadium. Now it's a city within the city, a haven for every un-hanged rogue on the Free Coast. At this archway we leave the confines of Taux City behind and join into the society of free men."

"Oh, is that how it works?"

"No law beyond the Black Gate but what you bring with you, my friend." Tohil hefted his sword. "So keep your weapons close and your purse even closer."

"Then it is truly a pool of anarchy?"

"No. Say rather this is a businessman's paradise and the inhabitants like to keep it that way. They stay clear of the law, but they have a deal with the Nightmen Guild to keep organized crime out. For a nominal monthly sum, the Nightmen stay out of the businesses beyond the Black Gate and watch that no one else moves in. All men profit – except the city fathers – and visitors are reasonably safe from harm, even without the presence of the city guards."

Matlal nodded, "An interesting arrangement."

They passed through the nearly empty walkways, the ramshackle structures, the closed tents of the infamous Raised Market, and reeking refuse piles in the streets. There were few people about at that hour and all gave them a wide berth as they traveled.

The building that hosted the Silk Purse had been crafted as part of the original city, a permanent structure of several stories. Before the smooth face of its polished, lindenwood doors stood a pair of delightfully-cast brass monkey figures bearing lamps which were burning brightly even at the late hour.

"Now here's the finest bordello in Taux," Tohil told him proudly. "In the Silk Purse your most basic needs may be fulfilled or your wildest fantasies will be explored, depending upon how much coinage you have to indulge your pleasures."

He hammered upon the door and it swung open after a moment. A massive giant of a man armed with a shortsword and a wide assortment of ugly knives stood before them. He smiled as he looked down at Tohil displaying lower canine teeth that were too large for a Human.

"Hammil!" Tohil greeted the Jai-Ruk guardian. "What's on special this morning?"

The guard laughed and patted the burly Sturgeon on a shoulder very carefully, as though he were afraid he might break him. "Tohil! Always joking." He waved them inside while displaying a huge, toothy grin.

After they had passed inside, Matlal whispered, "I didn't know a Jai-Ruk could grow that big."

"His size makes sure everyone stays friendly," Tohil told him with a smile. They walked down a hallway and pushed aside a white linen curtain, and Tohil heard Matlal draw breath.

The ancient stone walls were draped with hangings of emerald, saffron, and azure silk that tumbled to rainbow piles of luxurious pillows. Smoldering cressets of polished brass lent a gentle hint of spicy incense to the warm air, and a ring of low tables created a circle where a nimble dancer cavorted to the beat of drum, pipe, and lute.

"*Ueuecoyotl* be praised," Matlal murmured as he looked around. "This is an elegant playhouse."

Tohil laughed and waved the man to one of the many unoccupied tables. He doffed his helmet and the blue cloak of his office. Matlal swept off his own cloak and buckler. Beneath the garment, the man wore a simple skirt-like loincloth of white that draped to his knees in the front and was edged with a banding of woven purple braid. The room's many lamps revealed his coppery skin and a patterned headband that held his black, shoulder length hair from his face. No shirt covered his well muscled body, but studded leather straps terminating in a wide, gold medallion in the center of his chest secured a brilliant jaguar pelt to drape over his left shoulder. A vague recognition stirred within Tohil when he saw the pattern of the medallion. He knew he'd seen its likeness before, but couldn't remember where.

The pair sprawled out upon pillows to observe the dancer's undulating charms at closer range. She was a lithe woman, dressed in little more than a translucent breast band and a plethora of intricate jewelry that shimmered frostily in the lamplight as she moved.

"So, where are you from, Matlal?" Tohil asked.

"*Tehuantepec*," the man said while waving a hand vaguely to the North.

"Te- huan- te- pec," Tohil mouthed the curious word. "Is that a city or a country?"

"It is a place," the man replied with a shrug.

There were still various tribes living in the mountains beyond the poisonous swamps that bordered Taux. Although immigrants from various far-off nations had re-settled the city, an odd handful of locals occasionally dared to travel to the city. Before Tohil had time to importune Matlal further, soft fingers stole across the black tattoos that wound about his dark shoulders and a voice whispered, "Tohil". He looked up into the striking, green eyes of a buxom, olive-skinned matron gloriously draped in a gown of supple, emerald-colored silk that caressed her generous curves in a way that pleaded for a man's attention.

"Mama Serene!" The Sturgeon swept her into a possessive embrace with a laugh and a kiss. When they pulled apart, Tohil nodded toward Matlal and told her, "My friend needs a bed for the night and someone amicable to share it with him."

"Well then you've brought him to the right place," Serene clashed a pair of finger cymbals three times and a group of girls gathered from around the room. They stepped past the tables and paraded into the circle. Surrounding the dancer in the center, they circled slowly, stopping every few steps to turn and then resume their bold procession.

Matlal's eyes made his choice long before he admitted to it. His gaze passed over the buxom trio of haughty, blonde Thalonian's with their ice-blue eyes and ivory skin, it lingered upon Lan and Lin, the waifish, giggling twins from the T'ung, and he winked at the dusky, round-hipped beauties of Zimbolay. Yet it was a local mountain girl with her raven black hair chopped at her browned shoulders and crested with a tall spray of pheasant feathers who held his attention.

"I see that Teya has drawn your comrade's favor," Serene said as she waved the girl over. "And who shall it be for you good Tohil?"

"What about you, Serene?"

"Don't be foolish," she brushed off his suggestion coolly. "You know I never get involved with men of law. What about Zama, Melyne, Varvara— or perhaps the twins with a flask of spiced wine and a pot of warm oil?"

"Ah, you know me too well," Tohil laughed. "But it's late and there isn't time to do the skill of the twins justice. Is Plums-By-Midnight available?"

Serene shook her head, "No, I'm afraid not."

Tohil nodded, "Then I think I will make do with Ingitrude this evening."

The Thalonian girl overheard him and her pale eyes flashed with resentment. She approached the Sturgeon as though warming for bitter combat.

"Make do? Haughty swine," she snapped. "No one 'makes do' with Ingitrude! Bold suitors cut each other's throats for the favors of Ingitrude."

Tohil looked about at the scattering of patrons in the room and then back at her before saying with a laugh, "No one's cutting any throats over you tonight my fair dove. But I'll punch that little wine merchant over there in the corner if it would make you feel more important."

Even as he sparred with his choice for the evening, the odd reaction of the girl, Teya, caught Tohil's attention. Having approached the table, the object of Matlal's interest only stood, kohl-blackened eyes wide, staring at the man. Tohil saw her shaking finger raise as she inhaled and he looked to his new comrade just as the girl loosed a shrill scream of terror.

Every head in the room turned and the frantic woman yelled, "*Tezcatilpoca! Tezcatilpoca!*"

The room became chaos as a handful of patrons scrabbled for the exits. The hulking guard, Hammil, rushed into the room with sword drawn and cast about to see what was causing the commotion.

"Oh, shush, girl!" Serene ordered then turned to Matlal with an apologetic smile and told him, "I must beg your indulgence, Sir, she's just a superstitious mountain girl, unsettled at seeing someone wearing a medallion of the old Jaguar god."

Tezcatilpoca, the Jaguar god of rulers, sorcerers, and warriors. *That* was where Tohil had seen the emblem on the man's medallion before! It was boldly displayed upon the blood-stained stones of numerous old temples throughout Taux. *Tezcatilpoca,* whose insatiable thirst for Human blood had been fed throughout the long centuries with the dripping hearts of prisoners, slaves, and even shrieking citizens of the city. Tohil had heard that the murderous cult of the Jaguar god was long extinct.

"She is wise," Matlal said as he stood, "for I *am* a priest of *Tezcatilpoca.*" He reached into his wide wallet, withdrew an intricate bracelet of figured gold, and held it aloft to shine in the bright lamplight. Tohil saw then what old Kine, the trinket merchant, had sold the stranger in the dark alleyway. It was an artifact from the temple of *Tezcatilpoca.*

Matlal shouted, "The Jaguar god shall rise again!" and then wrapped the ornament about his wrist. At the instant of the shining gold encasing Human flesh, the room was filled with palpable horror. The silken hangings about the room were whipped and swept away as though by storm winds, and the ancient stones of the building walls howled to tormented life.

"*Xolotl*," Matlan cried, "help my brothers and sisters break free of their prison of stone. *Xolotl*, great traveler, lead your children home again!"

Before their eyes the wine merchant sitting in the corner of the room seemed suddenly drawn into the stones, almost as though he'd been yanked off his feet. He had barely time to scream before he'd vanished into the wall and a different man was pushed out into the room. The newcomer's shape was cloudy for a moment, then solidified. He was dressed as Matlal was, in a loin cloth of purple-edged white. His eyes were wide with wonder and he bowed to Matlal. Though his speech was strange, it was clear by his posture and gestures that he was thanking the priest for freeing him.

Tohil had seen mages use mystical artifacts in deeds of black sorcery before. The diabolical items magnified the paltry magical gifts of ordinary people to extraordinary levels of power, but he'd never seen anyone wield such a horribly potent artifact like this.

"Damnit, man," Tohil stood and cursed Matlal, "You can't just trade the lives of the living to resurrect those long dead!"

"*Itzli*, the god of sacrifice, must be paid," Matlal told him. "A life for a life. I will gladly sacrifice the lives of strangers to bring back the glories of my grandfathers."

Ingitrude ran wildly for the exit, though for all her unsteady haste, she lurched suddenly toward a wall and vanished into the stone with a wail. A different girl burst from the wall, stumbled and faded in to look about in confusion. She was dressed in a simple, white wrap edged with purple and she also bowed to Matlal.

"Keep away from the walls lest they draw us in!" Mother Serene shouted to those about. At her words, the patrons and employees of the Silk Purse eschewed the raving walls like the trap they were, and moved together into the center of the establishment.

"Saint Siegfried curse your elder gods, you cold-blooded bastard!" Tohil drew his sword and stepped between the group and the priest. "Their toll of passage shall not be paid with *my* people!"

In answer, Matlal thrust his hand toward Tohil and screamed, "*Atlacamani!*" and the world whirled about the big Sturgeon. He was flung, spinning like a doll in a hurricane to tumble across the floor.

He heard a frantic shrieking and was able to flop over in time to see Lin, one of the twins, pulled from her sister's desperate grip and vanish into a wall. No sooner had the girl disappeared than another of the city's lost inhabitants appeared in her place.

Hammil sprang to attack the priest with a roar but was sent spinning away in a whirlwind just as Tohil had been. The huge Jai-Ruk lay stunned a few feet from the Sturgeon. Still dazed, Tohil could hear the cacophony of the power-drunk Matlal laughing in victory.

Then, above all the rest of the noise, the strong, rich voice of a woman entreated, "Here beloved priest! I'm trapped here! Release me!"

Matlal walked boldly to a wall and waved his hand over it saying, "I divine that your spirit is strong. Who are you?"

"In life I was the Princess Yaretzi, a joy to my people," a melodic voice replied. "In death my heart has withered to stone."

"Then I shall give you the joy of life once again," Matlal promised. "And we shall overcome the curse of our people together and renew the former glory of our city." He looked around and waved a hand at the prostrate form of Hammil. "To bring back a spirit of your power, we'll need someone stronger than a usual sacrifice. This stalwart fellow should suffice." He waved a hand and Hammil began to be dragged toward a wall by unseen forces, but Tohil had gathered enough strength to throw himself forward and wrap his arms around the unconscious Jai-Ruk's leg, trying to anchor the guard with his own bodyweight.

He slowed the movement, but found himself dragged toward the wall along with the giant. He hung on dizzily with all his might as the hungry surface of the wall grew closer and closer. At the last moment, he was knocked rolling by another weight striking him from the side. He lost his desperate grasp on Hammil's leg and the Jai-Ruk slid into the wall as though he had slipped down an icy incline. Tohil looked down and found Serene's arms wrapped about his waist.

"I thought you never got involved with the law?" Tohil took the time to ask in his surprise.

"This isn't business," she told him with flushed cheeks. "He's insane! Don't you see, he's planning on destroying us all to bring back the people of the old Tolimic Empire!"

"But what can we…" Tohil hesitated as the figure of the Princess Yaretzi solidified within the Silk Purse.

A shroud of silence muffled the frightened exclamations of the people trapped in the establishment. Yaretzi's flowing, sea-green robe rustled before them upon a spectral breeze that touched nothing else in the room. The garment bore a cunningly-wrought emblem of a pale, white skull upon its breast and seemed to be woven of supple snakeskin. She wore no royal ornaments and her head was closely shrouded with a shading hood that hung low where her proud face would've been – if she'd had a face. Chalk-white bones poked through every undraped corner of her form and her skeletal hands spread as though in benevolent greeting to all before her.

"Blessings of Saint Shera," Serene whispered. "She's a *Civatateo!*"

All the people were frozen where they stood, though whether by some arcane power of the *Civatateo* or through the sheer horror of her presence Tohil couldn't tell. The monster moved with a gliding gate toward the door. Matlal thrust out a hand in a gesture of command, but the undead princess ignored it.

Nodding her shrouded head as she passed, she told him, "Thank you, little priest. I have been trapped in that stony prison for all these long years, tormented by the gnawing hunger of the ages. You have kindly resurrected me to feed at the breast of this lovely city of tens of thousands." She brushed her fingertips down the cringing cheek of the first man Matlal had resurrected as she passed by him. The poor fellow released a sort of strangled gasp and crumpled to the floor as a desiccated pile of bones. "Oh yes, I shall enjoy feeding here." The splayed bones of the monster's feet left puddling gore wherever she stepped.

"But this is our city," Matlal called to her. "You were a princess of our people. We can re-awaken our ancestors, resurrect not just their bodies, but their former glory as well."

"In life I was the Princess Yaretzi, a joy to my people," the monster intoned the words as though by simple rote. "In death my heart has withered to stone. Past glory means nothing. Only hunger remains."

"You shall not feed in *my* city, Princess!" Matlal ordered imperiously, and again gestured with the mystical bracelet. Nothing happened and he looked to the talisman with wondrous frustration.

"I am a servant of the Jaguar god also, little priest," the *Civatateo's* warm voice hissed merrily, though her skeletal mouth never moved. "I distribute his dooms among the nations. How then do you think to oppose me with a tool of *Tezcatilpoca's* power?"

"I shall stop you!" he promised.

But the Princess Yaretzi simply laughed and passed out of the Silk Purse to haunt the maze-like streets of Taux, leaving a trail of bloody footprints behind her.

Tohil's legs were still too unstable to stand, but he used Matlal's distraction to palm his dagger.

"No, Tohil," Serene shouted, "we need him to resurrect Ingitrude, Lin, and Hammil!"

But the knife was already in flight. Matlal's eyes widened as the blade bit deep into his kidney and he wheeled unsteadily to face Tohil.

"In the back?" Matlal said in a wheezy voice. "Again no rules, Sturgeon?"

"My city," Tohil told the man, "*My* rules!"

The priest of *Tezcatilpoca* drew a deep breath and thrust out his hand as though it held a weapon. The room seemed to swirl around Tohil as he was sent spinning to slam against a stone wall. Then he knew only blackness.

Tohil awoke in a bed with his body still aching with pain. He lurched upright to be dazzled by the steamy golden light of another morning in Taux. A hand upon his brawny shoulder restrained him and he turned to find Mama Serene sitting upon a bench next to him holding a wet rag.

"Be at ease, Sturgeon," she told him somberly. "You need to recover." She laid the wet cloth across his brow to comfort him.

"But the *Civatateo*, I have to warn people…" he argued. "And Matlal, there's a bastard I have to run down!"

"People already know," Serene told him. "She killed twice more last night and the city is in a panic. The Big Fish has called upon the Razors for reinforcements, and both Sturgeons and Duelists are out in-force to hunt the monster down. They're all busy following criss-crossing trails of bloody tracks throughout the Black Gate."

"If I ever find Matlal…" Tohil ground his teeth in fury as he thought about the priest.

"He's a corpse. Attacking you was his final act, but one of those that he resurrected took the bracelet from his body and fled. I need you to track her down and break her bones, one-by-one, until she agrees to release my friends from the walls of Taux…" she told him with a chill edge to her voice. "And do it *very* slowly."

AUTHORS

Lynn Flewelling grew up in northern Maine, United States, and has since lived on both coasts and traveled around the world, all experiences that are reflected in her writing. She has worked as a teacher, a house painter, a necropsy technician, and a free-lance editor and journalist. She has been married to Douglas Flewelling since 1981, and has two sons. She currently lives in Redlands, California, where she continues to write, and offers lectures and creative writing workshops at the University of Redlands. Her first Nightrunner novel, *Luck in the Shadows*, was a Locus Magazine Editor's Pick for Best First Novel and a finalist for the Compton Crook Award. Her novels *Traitor's Moon* (2000) and *Hidden Warrior* (2004) were both finalists for the Spectrum Award. Her novels are currently published in 13 countries, and in 2005, the first volume of the Japanese language version of *Luck in the Shadows* was published.

Harry Connolly is a longtime survivor of the publishing world, and that is no light task. He made his name in the urban fantasy genre with the creation of the character Ray Lilly and his *Twenty Palaces* Novels which have been listed on various years best lists.

Todd Lockwood's illustration work has appeared on NY Times best-selling novels, magazines, video games, collectible card games, and fantasy role-playing games. It has been honored with multiple appearances in Spectrum and the Communication Arts Illustration Annual, and with numerous industry awards. Always known for the narrative power of his paintings, Todd now turns his hand to writing, and is working on a novel to be published by DAW Books at a date still to be determined. You may view his art at his website, http://www.toddlockwood.com.

Juliet E. McKenna is a British fantasy author. She studied Greek and Roman history and literature at St Hilda's College, Oxford. McKenna has written three series of books, *The Tales of Einarinn*, *The Aldabreshin Compass* and *The Chronicles of the Lescari Revolution*, as well as many short stories and articles. She is currently working on a new series, *The Hadrumal Crisis*.

Michael Tousignant is a part-time college student, part-time library clerk living in Monroe County, Michigan. He occasionally tries his hand at writing, and is holding off on trying to be clever in his biography until after he's had a few more stories published. Michael is also the super hero Iron Fist... oops, I guess I shouldn't have said that...

Martha Wells is the author of fourteen SF/F novels, including *The Element of Fire*, *The Wizard Hunters*, *Wheel of the Infinite*, *City of Bones*, and the Nebula-nominated *The Death of the Necromancer*. Most recent are *The Cloud Roads* (2011) and *The Serpent Sea* (2012) published by Night Shade Books. Forthcoming novels are *The Siren Depths* (December 2012, Night Shade) and a YA fantasy *Emilie and the Hollow World* (Strange Chemistry, May 2013) She has short stories in *Realms of Fantasy*, *Black Gate*, *Lone Star Stories*, and *Elemental*, and essays in *Farscape Forever*, *Mapping the World of Harry Potter*, and *Chicks Unravel Time*. She also has two *Stargate Atlantis* novels *Reliquary* and *Entanglement*. Her books have been published in seven languages.

Julie E. Czerneda, Canadian author and editor, has transformed her love and knowledge of biology into science fiction novels (published by DAW Books NY) and short stories that have received international acclaim, multiple awards, and best-selling status. Her latest works include the Aurora-nominated *Tesseracts Fifteen: A Case of Quite Curious Tales*, co-edited with Susan MacGregor, and *Rift in the Sky*, latest installment in her SF series, The Clan Chronicles. Coming March 2013 to bookstores everywhere is Book One of her new Night's Edge series, Julie's debut (and really fat) fantasy novel, *A Turn of Light*. There are toads. Writing for *Tales* has been a wonderful experience. For more about Julie's work, please visit www.czerneda.com.

Scott Taylor is a horrible writer. When 'they' say you make it because you never give up, not because of overall talent, they are talking about Scott. In fact, he wasn't even supposed to appear in this anthology but was forced to activate his Microsoft Word program when other signed authors dropped out at the last minute. He currently runs the micro-publishing house Art of the Genre and produces art inspired 1980s throw-back novels like *The Burning City*, *The Gun Kingdoms*, and *The Cursed Legion*. Obviously, he also has a penchant for sticking 'the' at the beginning of all his titles.

Rob Mancebo helped build an orphanage in Mexico, stood watch on the cold war era border in Europe, put-down riots, toured in Ireland, installed and repaired all sorts of security hardware, delivered classified material, chased down thieves, and has helped the authorities put many very bad people in jail. He's read slush and edited books, sold guns and been a range officer. He currently assists the sick and injured in an urgent care facility and in his spare time writes the fantasy and adventure stories which have been featured in numerous magazines and anthologies.

CHARACTER DESCRIPTIONS

© JANET AUUSIO 2013.

ZHADA

Zhada is a Lowl at ease with his dual nature. He honors the divine power that blended superior canine senses with Humankind's abilities to walk upright and hold weapons and tools. Following in his father and grandfather's footsteps, he's quietly determined to be a trail-blazer; to rise in Taux society through his own merits and honorably-earned wealth until no one can gainsay his right to marry the Human woman he loves.

Bold when action is called for, he generally prefers to achieve his aims through negotiation and co-operation. Only a fool would assume his usual calm manner indicates a coward though. Physically strong and a skilled swordsman as well as a capable hunter, he sees no reason to yield to bullies or threats. He won't stand to see his more vulnerable kinfolk abused or exploited either, especially by deceitful tome mages offering 'cures' to turn Lowl fully Human. On the other side of that coin, he has no patience with those Lowl who boast of their bestial nature, denying their own Humanity.

With elemental fire woven into Lowl nature, he can use a little low magic for everyday cantrips. He is very wary of high wizardry's far more perilous powers.

CENOTE

Before coming to Taux to live as a humble maskmaker's assist, her face ever-masked, Cenote had been a powerful Wizard. She'd lived in the Star Tower, her task and talent to use water as a lens to watch for danger as well as wonders. Her magic let her touch the Afterglow and use its power. She was a teacher, a lover, one among many and safe.

Until the day came when she saw too much and too clearly. When disaster struck Taux, only Cenote saw the face behind it. Only she cried out in warning. And when the time came for that evil to rise again, its first act was to blind her forever.

Cut off from the Afterglow, no longer a Wizard, believed dead and lost by her kin, Cenote has found a way to keep her watch. Through the eyes of friends, through her own water magic, and, most of all, through her heart. She will find her nemesis. She will refuse its evil any foothold or gain. Regardless of the cost, ever in secret, she will fight where other Wizards cannot. Within the Black Gate.

EMIL LACOSTA

Emil Lacosta is a tome mage with a rather slim selection of spells: He is able to create and destroy love, and his talents lie with the creation of potions.

He is a black man from Zimbolay. While in Taux, he has taken a foreign name as his "public name." The people of Zimbolay value privacy very highly, and his private name will never be shared outside his family.

This cultural preference--never explained to outsiders--can create problems among the faux-European cultures. To that end, Emil has chosen a name common in Findalynn, a sea-faring nation that is predominantly white and has many immigrants in Taux. He doesn't hide the fact that he's Zimbolay (the name of the country and the name of the people are the same), but if people make the wrong assumption...

In fact, Emil does not much care what the people of Taux think of him, only that they pay him for his services. In part this is because he was raised to shun outsiders, and in part this is because years of work in the lab, creating potions, salves, and powders, have dulled his emotions.

Emil is slightly under average height and somewhat skinnier than most people. Physically impressive, he is not. His eyes have a slight squint and his shoulders a mild stoop from long hours spent in his lab. His clothes and manner are always modest and mild--he has a deep aversion to flamboyance or ostentatious display--and he never wears a sword.

TORRENT

Torrent is a Corsair, the sea-going, very Human-looking peoples attuned to a low affinity for elemental water. She has thick, wavy dark hair and dark eyes, and a heart-shaped face. Her hair is usually contained in some way, either in a bandana or tied back in a pony with the same bandana. Not tall—about 5'4", but with a lithe, athletic build and fluid, cat-like grace. She ordinarily wears breeches, soft, calf-high leather boots, a shirt with loose sleeves (allowing for ease of movement) and a leather vest or sleeveless doublet. She wears her sword on her left hip.

© JANET AULISIO 2013.

Torrent has a quick temper, but is introspective and wary. She thinks and acts quickly, occasionally with unfortunate haste. She has the rare ability to manipulate water in small volumes, in various ways. Most notably, she can attune herself to the flow of liquids in a person or animal she has touched and cause cramps; heart palpitations; blinding migraines; a sudden need or inability to eliminate body wastes; sweats; or spontaneous orgasm—or failure of same. She used some—but not all—of those abilities in the past at different times, in different ways, in order to keep herself fed and safe. She used to run scams with Savino, and isn't above cheating people out of money.

She has been a Jill-of-many-trades, none of them crafts, unless slicing people with a deadly, slender curved sword is a craft. She's not a duelist, and would never willingly enter into a duel herself. She doesn't like rules. She was most comfortable as a hired sword on the ships of various merchant fleets, where she was also an adept sailor, but has found herself stranded in Taux.

© JANETAULISIO 2013.

DETHOCRATES

Most citizens of Taux don't think of Jai-Ruk as unobtrusive; they think of them as dull, or brutish. This is how Dethocrates prefers things, as underestimation makes his job easier. Dethocrates – or Dethoc, or Deth, or occasionally 'Thock' – spends his evenings earning money in illegal pursuits, mainly burglary, smuggling, or swindling. He's rarely the mastermind behind a scheme, but he's able to find a way to pull it off.

As an archer, Dethoc prefers to be methodical on the job; he likes to find a secluded 'perch' from which he can keep an eye on things, and when the 'perfect shot' appears, to strike. Of course, in a city like Taux, there are few perfect shots, and Dethoc spends much of his time improvising when a plan falls apart.

Dethocrates sailed into Taux a decade ago, and immediately made his home within the busy streets of the Black Gate. He's fairly quiet about his earlier life; he'll mention on occasion an Aspara who taught him archery, and when drunk enough he'll hurl curses at the Wounded Land, but apart from that, he keeps his past in the past, and considers Taux to be the only place that matters.

SAVINO EMANTRA

Born in the mountain passes of Mistfin, Savino Emantra is a Korys, a product of low affinity for elemental air. This makes him both long-lived and a man of constant movement, be it from lover, city, or job. At his core, his is a charlatan, a man who understands all that he isn't, and yet strives to be so much better than he is, even if it is a grand deception.

©JANET AULISIO 2013.

His greatest fear is that at some point his house of cards will come crumbling down around him, but to this point he's managed to keep himself just above water, and his time in Taux has been both lucrative and dangerous, a combination that keeps him occupied enough to stay in the city as his wanderlust is always pressing him to move on.

Handsome to a fault, and trained to be a stage actor, he uses these skills to his advantage on any number of scheme he devises to gain money in a way that requires the least effort or reflection of an actual honest day's work. Toiling away at the same thing every day is anathema to Savino, and he's always looking for the next score, the next conquest, and the next move.

© JANET AULISIO 2013.

TOHIL

Tohil is a man of the Opal Gates, and relocated to Taux where his skill at hunting other men and work with a blade earned him the blue overcoat of a Sturgeon, the mercenary police arm of the city. Having spent years patrolling the streets, he was eventually drawn to the Black Gate, where he found friends among the people there.

One of the few Sturgeons who will venture inside the Black Gate alone, he is a known frequenter of the Silk Purse where the greatest percentage of his weekly pay goes without question.

Heavily tattooed with raised 'scar' markings, his face and arms have become an unforgettable site to behold, and his dark skin marks him as a foreigner even among the immigrants of the city. Still, although he may appear fierce, inside his large chest beats the heart of a man ready to defend the city he has come to love with his life.

JELITH

Jelith was born in the kin city of Madrean, far to the north among along the fringes of Gariny. There, when he came of age he was cast out by his Kin Sire, as all young male Kin are, to fend for themselves in the wild. Instead of staying in the mountain passes, he drifted south through Lowl lands and eventually settled in Taux.

He was small in stature and always preferred stories and scholarly pursuits to anything else, and so not considered to have much potential by his pride. But as he grew older, he became highly skilled at shaping stone. He knew this skill might have secured him a place inside his pride, perhaps even with a mate, but he decided not to return

© JANET AULISIO 2013.

to his people or his Thane. He has journeyed through various cities, supporting himself as a stonemason, while looking for scholars and centers of learning where he could feed his growing passion for knowledge of the past.

The mystery of Taux drew him to the city, where he met his Jai-Ruk partner Kryranen. Together, the duo has made a name for themselves as experience pot hunters inside the Black Gate.

SHAY

© JANET AULISIO 2013.

Is a twenty-four year old master duelist, aka Long Shay, Cold Shay, the Dark Angel of Death, and—to those who raised him—Cricket. Named at birth for St. Shay because of his dark-eyed beauty and circumstances of his birth, Shay and his first born twin sister Shayla are the children of Mama Serene, madam of the Silk Purse, and Esmer Serata, second in command of the Taux Razor Duelist Guild.

Shay is a stunning beauty, inspiring all the lust, deceit, and suffering of his namesake saint. Tall and slender, with soft, dark brown hair, dark brown eyes, smooth tanned skin the color of milk-slaked coffee, and the face of a stern young angel, Shay draws the eye of man and woman alike, and many unwanted advances. But Shay's heart is cold, and the chip on his shoulder is the size of the Gate itself.

Shay's heart is scarred and closed. He grew up petted and spoiled by his mother's people (some of whom still embarrass him by calling him by his childhood nickname, Cricket), and considered them as older brothers and sisters. Most he meets, given his looks and upbringing, assume he's a randy sex god, but the truth is, he's sealed that part of himself off. The only two people he is truly open with are his mother, whom he adores and resents in equal measure, and his twin, whom he worships almost to the point of incest. Both mother and sister despair of him and the path he's chosen.

THE CITY OF TAUX

TAUX

1

2

3

4

5

8

6

7

JAL
13

1. SERPENT WALL DISTRICT, 2. THE BLACK GATE DISTRICT,
3. GOLD JAGUAR DISTRICT, 4. SMOKE DRAGON DISTRICT
5. TURQUOISE TURTLE DISTRICT, 6. HARBOR DISTRICT,
7. HAUNTED TEMPLE DISTRICT, 8. STAR TOWER

THE CITY OF TAUX

*F*ormerly the Tolimic City of Taux, this stand alone metropolis rests at the tip of the Free Coast and once served as a way station between a dozen large nations all over the northern Halo Ocean. More than half a century before the current date, during the final days of the *Five Year War* that banished all the old gods from the world, the population of the city was destroyed by a necromantic surge of energy. The tale of that destruction is as follows:

> *Near a century ago in the Nameless Realms timeline a council of Moon Priests and a coven of Tome-Mages theorized that like the Afterglow Sea that resides beyond the Elemental Plane of Water, there should be another plane of existence behind each of the known Elemental Planes [Fire, Water, Earth, Air, Positive Radiance, and Negative Shadow]. Because Taux sat so close to the 'Ebon Swamp' which is known to bubble up with Negative Elemental energy, they decided to dedicate a portion of their resources to discovering this 'other plane' from the secret subterranean conduits in Taux. Years passed, and the two Orders built a series of tunnels beneath the surface of Taux that could be used as a kind of elemental broadcasting station. Then, on a night corresponding with the closest proximity of the Negative Elemental Plane to the planetary sphere, they broke into a huge magical ceremony that would 'ping' beyond the Negative Elemental Plane, hoping to find another source of raw magical power there. The theory was that some reverb would come back that proved its existence and they could use that for further contact. Nine hours after the magical ping, just as the city woke in the predawn gloom for work, a nightmare scream struck the city with an apocalyptic wave. Every living thing within a hundred miles was obliterated; all souls flash-burned into the stone of the landscape around it. Since that day the city and surrounding lands have been quiet, but the souls still remember, now trapped forever in the walls of their cursed city...*

Today, Taux is once again a thriving port city, although instead of Tolimic Humans, it is populated from many cultures all over the Halo and beyond, each trying to make a profit on the mass of cargo that moves through the free city without taxation. Although still haunted by the spirits of the past, the current inhabitants try to quiet the stone and live with strange whispers at night or the sounds of cries from rooms no one is currently in.

City Size: Population: 60,000+ [15% are non-Human]

Districts:

Black Gate District: The Ullamalitzli Stadium that once housed 75,000 fans and is now home to perhaps 7,000 squatters who have built tenements in the stadium proper.

Gold Jaguar District: The high class district cut by the prestigious Ruby Lane. Here is where the very wealthy of Taux live and play in the former homes of the greatest nobility the Tolimic every possessed.

Turquoise Tortoise District: A middle to upper class merchant district of the city and home to the Grand Bazaar of Taux.

Harbor District: The port, docks, and wharfs of Taux. Here is the lifeblood of the city, the place where all cultures meet as ships from the entire Halo Ocean trade cargo for shipment all over the world.

The Haunted Temple District [Ghost Towers]: This little populated district is the home to the poor of Taux. With no place else to go, the destitute gather among the screaming stones of the former Tolimic Temple District.

Serpent Wall District: Situated against the outer wall of the city, and thus wrapping it in a large crescent, this outer district is home to the mass of the middle to lower working class of Taux.

Ebon Fields District: Located outside the main wall of the city, this tangled group of farmland is the only true source of local food Taux possesses. Farmer and cattle-folk work to stave off incursion from the Ebon Swamp as they cling to a meager existence among the lowland marshes that now serve as livestock fields and in some areas rice patties.

The Smoke Dragon District: This district is the home of the base production elements of Taux with some industry having sprung up to use cheap raw materials taken from incoming trade ships and turning them into more expensive trade goods to be shipped out. It is also the home of the Sturgeon Keep, where the mercenary army of the city is housed.

RACES

All races in the world are bound to an elemental spark, that binding element influencing their nature and depending on your affinity [subtle/medium/high] you can also have the power to wield that element in some form. This affinity doesn't necessarily mean an Eldaryn [High Fire] can set a street aflame with a twitch of his nose, but if he's a Tome-Mage Pyromancer his spark's power would be additionally lethal. Examples of elemental manifestation might be that Aspara [High Air] seem to having a phantom breeze blow through their hair when they're thinking hard, or when a Human [Subtle Fire] gets mad the temperature around him goes up a couple of degrees.

Writers gathered together to tell a tale of a single race born into the world, the Byrin, that all races, once touched by the elemental link to the gods, evolved from as they slowly formed to the will of the element of their deity. In this fashion, all the sentient races of the world developed.

Aspara: [High Affinity Air] 6 to 6 ½ feet in height. These are rather ethereal looking Humans with a personality that can change as quickly as the breeze. The opposite of the Kin in most ways, the Aspara are known to be flighty, pulled in various directions, and hard to negotiate long-term contracts with. They live free lives, rarely settling down for more than a few years at a time, and tend to shun most other races in an almost xenophobic way. In the Opal Gates, Hilani Plains, or Zimbolay, the Aspara are a chocolate-skinned and ebon-haired with sapphire blue eyes. They are a mystical people who travel the savannah and disappear from the site of Humans when pressed. They are immortal creatures, age never touching them, and so they have no need for haste unless provoked. As they are inherently detached, marriage is almost unheard of among their people, and children are scarce because mothers hate being tied down to their offspring for any length of time. Some in the world see the Aspara as inherently uncaring, but that isn't the case. They can be both passionate and heartfelt if the mood strikes them, and are capable of beautiful crafts that might take decades to finish, assuming the items the craft can be carried with them as they travel.

Farian: [Medium Affinity Air] 6 to 6 ½ feet height. Often thought to be the product of Aspara and Korys mating, the Farian race is an incredibly long-lived and secretive one. They tend to stay removed from society much like their Aspara cousins, but instead of living in the windswept plains of the world, they are people of the high mountain. In the heights of the world, the Farians dwell among the cliffs and snow as close to the heavens as they can reach. These air-born are sky sailors, builders of winged craft, and tethers of the mighty wind. They are fair-skinned and blond-haired with eyes as blue as the open sky. They live at such heights that most Humans can't climb to their lofty eyries. Farians tend to be more 'settled' than Aspara and congregate seasonally for trade and ritual feasts before heading back to solo dwellings along the cliffs.

Korys: [Subtle Affinity Air] 6 feet. Unmistakable from Humans, the Korys are often flighty, rarely bound to a single local, and yet possess an increased lifespan that's keeps them looking young for up to three hundred years. They are very few in number, mostly because they don't congregate as a unified race, instead flitting away with the wind and often having progeny with Humans or Corsairs rather than seek out other Korys who they typically find impossible to deal with because they can never agree on any one thing for long.

Kin: [High Affinity Earth] 4 ½ to 5 feet height. They are a hard race, intractable and fierce, but are also master builders and shape stone with deft hands. Sometimes this race lives within mountains, but their greatest creations come from shaping cities from stone on the surface, molding it in the passing of years. This unique connection with the earth plays out in the nature of  the Kin's coloring. Whatever natural stone they are around 'bleeds' into the Kin's pigmentation, and like a Flamingo turns pink eating pink shrimp, the Kin take on the aspect of the stone in which they live. In this fashion they marbleize, sometimes looking to have metallic veins running through the rich tones of their flesh.

They are small in stature compared to Humanity, averaging no more than five feet in height. This smaller size helps them navigate natural passages in the earth, and it is often whispered among other races that Kin can actually pass through stone, although this is unproven. The Kin also have very limited eyesight, and direct sunlight is a constant irritation. In standard daylight they wear masks or eyeshades. Under the ground, the Kin can go without any light and use echolocation to sense where they are, large ears helping to capture the sound of their incessant clicking when they travel.

No Kin have hair anywhere on their bodies, but Female Kin are known to decorate their heads with specially cultivated moss, fungus, or grass to make a kind of hair-like crown.

Jai-Ruk: [Medium Affinity Earth] 6 to 7 foot in height. They are something like the civilization's definition of brutes, tan-skinned, dark haired, and yet more muscular and square-jawed than most Humans would look. They also have slightly enlarged lower canine teeth that might just peak out of their lips on occasion. Again, otherwise they are pretty close to Humans in appearance. Jai-Ruks are large, sometimes standing as tall as seven feet, and broad at the shoulder. They are heavily muscled, but not so much it distorts their body shape, as their true strength comes from their association with the Earth. Their skin tends toward grey hues, and their hair is usually dark although some have been known to have coppery hair and their eyes are deep brown and flecked with gold or silver.

Loam: [Subtle Affinity Earth: 6 feet in height. Some say that the Loam are the product of Human and Jai-Ruk mating, but that is unproven. It is more likely that rogue bands of Humanity that settled far in the mountains or grew tied to the earth as farmers shed their fire spark for that of a subtle earth affinity. However, there are known to be more Loam in the nation of Aflyr than any other, and it boards on the Broken Land, a nation populated almost exclusively by Jai-Ruks and their Delver servants. Whatever the case, Loam are a sturdy hill folk, a people bound to the earth and steadfast in its defense.

Delver: [Subtle Affinity Earth]: This cursed race was once Human-like as well, but was corrupted by Arcxas, the God of Night. They have become a harsh barbaric race, sloped at the neck, and beast-like in their face. They live in loose bands away from most civilizations until they are roused by a leader who seeks plunder among local populations of other races.

Eldaryn: [High Affinity Fire] 3 ½ to 4 feet. This small race is bound to the pure fire and always has red hair sometimes touched with blue on the tips.

As they age, and they age quickly, their hair can turn to yellow, orange, and sometimes copper, especially with facial hair. They are known as tricksters, merchants, and sometimes pyromancers, and they are considered attractive little fellows by most other races. They live fast lives, and have a standard lifespan of no more than 60 years at the most, with the bulk living less than 50. The fire of this

race burns so bright that when angry they can be extremely dangerous, especially if they are in possession of 'Eldaryn Powder'. This explosive has been harnessed by the race in what they sometimes call 'Dragon Wands'. It is basically a flintlock pistol without the need of hammer or flint. Eldaryn can ignite the power simply by using their spark which makes the weapon completely attuned to them. It has been said that properly trained Lowl, and sometimes even Humans, are capable of setting off Dragon Wands, but this is unproven. Males are known for loving to have coppery-colored mustaches which they take great pride in, and females are notorious flirts who are said to have the ability to shape-shift for limited amounts of time. Many are the tales of Humans seduced by a lovely female of their own race only to awake the next morning in bed with a diminutive female Eldaryn.

Lowl: [Medium Affinity Fire] 6 ½ feet in height. These 'Dog-headed' Humans are one of the most 'odd' of races of the Nameless Realms next to the reptilian Candon. The Lowl can be quick to anger, and use their element to their advantage as it can fuel a powerful strength common to the species. They are known to be valuable mercenaries, and have a highly attuned sense of smell and a keen sense of hearing. In their own communities, they tend to run in tribal packs, but in Human society, they adapt quickly and are more respected in common company than Jai-Ruks.

Human: [Subtle Affinity Fire] Much like we are Humanity in our own world, save that they have a simple affinity with fire which manifests as increased temperature when they are excited in some fashion. By far the largest contingent of the Nameless Realms population, the Human race consists of more than 60% of all sentient souls in the world. Their patron of creation has long been the Sun, and although old world deities no longer hold power in the Taux and much of the rest of the world, Humanity's spark is still tied to the rising and falling of the sun.

Wizard: [High Affinity Water] Usually above 6 and a half feet in height. Human-like in most cases, although bound completely to the plane of water, they tend to 'flow' as they move about, having long hair and wearing clothing that resembles the ocean waves [mostly robes]. They are high sorcerers, their elemental plane bound closely to the Afterglow Sea of magic where they draw their power. Tall and proud, this race is sometimes considered dour, often harsh, and certainly foreboding, but like the depth of their element, there is more below the surface than can ever be perceived. They tend toward dark hair, sometimes touched with green or even more rarely violet, and their eyes are like polished emeralds. Their skin is pale *like a pristine cloud unless* they are emotional when violet and blue washes along cheekbones, or sets into the tips of their fingers. Power flows through them, not from the water that is inherently theirs, but instead from the connection

that water brings pure raw energy of the Afterglow. For this reason and powerful connection, the race of High Water are referred to as Wizards.

Wizards are more artists than sorcerers, the true power inside them tied to their ability to visualize and 'paint' pictures with the *Afterglow* energy they siphon through the plane of water and into the mundane world. Certainly, there is no doubt they are powerful, but to master what they do takes countless years of exercise and dedication to their craft. Like a master of oil painting, there are too few Michelangelos or Da Vincis in the world, and so too is it with Wizards.

Candon: [Medium Affinity Water] 5+ foot tall 'Lizardmen' with Alien-like heads, scales, and all that. They have long ago moved into swamps, marshes, and secluded rivers where their medium water affinity makes them hard to pursue or fight. They don't hold a dedicated connection with *Afterglow*, having never studied it like Wizards, but sometimes shaman in the culture to have a way with magic not seen in other races.

Corsair: [Subtle Affinity Water] Roughly 6 feet in height. These are standard 'water humans'. Corsairs wouldn't be picked out from a crowd of Humans, although they do sometimes become lesser tome mages, and thus have power that isn't seen in most races. They are bound to the sea, most never leaving the coasts, and make fine sailors.

RELIGION

There are six 'High Saints' that comprise the worshipped pantheon of the Taux settlers from the New Kingdoms across the Shining Sea to the west and over the full Halo Ocean to Dragmarsh in the east. Their power and influence has all but overwhelmed the ancient temples of the previous inhabitants who had elemental gods like sun, moon, stars, sky, etc...

All of these Saints were actual living people in the Realms and were raised to the level of 'sainthood' by the will of world cultures desperately looking for something to follow in the wake of the Five Year War and the banishment of the Old Gods from the world.

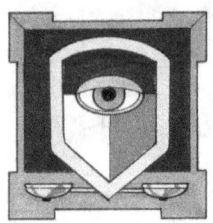

Saint Siegfried the Brave, Patron of Knights, Warriors, and the Just. Siegfried was a fabled Knight of Gariny who renounced his claim to the Ducal Throne of the nation so that he could pursue a life of unencumbered justice against all evil that still walked the world once the Five Year War ended. His deeds quickly became legend, and soon, people were praying to him for guidance which elevated him to the role of saint.

Saint Erik of the Thousand Faces, Parton of Rogues, Charlatans, and Gamblers. Erik was the leader of the rebel armies that allied against the tyranny of his brother Gorwin, King of Thalonia, as he tried to take over the globe under a single unified banner. He was a known thief and womanizer, many saying he stole his first crown in the Old Kingdoms by committing regicide. Still, when the world needed a hero, he answered the call before he was finally killed during the Battle of the Realms Gate that helped seal the world off from the Old Gods. However, some whispered that he hadn't died, but once again taken on a new form, and so the rumors of his rise from the ashes helped him gain sainthood.

Saint Shera of the Happy Hall, Parton of Hearth and Home, Travelers, and Lovers. Shera is the counterbalance to Erik, and many say the two were lovers before the Five Year War, and even more tell tales that Erik came back from the dead to find his love once more. One thing is clear, Shera was once the owner of the infamous Emerald Serpent Inn that lies at the heart of the Black Gate in Taux and was one of the first to enter the city after its fateful apocalypse. Her service was legendary, and it is said she was instrumental in the final victory of the Five Year War.

Saint Amanda of Virgins, Parton of Nobility, Good, Healers, and Radiant Light. Sister to Erik and Gorwin, she was the only relation that could claim the throne of the new World Empire once the two brothers were lost in the Battle of the Realms Gate. She was the first World Empress, and was beyond reproach as she never took a husband and was known as the Virgin Empress until the day of her assent into the ranks of sainthood.

Saint Shay of the Dark Beauty, Parton of Lust, Deceit, and Suffering. Birthed from the fabled Burning City, Saint Shay was once a Human woman like any other, but after confinement in that cursed otherworld she emerged something entirely different. Taking up the mantel of suffering that swept the world in the aftermath of the first great plagues once the Old Gods were lost, Shay plied her dark talents to any who would listen until word of her power spread over the world and she took on the form of a saint of darkness.

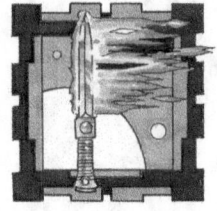 *Saint Colin of the Flaming Blade, Patron of Warriors, Doom, and Battle.* Many are the tales of Saint Colin, some say that he is the son of Saint Erik, and that he followed his love into the Burning City of his own volition, only to return again as an avenging blade of destruction. He is also claimed by the Jai-Ruk's of the both the Wounded and Broken Land as a patron of battle, and their legends tell that he is one of their race, a friend to the elemental earth, and that his power comes from the heart of their people. Whatever the truth, it is known he is a consort of the Saint Shay, and that the two are said to be seen in the aftermath of great wars or terrible disasters, either as collectors of souls or specters feeding off the flesh of the dead.

MAGIC

Magic in the Nameless Realms, and therefore in Taux can be a confusing thing. In essence, there are two distinct kinds of magic in the world, Faith-Born Miracles delivered by the Old Gods or even the new Saints which is sometimes 'perceived' magic and certainly far from potent, and Afterglow magic, which is the more functional type employed by Wizards and to a lesser degree Tome-Mages.

Faith-Born Miracles: These are gifts and blessings of the Gods and Saints. They manifest inside people of faith, typically priests, prophets, or hospitalers, and produce effects that might sway the outcome of a game of chance, heal minor injury, or ease the suffering of a troubled mind. They are rarely dramatic, and should be perceived as a very passive type of magic.

Afterglow Magic: There are six known Elemental Planes, a dozen Para-Elemental Planes, and of course the Planar Archipelago where the Old Gods dwell, but none of these directly accounts for magic in its purest form. Long ago, Wizards, being of the High Water, found that if they delved deeply enough into their element, they could piece the membrane of the Elemental Plane of Water and connect another yet unknown plane of existence, something they called the Afterglow Sea. This veritable ocean of raw energy was a place where they slowly learned to draw power from, shaping the 'magic' of its essence like an artist moves paint on a canvas Afterglow, therefore, has nothing to do with Elemental Water, it simply exists on the far side of that plane. Because of this, only Wizards have direct access to it, all other races too far removed from the connection needed to penetrate the Elemental membrane. This Afterglow magic is hard to control, and deadly in the extreme, but as a master artist can make masterworks with a brush, so can a Wizard wield terrible power with his will. Wizards don't need spell-books or such simple trappings to play with Afterglow, but there are others who have learned to siphon Afterglow and store it, typically in items or foci, for later use. These magical practitioners are called Tome Mages and they can manipulate Afterglow with elaborate storage foci and intricate spell formulas. To a Wizard, such people are simple charlatans, but to the general populace they are powerful and dedicated individuals who are to be taken seriously. Also, it has been documented by Tome Mages that Afterglow can often 'bleed' into this world through the elemental connection of all things. In this fashion, common items can sometimes 'become' magical foci just because of the situations in which they are used. This effect is called 'imprinting', and many fabled magical relics are known to exist simply from this connection and not from the forging of Wizards.

The Star Tower: The race of Wizards is a breed apart, and even though a coven of them [known as the Order of Towers] are housed within the harbor of Taux, they're secluded on a magnificent 'Star Tower' that dominates a central harbor of the city, and looks much like a larger version of Rapunzel's tower, the middle becoming precariously thin while the top houses seven massive towers that hang off the central spire. People of Taux often see the top of this structure shrouded in mist, and that mist is known to populate the city streets on nights when the Ghost and Blood Moons are full. It is said that the water magic of the Star Tower keeps the harbor clean and fresh, as well as the city's canals. One thing that is certain, however, is that any boat approaching the tower is turned away by a mysterious tide, and even the strongest rowers will break their backs before coming within a hundred yards of the circular reefs that ring it… unless the Wizards wish them to make landfall.

GLOSSARY

Baymourn Bridge: Ancient and normally non-utilized dueling bridge that connects the city to the Sun Arm of the southwest breakwater island in the bay.

Champurrado: A thick, hot drink made with milk, masa harina, chocolate, and anise, usually served in colorfully glazed cups.

Coins: Silver Coatl is the most common coin in the city, followed by standard coppers and then the Gold Jaguar [and that reflects the wealth of the Gold Jaguar District, as well as the Gold Jaguar Ulama Ball team, which is to say the wealthy aren't always the most imaginative people]

Death's Kiss: A crimson flower that grows deep in the Black Swamp and is deadly beyond measure if distilled and consumed by that intelligent races of the world. They are so deadly, in fact, that rumor has it that while still on the vine, the flowers can emit dark magic that will strike a living soul dead an arm's length from the blossom.

Ebon Swamp: Also called the 'Black Swamp', this is the massive corrupted delta that surrounds the city of Taux which eventually gives way to uncharted rainforest to the east and the Lowl plains to the north.

Golden Jaguar District: The highest class district in the city of Taux.

Gold Monkey: The highest class eatery in the Black Gate, situated just across Circle Street from the Emerald Serpent.

Hairyfist Spider: Tarantula-like spiders that frequent the dark friezes of the cities walls and often prey on birds.

Hospitaler's Guild: A league of physicians and petty healing priests mostly dedicated to Saint Amanda, although all faiths are welcome as healers inside the various guild halls and clinics.

Haunted Temple District: Also known as the 'Ghost Quarters', 'Pauper's Quarter' and 'Ghost Towers', this is a section of the city where the most downtrodden live. It is located on the western side of the city.

Moon Isle: This is the twin island to the Sun Isle, also called the Moon Arm, and it shields the eastern side of the city harbor.

Nightmen Guild: The thieves' guild of Taux

Razor Duelist Guild: The renowned duelist's guild in the city. Although open dueling is illegal, this guild moonlights as a secondary police force and also hires out as a mercenary force for the wealthy of the city.

Red Pillar: A ruling council of mostly secret, wealthy, and powerful men and women who control the government of Taux. They few of the council who let the city known their position walk around with crimson scarves about their neck, the most notable of these being Tlacolotl Vash.

Ruby Lane: The great road that leads through the Golden Jaguar District and ends at the gates of the Black Gate District.

Sepak Ball: A game much like real world Hacky Sack

Serpent's Head: A game much like modern badminton, with a feathered cock and open palms.

The Shining Sea: The great reach of the sea stretching out from the sheltered bay of Taux, and is part of the larger Halo Ocean.

Sons of the Moon: A local street gang that has been growing in power and has territory in Haunted Temple District.

Smoke Dragon District: The industrial quarter of the city where the bulk of the workforce goes each day via canal barges.

The Silver Circle: The main oval street that runs the full circumference of the Black Gate's inner floor.

Sun Isle: This is the old ceremonial island that is often referred to as an 'arm' as it shields the western side of the harbor.

Tolimic Empire: The fallen and cursed society that created Taux and was destroyed by the dark magic apocalypse.

Ullamalitzli: A Tolimic game set between two, four man, teams, that utilizes a heavy rubber ball called a Ulama. The purpose is to get the ball inside an open stone hole set high in a kind of goal on each side of a sunken field of play. Notable professional teams within the city include the Black Gate Snakes and the Gold Jaguar Jaguars [coached by Gamemaster Ixchel a Human female].

WayNside Bridge: Ancient and normally unused bridge that connects the city to the Moon's Arm island that surrounds half of the bay. Beneath this bridge, Jai-Ruk longshoremen sleep in hammocks to avoid fees from local dives while still staying close to their work.

Whispering Shoals: The shoreline of the Moon Isle that surrounds northeast section of the bay, also known for its Jai-Ruk squatters and breakwater that often gets valuable flotsam from the deep ocean.

Zimbolay: A city the lies far across the ocean to the south of Taux and resides among the fabled cities of the Opal Gates. Zimbolay is not the largest of these coastal city-states, Ulandm holding that honor, but it is known for producing the most tome mages in the southern hemisphere.

Cast of Characters

Balthazar Della Nova: Male Human dueling partner of Shay Gatewell of the Silk Purse, Balthazar is often the calm rational voice of reason to the brazen young Shay, although technically only two years his elder.

Esmeralda Serata: A young female Human duelist and former noble, she has attained the silver badge of a 2nd degree duelist in the Razor's Guild of Taux and is always looking to learn new techniques with the blade.

Emil Lacosta & Mariella: Emil is a Human tome mage practitioner and maker of potions from the dark coasts of Zimbolay who has taken Mariella, as seventeen year-old Human female, as his apprentice in all matters of magical elixirs, including his trademark love potions.

Fynn & Analyse: Eldaryn street performers and petty rogues with a trained monkey inside the Black Gate.

Increase Coin: Male of Zimbolay, Human with various scars about his deeply black face. He is a bodyguard, and sometimes cutpurse who is often employed as a guide to the Black Gate by outsiders with plenty of coin.

Oswald Burgunzi: One of the three richest men in Taux, and fat beyond measure. His family is only pressed for full mercantile control by the Vash and Dharn clans respectively, although the Dharn family's power is waning after several recent deaths including that of their patriarch.

Quilan: The tavernkeeper at the Emerald Serpent

Shayla Gatewell: Twin to Shay Gatewell and daughter to Mama Serene of the Silk Purse, Shayla is a Human female and devout worshiper of Saint Amanda as well as a practiced surgeon and member of the Hospitaler's Guild.

Serene Gatewell: Known as 'Mama Serene' this Human woman is the madam of the infamous Silk Purse, the finest brothel in the Black Gate, and arguably all of Taux. She is also one of the Red Pillars, a secret ruling council of twelve that makes most of the decisions concerning the running of the city of Taux.

Tlacolotl Vash: The patriarch of the wealthiest family on Taux, the Vash Clan. His family employees commonly wear black livery while 'off duty' and black and gold when serving the family in public.

Xavier Craine: A Human and former duelist of the Ebontra Cross style, he is now the sole teacher of the craft of swordplay inside the Black Gate District.

www.ingramcontent.com/pod-product-compliance
Lightning Source LLC
Chambersburg PA
CBHW070702280626
47159CB00022B/1765